Sunland

WEST WORD FICTION

A NOVEL

Sunland

DON WATERS

UNIVERSITY OF NEVADA PRESS ▲▲ RENO & LAS VEGAS

West Word Fiction

University of Nevada Press, Reno, Nevada 89557 USA

Manufactured in the United States of America
Design by Kathleen Szawiola

Library of Congress Cataloging-in-Publication Data

Waters, Don, 1974-
Sunland : a novel / Don Waters.
pages cm. — (West Word Fiction)
ISBN 978-0-87417-921-7 (cloth : alk. paper) —
ISBN 978-0-87417-922-4 (e-book)
1. Grandmother—Fiction. 2. Drug traffic—Mexico.
3. Older people—Pharmaceutical assistance—Fiction.
4. Drugs—Prices—Fiction. I. Title.
PS3623.A8688S86   2013
813'.6—dc23   2013007119

The paper used in this book meets the requirements of
American National Standard for Information Sciences—
Permanence of Paper for Printed Library Materials,
ANSI/NISO Z39.48-1992 (R2002).
Binding materials were selected
for strength and durability.

22   21   20   19   18   17   16   15   14   13
5   4   3   2

For Robin

Acknowledgments

I'm indebted to many people and organizations that have helped me along the way. Josh Benke, Don Lee, Robert Boswell, Julian Rubinstein, and Pauls Toutonghi read early drafts and offered sound advice. For their insights, humor, and friendship, big thanks to Willy Vlautin, Ralph Morgan, Nicole Tourtelot, Scott Benke, Dan Engber, Blake Nelson, Sam Moulton, Rus Bradburd, Josh Weil, Dana Levin, Mario Zambrano, Clifton Spargo, Andrés Carlstein, Liz Weiss, Caleb Cage, and Piera Willner. For the gift of time, space, and support, thanks to the Lannan Foundation, Casa Libre en la Solana in Tucson, the Christopher Isherwood Foundation, and the Iowa Writers' Workshop. At the Workshop, thanks to Deb West, Jan Zenisek, Connie Brothers, Sam Chang, Ethan Canin, Marilynne Robinson, and Andy Greer. It's a true pleasure to work with the University of Nevada Press, and I'm immensely grateful to Joanne O'Hare, Mike Campbell, Margaret Dalrymple, Kathleen Szawiola, and Jan McInroy. Huge thanks also to my agent, Maria Massie. I'm supremely thankful to Humane Borders for allowing me to tag along in the desert borderlands. The staff at the Oakland Zoo were really helpful and taught me everything I needed to know about the sex lives of zoo animals. Thank you, KJ Page, and Chaparral House, for showing me, at 26, that compassion coexists alongside laughter. Thanks to my mom, my stepdad, and my entire family for their love and support. Special thanks to Ben Fountain and the *Southwest Review* for encouraging my earliest work. And of course, I would be nowhere without Robin Romm—thank you for everything, always.

SUNLAND

Part One

1 And here they were, the walkers and canes and Panama hats under the parrot-green Arizona sky. I checked my watch. Four thirty was dinner hour, the fever-rush to the dining commons. In the shimmery heat of the summer afternoon, everyone prepared for gossip and spoons. Elevators in the whitewashed towers opened with a pneumatic hiss, spilling groups of twos and threes onto the central brick quad, where men in oversized Hawaiian shirts mingled with elderly women who stood bent, and tiny, and fragile underneath the hook-armed, hundred-year-old saguaro.

Ms. Haybroke, one of my septuagenarians, led the charge with a sleek new cell phone to her ear. Her heavy blue eye shadow looked applied via paint gun. She sauntered my way and pinched the phone shut.

"Just get me the same," she said and passed me a silky envelope. I handed her a white paper bag. My finger grazed her ring as she moved on, but for a moment I felt comradeship—that we were spies trading information, that we were children exchanging notes. Inside her envelope was her monthly payment, in cash.

I stood at my usual bench by the lake, my granddad's old, tattered U.S. postal bag looped over my shoulder, distributing white paper bags with gold stickers over the flaps. I worked for my clients. We whispered about dollar amounts, doses.

I hitched the bag to my other shoulder, feeling a sting in my rotator cuff, and kept my eye on a stranger leaning on a YIELD FOR WHEELCHAIRS signpost. A white Stetson shaded the stranger's face. The man was watching with interest. I was unable to connect him to any of my clients. I knew faces around Paseo del Sol. And they knew mine. I watched him snuggle his thumb in his jeans pocket and study me as though he wanted to know me. I was always interested in men who wanted to know me, in men I didn't know. Any day, at any hour, a police baton could tap at my door, and the work would come to an end. The man's eyes shifted overhead when aquamarine drapes slashed shut inside one of the assisted-living towers. Some old folks enjoyed watching brilliant, slow-moving sunsets filled with dramatic cloudbursts. Others hid behind thick drapes.

People on campus knew my grandma as Miss Mary Beth, as Ms. Dulaney, as Bethie, but to me she was Nana—just Nana, my nana, whom I adored—and Nana was late for the dinnertime sprint.

When Nana finally appeared she had an argyle scarf around her neck. A puffy, hand-knit wool sweater concealed her curved back. It embarrassed me when Nana wore wool in this kind of heat.

"Scrubbing the grout stains again," she said, rolling out her usual routine. "You should see the caulking," she went on. She pulled two fingers through short gray hair with black strings in the mix. "Goes white to brown in minutes. Minutes! We need bleach. A big bottle. The biggest. The kitchen is under attack, Sidney. I thought you were supposed to help with the cleaning." Her tongue slid over specially ordered dentures. "And what are you doing out in the sun again?"

"We're having dinner. Remember?"

"Is it Tuesday?" she said.

Beside her I felt like a hovering giant. As a teenager, as I grew, she shrank. Now she was a slight eighty-eight-year-old with large purple veins, thick as earthworms, lining the tops of her hands.

As we walked to the dining commons, I watched the stranger unhitch his thumb from his jeans and right himself like an impertinent bowling pin. I ignored the man's stare and showed Nana the loot inside Grandpa's bag: celecoxib for her arthritis, lisinopril for hypertension, sertraline for mood stability, and so on. A small pharmacy.

"All of it illegal, I suppose," she said.

"Cheaper," I said. "I'm trying to keep ahead of your bills. The cost of managed care is astronomical."

"Oh, save it." Nana drilled me with her stare. I knew she didn't approve of the side business I'd carved from her living situation—she worried about my safety, the law, especially the violence along the border. "I just never thought Frederick would sire a criminal son," she said.

"Enough with the guilt trip, Nan."

"Don't sass your grandma." She wiped at the corners of my mouth with a wet thumb. "I just wish you'd find something better to do with your time."

In the distance thick black fingers dropped from the sky and touched the thirsty soil. It was raining far off. I felt a rush and grabbed my grandmother's hand. Lightning veins appeared, flickering like broken neon. Black rain clouds looked like pulled dirty cotton. Thin strands of sunlight shot through the clouds and caressed my neck. During monsoon season, the days were long, superheated, and oppressive. In the late afternoons I liked watching for rare skies and meteorological dramas, scanning the outlying horizons for signs of pregnant, silver-blue rain clouds, hoping and praying for clouds that would strain and heave and cry before blowing off, so that nothing was left but the good, sodden smell of oiled creosote and wet earth, that welcome and needed relief under the windy clapping of acacia leaves.

"You did the same as a boy," Nana said, gripping my hand tighter. "Always skygazing. Must be something up there you like."

2   Questions I overheard at the surrounding dinner tables: Why was Saul Berger's left eye so droopy? Anyone hear about Jane Munro biting a nurse? Who was excited about the upcoming Elvis Presley Impersonation Show, to be performed by a man named Eli Presley?

Nana nibbled down five buttered wheat crackers, threw her hands up at me, and called it a night. She looked exhausted from all the chewing. Due to how her dentures fit, she chewed roundly, as though she had a horse bit in her mouth.

"You need to eat more than five crackers," I said.

Nana slit her eyes. "Stop telling me what to do."

Tuesday was Buffet Night, and for the money I paid Pasco del Sol, I disliked Buffet Night. It should have been renamed Cheapskate Night. I was not a fan of elementary school food dressed up with gold-embossed placards that made each dish sound well traveled: "Moscow" beef Stroganoff (soupy), "Southern" green beans (bland), and "Washington State" applesauce (too sweet).

Nana's dinner crew claimed the corner table, near a soft-serve machine that squirted ropes of diabetic ice cream, and I sat with them like a cornered prisoner.

Leaning back, fingers behind my neck, I attempted to lift the boredom from my soul by flapping elbows at Ms. Bunny Vallance, who was sitting beside Nana. Ms. Vallance was one of my favorite clients. She broadcast her flirty smile at me.

"Mary Beth tells us you're still unmarried," Ms. Haybroke said to me, halving a green bean with a dull knife. "At your age, Sid, and still unmarried. How old, these days, are you?"

"Thirty-three, these days," I said.

"And still unmarried," she said and shook her head.

"Sidney had a lady friend in Massachusetts," Nana said. "Then he moves back here, I don't know why, and he hasn't told me what happened."

"Let's not mention that," I said.

"Sidney enjoys playing the bachelor," Nana said.

Ms. Bunny Vallance pushed away her salad bowl with a chromium lipstick tube. She twisted the cylinder. Fiery red lipstick popped out.

"Nothing shameful with the unwed approach," she said in her California voice. Bunny Vallance didn't speak; she cooed. She reached across the table to touch my knuckle. "So you're playing the field. There's nothing wrong with that. Wouldn't we all, if we owned those eyes?"

The rims of my ears burned. "I'd like to change the channel, if nobody minds."

Ms. Haybroke rolled her eyes. "You should be with someone, kiddo. Share your one life. People need other people, after all. Look at us."

"Working on that," I said, feet crossed, arms crossed, leaning back, ready to go. Other than pushing my "Tuscan" macaroni around with a spoon, I hadn't touched dinner.

"Oh, let the man enjoy himself," Ms. Vallance said. She studied a pocket mirror and painted her bottom lip red. "Get out there and sow your oats."

Ms. Vallance's suggestion seemed to hang in the air before Ms. Haybroke batted it away and said, meddling with her big silver bracelet, "That's not advice. Let's don't listen to Bunny. Find a nice girl, like my Jeremy did," she said. "Get down on a knee. Make your grandmother happy."

"Are you unhappy?" I asked Nana.

"You do need someone," she said.

"A nice lady," Ms. Haybroke said.

"Plus, think about the regular *release*," Ms. Vallance said. Her lips came together as she spread the red to her upper lip. "Me, I like it in the morning, before dawn, in that haze before I'm fully awake."

My grandmother coughed, bunched her napkin, threw it on her crackers, and fished an envelope from her old leather purse. She heaved the envelope at me. "I found this while cleaning."

It was a bill. Pink paper behind a cellophane window. I faked a smile at Nana's companions. "Why didn't you give me this?"

"It's been under a pillow for months. I hope this doesn't botch the accounting."

Pink meant past due. Past due meant cutting down her bank account even further.

Across the dining hall, an elderly man stood, raised his arms, and shouted, "Bingo! Bingo! Bingo!" We watched a nurse quickly attach herself to the man's arm and guide him out a side door.

After dinner, I escorted my grandmother to her one-bedroom apartment on the third floor of her assisted-living tower, La Catalina. Nana took her time unfurling her silk scarf, folding it into a square, and setting it on top of others with the same impeccable fold. She ladled water from the kitchenette faucet and dabbed her face. Beads swam down her nose. Another night accomplished.

"That Bunny Vallance," Nana said with a slow head shake.

"She's a firecracker, all right," I said.

"I wouldn't mind stepping into her shoes for a night or two. Expensive shoes, too, by the shine. Some days I wish I could be more like her. She has her way with men. Tell you. And don't get me started about how she dresses. Every time she walks into a room the lights glow brighter."

"She is special," I said.

"Special?" Nana tittered. "She's the reason rumors were invented. When she walks through campus, there go the busy lips. Another rumor is born." Nana leaned on the counter and looked at the ceiling absentmindedly. "I'd very much like someone to start a rumor about me someday."

"I could try."

"*Pfft*. You're biased. Besides, I'd like something good. Something tantalizing that will only get back to me when I least expect it. Look at me," she said, swiping her hands with a dish towel. "I'm an old woman who finds comfort in clean kitchens."

Her apartment, you had to admit, was grandmotherly. Coffee-colored walls clashed with a gold sofa with frayed tassels down the sides. Tacked to her bedroom wall was a decorative chile pepper ristra. Cool air pulsed from a vent, rustling a set of pink drapes. Nana fit with her age. She was set in her ways. But the yellow Post-it notes put me off. They were affixed to nearly every item in her apartment, detailed instructions on *what was to be done* after she was gone. I despised these little reminders. Nana had once given me several Post-it note pads—bright pink ones—and asked me to write my name on them and stick them on whatever caught my eye. I never carried out her wish.

"I trust you're caring for the yard," Nana said.

"Don't worry. Your casita is fine. Everything's tip-top."

"You need to remember to water out back."

"There's nothing out back but weeds."

"You need to water them. They add green to the view. Makes the house look lived in."

I saw an opportunity. I quickly nudged the opening wider. "About that, since you brought it up. About your casita," I said, and for the umpteenth time I took out the financial durable power of attorney forms from my bag. Nana had designated me as her health-care proxy. But she refused to sign the financial paperwork. The papers had been in the bag so long that the tips were soft and curled. "I need your signature on that last page." I creased the papers back. "Look it over. The lawyer prepared everything accordingly."

"Not again," Nana said.

"Not again what?"

"This talk."

"I need your signature to sell the casita. Make me your financial power of attorney."

"Absolutely not," she said.

"You said so yourself. You want me to stop running prescriptions. We sell the casita and we'll have enough to afford this place."

"That's not an option," she said. "That's *our* house. It's where Bubba and I took care of you when your mama left. Besides, what if I want to move back someday?"

As much as I disliked the idea, there was no other option. I was the only child of an only child, and my father was dead. Hanged, via rope. So I was the last in line to assume responsibility for the direction of Nana's care. "It's just a signature." I held out a ballpoint pen. "I'll forge it if you don't sign."

"Banks look closely at that," she said.

"I sign your other checks."

"Because I allow it."

"Please, Grandma."

Nana nailed me with her stare, as though a stranger had commandeered her home. Then she struck her pose, her frightening pose: fists on hips. "Now listen to me, Sidney Joseph, and you listen carefully—"

I did. I listened. And listened. Nana talked in circles and tied her words into a bow around my neck. I felt my cheeks heat up. My relationship with her was based on patterns, routines. Nana talked, and talked. I listened. Like my grandfather, I listened. Moments like these I understood why my granddad found ways to distance his mind from his wife's jawing. After a long sweaty day of delivering mail, Bubba would return home, fork down dinner, and spend many nights in the backyard shed, where he made wooden rocking horses. Bubba even constructed one in the hope that I might someday give him a great-grandchild. It was still back there, collecting dust.

"And that's my home, your grandfather's home, *our* home. And I won't have people that I don't know buying it," Nana said, and in conclusion, "that's *final*."

We looked at each other from across the room. There was nothing more I could say when she got like this. I shoved the paperwork into my bag and dumped her medicine bottles on the glass table. "We'll discuss this later," I said and went for the door.

My grandmother's tower connected to its sister tower, La Santa Rita, via an indoor glass walkway that passed over a Japanese rock garden thirty feet below. I strode through the halls on a mission. Paseo del Sol was nice. Expensive. And it showed. The building's floors were marked with alphabetical signage, and Management kept the towers smelling interesting with plug-in, time-released deodorizers. Tonight La Santa Rita was pure pine needles. At the end of each hall, on every floor, the bookshelves were packed—more specifically, they were packed with romance novels: thick, dog-eared, bodice-ripping paperbacks. I'd never seen anyone reading the books in public, but judging by the number of paperbacks crammed into the overflowing bookcases, the books were consumed at an astonishing rate.

At first, I had trouble accepting the little amounts people could pay me for delivering drugs. My problem was that I liked these old folks too much. I liked their unending kindness, their teary eyes, and their crazy fashion sensibilities—elastic-band jeans, non-slip-sole shoes, durable fabrics, what have you. Very few people had the time to sit down, prepare a pot of tea, and talk to you, and care about you, truly care, but these people did.

Still, a few bad seeds eventually spoiled things for everyone. Old-timers could be cheap, sure, always locating ways to cut corners, their wallets and purses stuffed with coupons. Some would rather skip dinner altogether than miss the early-bird special. After several clients began ripping me off, "forgetting" to pay, claiming early-onset dementia, or worse, I was forced to set down rules.

There was one resident above all others who gave me unlimited amounts of grief. Ms. Gwendolyn Wetherbee, of unit 63G, was the only woman that I'd ever met with a receding hairline. Not that I should judge, with a donut-sized hole in my scalp, but hers was remarkable, as though she'd worked on it. Above her flesh-squat body her pinched face rose into an elongated forehead, where her gray hair was accelerating backward.

"Oh, how extra nice," she said upon opening her door. Sweat glistened on the crown of her head. It was cotton candy hair, delicate as a dry dandelion, as though it could blow away with the faintest breeze. "Now, isn't this a delicious surprise?" she said to me. "And look. You're on time."

"My money," I said. "I need it. I'm tired of playing your games."

Ms. Gwendolyn Wetherbee outstretched her fingers against her chest. "*My*. Heavens word. You call *that* a greeting?"

She was incredible. Standing there, pretending she didn't owe me $782. Ms. Wetherbee looked over my shoulder and eyeballed the hallway. All around, oversized red EXIT signs indicated the direction of traffic flow in case of emergency. The hall was quiet except for the faint murmur of TVs behind closed, locked doors.

"I'm waiting," I said.

"Shush down," she said.

I tapped the face on my plastic watch.

"About that," Ms. Wetherbee said, backing farther into her pack-rat lair. I followed her in. "About your money," she said.

"That's right, it's *my* money. I am owed. Five bills now and I'll forget last week's nonexistent payment. I knocked on your door for half an hour."

"I was at Feldenkrais class," she told me. The lie quivered in her eyeball.

"I heard your television."

"You heard the TV because the TV is always on."

Wafting around her apartment was a burnt-nacho smell. A TV blared on a chipped wood stand. Dirty dishes plugged her sink. Torn-open brown shipping bags littered the light gray industrial carpet.

From her upper-floor apartment I was afforded a view of campus, and for a moment I stood at the window and looked out over my domain. Wild yellow grasses swayed along the banks of a man-made, stroll-around lake, where fountains spouted in the shape of flower petals. It was a self-contained city that lent the illusion there was safety within borders. Miles of wrought-iron fence line, looped with fragrant honeysuckle, enclosed twenty acres cut through with wide pedestrian-friendly lanes adorned with fake street signs. The community center and dining commons curved around a central quad presided over by the two grand towers. And tucked neatly between them, camouflaged by a copse of desert willows, I saw the flat-roofed, single-story building at the end.

I turned from the window. Ms. Wetherbee was shifting her weight from one foot to the other. Her apartment was stuffy, her windows were locked, and she didn't have her AC going, like any normal person. Summers in the Sonoran Desert were torturous, and if it weren't baseball season, I'd pop a fuse. Searing daytime temps had a curious way of turning my happy moods to misery. And now this.

"Look, you don't have to pay in full," I told her. "We can set up a plan. A payment plan or something. I'm just asking for—"

"God almighty I'm depressed!" Ms. Wetherbee cried. A finger trembled into her mouth. She tugged down her lip, revealing a crooked line of stained teeth. "Sidney, hold me. Please, hold me. I need someone to hold me. You can't imagine how lonely a girl gets." She shuffled closer.

The old prune's ability to frustrate me was colossal. Make no mention of this evening's display. Still, her tears won, and I landed a few pats on her emaciated shoulder. She yanked a polka-dotted shawl off a velvet recliner, shrugged my hand off, and collapsed in a chair. Now came the soft weeping, the sniffling and carrying on. She bunched the shawl and blew a hefty wad into it. By now I was used to her erratic behavior. So much jazz flowed through her veins that just standing near her was enough to catch a contact buzz. I knew I oughtn't deal to her, but I did.

When Ms. Wetherbee settled down, she offered me this week's explanation. You see, Sidney, you see. She would have the cash in her hand, if.

"If?"

"If I hadn't spent it." She shrugged.

The old woman's apartment was a remarkable achievement in controlled chaos. Pills were not her only vice. I knew Ms. Wetherbee was a full-blown Shopping Channel addict, and each week her tiny apartment filled with more rubbish: cuckoo clocks, coffee table books, silk pillows, teddy bears, baskets. A regulation NBA basketball was on the counter. I'd once considered swapping her regular meds with an antidepressant, which can help with obsessive-compulsive disorder. At least it could help tamp down her habit. Hoarding was a symptom of misfiring synapses. Not curable, but manageable.

"I understand that your husband died, and you're alone," I said. "But I need to get paid. I front the cash. I bring you the meds. The deal is, you pay me back, plus the fee. It's an easy arrangement to understand."

Ms. Wetherbee bit down on a fingernail. Her cuticles looked ravaged. "I promise to pay next week." She looked up from the recliner with nervous, wide-open eyes.

I reluctantly opened my bag. Even though I knew better, I dug out her bottles—pills for osteoporosis, arthritis, acid reflux, hypothyroidism, insomnia—and stacked them end on end until the sculpture was five bottles tall. The surprising thing was that compared with my other clients, she was fairly healthy.

She rose from the chair to study the labeling. "And?"

I brought out one last bottle, twisted the lid, and shook a 40-milligram Schedule II narcotic into my palm. Ms. Wetherbee stared greedily at the fat white pill. By my count she was up to three 40-milligram tabs several times a day. "Cash," I said.

"Take this watch," she said rapidly. She bent her wrist, lifted it. "Diamonds nestled around the sides. See? Roll it through your fingers. Scratch glass," she said. "They're not the best diamonds, but it's certainly worth more than I owe you. Here. Take it. It belonged to my sister." She unclasped the watch and it slid down into her fingers. "Take it. It's yours." Her eyes were big, jumpy, pin-striped red. My stomach sank as the old woman bounced anxiously on her heels.

From what others had told me, Ms. Wetherbee had developed her habit while watching her husband waste away from emphysema, his body melted into a mattress. To dull her anguish she began knocking back his meds. She was hooked long before his fade-out. She had even been high at his funeral, I was told. She went around tapping shoulders, asking people about the weather. When I took her on as a client, she told me, "Forty-two years of marriage, kiddo. That's longer than you've been alive. Think about that. Take a long, long moment, and think over that kind of pain." I was conflicted, sure. That I supplied drugs to a mid-seventies, retired middle school geometry teacher with two sons and five grandchildren.

"Look how you're living, Ms. Wetherbee. A bomb may as well have gone off. Don't your sons ever visit? Where are your sons? Who's taking care of you?"

Ms. Wetherbee inhaled gigantically. Then she began weeping again, smearing tears into her cheeks, swiping her wet hand through her vanishing hairline. It was hard for me to stay angry for long. She was just a wobbly old woman whose face resembled a sun-dried apple. But I would have loved to get a firm grip around her sons' throats. They did nothing for their mother.

I closed my hand around the pill, considering. At this time of day, normally, I wouldn't even think about it. Usually I kept business and pleasure separate. But it had been a long, hot afternoon—105 degrees in the shade, and even hotter in my crappy, non-air-conditioned car. I'd driven south out of Tucson to Mexico (Green Valley, Tubac, Rio Rico) and then returned (Rio Rico, Tubac, Green Valley). Not to mention, an interstate trucker hadn't bothered with his blinker, nearly jackknifing the rig and wiping me off the map.

I opened my fingers and inspected the delicate little nugget. The scored section was so precise. Without thinking too hard about it, I popped it. The pill stuck to the back of my throat, the way aspirin did. "I'm not taking that watch," I said, massaging my Adam's apple, trying to clear it. "That's not in our agreement. This is a cash-only business." The pill refused to drop.

I was at the door when Ms. Wetherbee shuffled across the room and wrapped her sweaty hand around my wrist. Her strength surprised me.

"You take this watch," she said, and the vibration in her voice convinced me of something true. "You hand over that bottle and I won't call the front office and tattle. I could tell them about your business. I could push the emergency call button. I'm a storyteller. He touched me, officer. He *touched* me." Her cried-out eyes narrowed. "I've already been weeping. Who will they believe? Hand me that bottle."

The old girl had me, and my opinion of her took a sudden, interesting shift. I looked at a sack of baggy skin under her chin. I smiled at her more kindly than ever before. I allowed Ms. Wetherbee to place her sister's antique watch in my hand and take the pills.

"And next time you're down there, get the patches," she said. "Try for the Duragesic patches. You stick them on your bicep." The pill finally loosened. I swallowed. She pointed at my throat. "I'm deducting that," she said. "Now you owe me."

FOUR DOORS, four stops, four white bags.

Quarter till nine, I stopped by the last door on my route, Mr. Garland Bills, unit 45D, the campus phantom. Few residents knew his first name because the man rarely socialized. Folks loved gossip, especially old folks. Invention bloomed when allowed space and time. Rumor was that Mr. Garland Bills was a former con man, or some Mafia relic. Depending on the week, he was a bank robber in hiding. Bunny Vallance had nearly convinced me that he had been a college dean, exiled from academia with full pension after he'd been caught playing grab-ass with a series of eighteen-year-olds. Whenever Mr. Garland Bills did show his face around campus, he wore different-colored tracksuits with zippers up the legs. And he was always tied into running shoes. He was younger than the others by decades, out of shape, with some respectable weight around his midsection. His posture wasn't the straightest but his teeth were his. Regardless of his reasons, he was here. Warehoused, like everyone.

I pulled a brass knocker in the shape of a howling coyote and, like always, listened for the sound of three locks. The door cracked open. A hand with clean, filed nails appeared. The hand took the white paper bag. The door closed. Then the rasp of locks again. Mr. Garland Bills was my most unproblematic customer.

I was unsure, for some time, what medications I was smuggling for him. I couldn't match the names of his meds with the long list of meds I'd become familiar with. Garland Bills's detailed instructions had come on a torn sheet of yellow binder paper: 250 milligrams of tipranavir with 100-mil boosts of ritonavir soft gelcaps, among many, many others. When I'd handed my Mexican pharmacist the long list, she'd given me a pained look.

"What?" I'd asked.

"SIDA," Amelia had told me. "AIDS medicine."

"Oh," I'd said.

Oxycodone hydrochloride folded the world into manageable, semi-humorous parts, first numbing the tissue beneath my fingertips, spreading to my cheeks, my back, my legs, but most importantly dulling an ache that occasionally bloomed at the bottom of my throat. I walked through the silent halls. The only cars in the parking lot were the overnighters and nurses working in the building at the end. I found my car and proceeded through the gate.

The hypnotic tracery of red taillights smoothed out the warm night streets. I cracked my window and breathed the clean, wonderful smell of wet pavement. Storm clouds had passed over earlier, spitting a little, but unfortunately they'd restrained themselves.

THINGS JUST UNFURLED THIS WAY. One minute I was teaching high school English in Massachusetts, and the next I was a mule for the elderly. I'd like to return to teaching, and I will—someday. I missed chalkboards and curious students. I missed bells and order. The trouble was: the bills. Plus, I knew I was good with the elderly. A great portion of my success was my ability to listen.

Before landing back in Tucson, I'd left my own set of tracks. I floated around this big weird country for twelve years, subsidized by odd jobs, picking up credits toward a degree in education, first in Indiana, later in Albany. Wanderlust eventually brought me to Northampton, Massachusetts, where I met Juliet, a successful trial lawyer with high doll-like cheekbones and exquisite feet. Then, life as I knew it fell completely and perfectly apart. I left Northampton around 2:00 AM on a cold winter morning. A light drizzle was falling from an iron-gray Massachusetts sky. The driveway was a sheet of black ice. I didn't leave a note, no forwarding address, nothing. Just took my jacket, three pairs of boxer shorts, and my wallet. That morning, I jumped in my car, shivered, turned the heat on high, and drove back to the city that raised me. And now, eight months later, still driving, I swung a right onto my warm, dead street, feeling the opiate really working now, spreading like salve and slowing my breath. I tapped my thumb to Waylon on the stereo. I turned into the dirt driveway and pumped the brakes.

There, tipped on its side, in the middle of the driveway, was a child's car seat. My car beams were trained on it. Dust floated through the headlights. I switched to high beams and the thing only glowed brighter. A beige car seat. A fucking beige child's car seat sitting in my driveway. I sat for a moment in idle, scrutinizing the five-point harness and adjustable canopy.

Someone had to be playing a massive joke on me, screwing with my medicated head. Someone had to be out there, watching and snickering and taunting me from the gathered shadows. Would Juliet do something like this? Another lash across my back? It was impossible, yet here it was, ten feet from my bumper. There had to be cameras in the streetlamps, a guy with a microphone about to jump from behind a tree.

I stepped out of the car watchfully, looking up and down the street. A quiet night, desolate. The only thing playing was the cicadas, humming along with the buzz in my ears.

I approached the seat and rolled it upright with my shoe. An infant belonged in it. I looked up and down the street. The deep smell of horse manure wafted over from nearby horse paddocks. It appeared that someone had pulled over to the curb, thrown the seat out, and it had come to rest here, in my driveway.

For a moment I pictured a sleeping child, a blanket tucked to its chin, its balled fists as tight as rosebuds. The baby shuddered awake. Its heavy head lolled about, trying to isolate a point of focus. The seat was stained with bits of dried food, but otherwise it was in reasonable shape.

Again, I looked up, then down, the street.

Contemplating it wasn't necessary. I rooted through my car and tossed jumper cables and Styrofoam coffee cups and loose papers into the hatch. I quickly wrestled the plastic contraption into the back. I didn't want to be spotted by a neighbor on a late-night dog walk. I ran the seat belt through the loops. I locked the door and flung my hands away, as though the car was now hot. Then I circled, peering through the window—stunned by the sight of a child's car seat in the back of my car.

3   Our financial tightrope was getting wobbly and there wasn't much room for maneuvering. So I'd laid an application on the local school district.

I was up early, shaved, fingernails clipped, socked-up, considering whether or not to wear, in this strangulating heat, my grandpa's long-sleeve blue oxford. It had been one of my grandfather's nicest. My first interview in over a year, and I was actually looking forward to the event. I hadn't had a proper job in so long that the meager academic accomplishments on my résumé—twelve years and three institutions to earn an undergraduate degree—struck me as belonging to another person.

Outside, the midmorning sun cut through the haze, burrowing through the dusty obscuration and brightening the dullest surfaces. Even the hairs on my arms, as I started the car and backed out, felt tinged. I drove to the local community college—a large, friendly, urban campus—and the office, when I found it, was nothing more than a double-wide trailer in the rear lot. A steel air-con unit hung off the building like a metallic growth. I'd been informed that District Admin had been temporarily relocated.

I checked my watch. I was early. So I waited in the heat and left my mother another voice mail. I had questions about the casita, and when I hung up I made a home on a bench, watching summer school students roam between buildings.

It happened several months after my father's suicide, when I was eight, when the environment at home was already confusing and charged. The event was a hiccup, I was sure, in my mother's life, so I found it weird that I would now file this particular memo under IMPORTANT. Oh, but oh those excruciating minutes of waiting in the classroom with Mrs. Candelaria—I remembered both of us watching a round white clock on the wall as big as the moon, both of us listening for the clip of my mother's heels to come hurrying down the hall. But they never came. And me, my shame leaking from my face and into Mrs. Candelaria's, into a room deadened into silence while hurt and disappointment ran hot and hummed through my veins. Eventually, Nana appeared. From that day on Nana picked up more of the slack, looking after me in ways my mother could not.

Two students walked past. They were talking about Charles Darwin. I lifted my arms. Oval sweat stains had formed around my armpits. They were horrible. They were embarrassing. I considered calling to reschedule. Instead I knocked on the aluminum door.

Inside, the makeshift office smelled like a mechanic's garage, as though the computers and printers had been expertly lubricated. My interviewer was a pretty young lady named Katie-Anne, about a decade younger than me, with eager eyes. She brought to mind an Olympian: good skin, perfect teeth, and dense thatch of hair.

Katie-Anne guided me to her cubicle and fell into a well-oiled chair, sitting perfectly upright. Her eyes narrowed when she saw my sweat stains. She motioned with my résumé, telling me to take a seat.

"They've been giving me your messages," Katie-Anne said to me. "You've been calling the office for the past month. Why do you want to substitute teach so badly?"

I tried to laugh. "I'm a teacher. Once I pass the state's exam I'll be applying for work through your office."

"Substitute teaching is a different beast," she said. "You're considered a floater and, in the eyes of this office, dispensable."

I was taken aback by Katie-Anne's candor. Katie-Anne asked about my qualifications, even though she already held everything with her French-manicured nails.

So I laid down the facts. Seven semesters at Ball State, several more in Albany, finished up at UMass-Amherst, plus two semesters teaching. "I worked with high schoolers," I told her. "I also have some, not much, really, but some experience with elementary school children. But my subject is high school English. That's what I taught in Northampton."

I watched her click a keypad. "Well, then, you know how this works. Let's see." Her computer monitor filled with schedules. "We have a teacher out this fall because she's having a baby."

"I'll take it," I said.

"I haven't offered."

"According to the advertisement in the paper, I'm qualified."

"We do have other applicants," she said.

Katie-Anne seemed to be judging my sweat stains. She was a hard person to budge. She touched her cleft chin, as though confirming that the cute indentation was still there. Her work space startled me. Pens vertical in a cup, paper aligned at a ninety-degree angle with the edge of her desk. Not one errant object. She kept paper clips stacked atop each other in a little aluminum tray. "I'm curious," Katie-Anne said. "What exactly have you been doing for the past year?"

"Studying," I said.

"Studying what?"

"I was thinking of pursuing work in pharmaceuticals but changed my mind." I watched her bite her lip. "It's an interesting field," I added.

"Subbing, anyway, is a temp position," she said. "There are no benefits and no voting rights in the union. But back to you," she said. "You haven't been employed in over a year."

Her finger caressed the edge of my résumé, her pretty eyes glistening. A clock on her desk ticked loudly.

"I've been taking care of my grandmother," I told her. "She lives in a residential village. She's old, needs help. I moved back to care for her. There was no one left. It was either me or God."

The soft, inquisitive lines on Katie-Anne's forehead dissolved, and her eyes warmed, and her hand tenderly touched my forearm. It was the right door, the shot to the heart. I watched her lips open into a wet smile. Her eyes zoomed in on my marriage finger. Bare, as always.

"I'm close with my grandma too," she said.

As I finished filling out the new-employee forms, Katie-Anne returned to the portable office trailer with two iced coffees. She placed one cup on the desk for me and folded herself, gracefully, into her chair, perfectly upright again. She grabbed the desk, pulled herself closer, and watched me over the lip of her cup. Then she carefully placed her business card on my knee.

"If you need anything, please call," Katie-Anne said. "I wrote my mobile number in the event you need it. Substitutes can and do run into problems. You know, it's there, if you need it. If you need me." Her number was drawn in red ink and twice circled.

DUST SWEPT OVER the cemetery's roadway like snow over ice. The Polack was already waiting for me, idling in his old Ford pickup. I pulled up to my friend's dented bumper and noticed a fresh scratch on the tailgate in the shape of a lightning bolt. I honked the horn and Warsaw extended a special finger from his window, showing me his feelings.

It was Warsaw's day off, but he piled out dressed for work anyway, wearing steel-toed Carolina boots and heavy-duty canvas pants. He'd complemented the look with a faded yellow T-shirt that said, in black print, I ♥ JOHN WAYNE.

"You're late," Warsaw said, pointing a half-eaten banana at me.

"Interview went long."

"Nice pants."

"My grandpa's."

"So you ask me to meet," Warsaw said. "And I wait in a cemetery. In a *cemetery*. And you show up late wearing grandpa pants."

"Did you remember the tape measure?" I asked, already annoyed by him.

My friend tossed the banana peel in the bed of his truck, unzipped a bulging compartment on his pants, and extracted a tape measure. Inside the same pocket I also noticed a book. The Book. Warsaw had been lugging the paperback book around for months. "So you managed to get me here," he said.

I counted fifteen paces from the curb. I dropped a penny on the spot and asked Warsaw to stand on it and hold the end of the tape. At a cottonwood sapling propped up by rubber straps, I pivoted and counted another eight. The sunburned grass crunched under my tennies. From a crouch I scanned the yellowed plane. Stone to the right, stone on the left. It was a prime location, partially shaded by two grown cottonwoods.

"This is it," I said. "I'm only one payment away. It will soon be mine. They add feet on all four sides to account for casket size," I said. "So, what do you think?"

"You bought a *gravesite*?" Warsaw asked me. He released the tape and it recoiled back at me like a pulsating tail.

"First piece of property I've ever owned."

"Macabre," Warsaw said.

"I didn't want to buy it, but Nana wants to prepare. I walked every inch of this cemetery with the lady from the office. This is the best plot we could afford. What do you think?"

Sighing, Warsaw swiped hair from his raccoon eyes. My friend worked outdoors, and his protective goggles had left white ovals around his eyes. Some days he looked to me like a disheveled tweaker. Lean-bodied, same height, he'd always done better in school than me, but he was lazy. Warsaw walked the gravesite's perimeter, his sunburned nose twitching as he thought over my question.

"There's a nice view of the Rincons," I said.

"Sure, because views are really important when you're dead," Warsaw responded. He dabbed his forehead with his shirt. That sun was inescapable, bright as a camera flash.

From where we stood, I could make out the top of a golf pin. A triangular red flag snapped on a pole. Headstones peppered the lawn to the east and ended at a grassy hill pocked on the downslope by white-sand bunkers. Three men with golf bags over their shoulders ascended a distant knoll, one man pointing with the tip of his club. The men's tan, birdlike legs contrasted with their white bleached shorts.

"This place is really creeping me out," Warsaw said. "Dudes are golfing over there."

The Family Services Officer who sold me the plot said that Ajo Cemetery shared lawn with Del Sur Community Country Club. The fifty-acre cemetery was heavily irrigated, and up to a point the grounds were dotted with headstones, dark and white granite, rounded, cubed, but the headstones ended at an invisible barrier, giving way to a swath of grass used by golfers. I now wondered what would happen when bodies started populating the ninth fairway.

"So is this why you brought me here?" Warsaw said. "To show me this carnival?"

"Just give me your opinion. Do you like the spot or not? They said I could always upgrade."

Warsaw released a comprehensive exhale. "It's a patch of grass like any other patch of cemetery grass. Sure. It's terrific. A delightful place to spend forever." Sunlight shot through the fluttering leaves of a tree, catching him. He squinted.

"My interview went well," I said. "So I'm getting out, like we discussed."

"Don't say that if you don't mean it."

"I want to get back to teaching," I said. "Now's your chance."

A small smile spread across my friend's face. Warsaw had been asking me for months. He wanted to be involved in my pharmaceutical business, not because he liked caring for people, but because he was bored.

"You know I'm in," Warsaw said.

"It's not for everyone," I said.

"Let me try," he said.

I knew Warsaw wasn't after money. Money to him was theoretical. The knowledge that he was in for a large inheritance down the line had taken the wind out of his sails. His father built shopping malls, and for as long as I'd known him, a steady flow of those profits found their way into my friend's bank account. Warsaw, anyway, had yet to decide who he was, who he wanted to be, but I knew he was unwilling to pursue anything that required manning a desk. Even though he'd earned a fancy graduate degree, these days he worked Mondays and Tuesdays and Fridays driving an asphalt roller for the Arizona Highway Department.

"So," Warsaw said. "You bring me the stuff?"

"I wish I didn't," I said.

"But you did."

Indeed, I did. Warsaw gave me cash to buy him magazines that were only sold on the other side. Mexican magazines. Spanish-only. Warsaw didn't speak the language particularly well, but that didn't matter. He was after photos.

I opened the rear hatch of my car and slid out a shoebox teeming with Mexican gore tabloids—magazines with gruesome depictions of death in all its absurd forms. I couldn't stomach them. The photos were horrific, some of the most disturbing stuff I'd ever turned eyes upon. And as far as I could tell, Warsaw had trouble looking at the pictures, too. Insisting that I buy them was a recent thing. Warsaw had stopped reading books, except one: The Book. He carried The Book with him everywhere—either stuffed in his pocket or curled in his hand—a best-selling self-help tract written by a man named George Greg, some guru with big ideas.

Warsaw dove into a copy of ¡Alarma! and I watched his eyes toughen. "George Greg has one golden rule," Warsaw told me, yet again. "Scare yourself. Prove you're alive by scaring yourself. I look at these and I see what the man's talking about. My heart. My heart's really going right now." He held up the magazine, but I refused to look. "Mexican culture is on top of it. In awe of it. They either celebrate it or make fun of it. You should ask your pretty little chica about it. She probably knows a lot."

"She's not my chica," I said.

"You want her to be your chica."

"Stop calling her chica."

A social worker at Paseo del Sol had caught my attention. No man with functioning brain cells could miss her pretty face. "She works inside the building at the end," I said and closed the hatch. "I don't even know her name. That's everything I know."

"Well, go inside," Warsaw said. "Introduce yourself."

"You don't understand what it means to go inside the building at the end. I've never *been* inside. They lock the doors. Visitors need a special code."

"Oh, Jesus Cristo. Look at you. You're blushing," Warsaw said.

"The heat."

"You think this woman hung the moon. Grow a pair," Warsaw said. "Man up. Introduce yourself."

"And what incredible things do I have to say to a social worker?"

"I don't know. Maybe you should read George Greg's book. Scare yourself. You might be surprised."

DANNI ZEPEDA'S reservation was awash in black market goods, and that's why I loved it. Tax-free cigarettes and legalized gambling were merely the veneer. Tohono O'odham territory was a quote-unquote huge foreign shipping zone forty miles west of Tucson, accessed by Highway 86. Her rez was so big that it spilled over the border into Mexico. The things that happened on her reservation were frequently mentioned in the paper, and I paid attention when they were. Every day and every night people came rushing across this section of borderland. Convoys of 4x4s raced north during the night. Mexican mules, paid by the kilo, jogged across alkali wastelands with parcels of marijuana, coke, and meth strapped on their backs. These days the rez was a dangerous place to call home, but it also happened to be an excellent place for me to bump into cheap pharmaceuticals.

Sitting in her home office, I watched Danni arch back in her executive leather swivel and tug back a thick rubber band. She was aiming at the lowest shelf on her freshly painted, lemon-colored wall. I held in a breath, and prepared for it. Handwoven bear-grass and yucca baskets embellished the uppermost shelf. Danni's office reeked of plastic sheeting, and a swamp cooler, shoved into a crude hole, blew semi-cool air into her black, tousled hair. At last she released the rubber band, struck a fine mesh of web, and tumbled forward in her chair.

"There's no design to black widow webs," she told me. "The insects live in chaos." Danni, who enjoyed taking her time with things, dipped a pinkie into a turquoise choker. Her V-neck plunged.

"Where is she?" I asked. I didn't see a spider, only a web.

"Trust me, she's around," Danni said. "She's probably hanging inverted somewhere close. She won't leave her web. She found her spot. She'll hold on. She'll fight to the death." Danni plopped a ballpoint pen in her mouth and chewed the end. "So, la la, how's your granny?"

"She found her spot. She's holding on."

I followed her through a set of French doors that opened onto a cement patio. The patio had been painted alarmingly white. Light filled my eyes, and I went teary.

"Like I always say, prettier than a baby seal," Danni said to me and latched a tuft of black hair over her ear. "Your eyelashes, I mean." She rubbed a sun tear into my cheek, as she'd done when I was a boy. Danni was a woman of volume, not fat, just powerful. She was inches taller and several years older and had a burly but feminine quality that I'd always found dimly attractive. Veins in her forearms were proof that she spent her nights curling dumbbells. I never knew arms could have such sculpted muscles at the wrist, but hers did.

We walked over washed-stone gravel toward a sizable work shed. The tin roof was rusty and the exterior was splintered. A large propane tank sat beside it. Danni palmed a metallic door lock and scrolled through the combo until, at last, it popped. The interior was completely refurbished with white tiled floors, stainless-steel counters, and dozens of house-plants. Greenery hung from ceiling hooks and gave the shed a tropical atmosphere. The restaurant-sized refrigerator made a thick sucking sound when Danni opened it. Inside, I saw tiny vials of liquid Epogen standing neat and upright next to a jar of fat-free mayonnaise.

"Exactly what I need," I said.

"I've been asking around for weeks. Finally got some for you."

"One of my clients. Her grandkid," I said. "Diagnosed with leukemia." On Clam Bake Night, during dinner, the elderly woman had tugged my pant leg and whispered her special request.

"Well," Danni said, picking up a plastic squirt bottle, "glad I can help." She squeezed and mist settled on our necks. As I watched her caress the plants, it occurred to me, especially when I saw her kiss a leaf, that there wasn't much excitement out here other than her plants. Plenty of white light and blue sky and brown shades and warmth and clean distances, but also, as it happened, too much time for a person to reflect upon loneliness. "If I keep my ladies outside, forget it," she told me. "Inside," she said, gesturing at the domed skylight, "look how they grow."

I lifted a cold vial from its container. "Just as it should be."

"I follow instructions," she said.

"Hard to come across this stuff down Mexico way. At least in Nogales."

"You need to dig deeper." She returned the pen to her mouth. "Every-thing's down there. You just need to know under which rocks to peek." The pen sat in her mouth as though she was smoking it. "Anything you want can be found in Mexico City, particularly Tepito. Tepito is the swollen teat."

My cut from the vials would cover the month's gas and electric with a little left over. Also inside the fridge, in the egg compartment, was an army of small insulin bottles. Danni was unlucky. Like many of my clients, she had the sugar disease. It was the reason she'd fallen into this work. And whenever I couldn't find something special, I rang her up.

We'd met long ago, twenty or so years in the past, when as a teen Danni relocated from the rez to her father's house two doors down from Nana.

Throughout her teens Danni bounced between rez and town. We had for the longest time a quasi-friendship that flirted with becoming something true, but she was older, with different concerns. Later, when I'd return from Northampton to visit my grandmother, we'd have a beer and then break contact. This time our friendship stuck, and we'd even tried going on a date, but rather than romance Danni spent the evening teaching me the finer details of moving pharmaceuticals, telling me how she'd become the unofficial pharmacist to the O'odham people, and it occurred to me, as I arranged vials inside a Styrofoam cooler, that I owed Danni a nice dinner, a movie, drinks.

She watched me affix ice packs to the tray with rubber bands, and when I stood, she stepped closer. Freckles sprinkled her smooth brown neck. A few faint black hairs decorated her upper lip—barely noticeable, but there. For a moment I imagined touching my tongue to them. She smelled like cement, and she blinked, and something in her eyes shifted, the light growing deeper. "You must be doing okay with the older folks," she said softly. The pen bobbed in her mouth.

"I don't charge markup. I keep business fair."

"Wait, what? You sell at cost?" she asked.

"Just the service fee. That's it."

"Well, shit, you can't be clearing much."

"The money I make carries me," I said. "Besides, I never thought I'd be doing it for this long. Fact is, I'm getting out."

Danni winced. "And what, get a job? A real job? That would be a shame. You open shop, create a niche, only to abandon it? People like you, Sid."

"I offer a service. Low risk and win-win. Everyone saves money."

"Listen." She tapped my nose with her pen. A thin string of saliva momentarily connected us. "I know about other opportunities. We could go in together."

"What kind of quantities?" I asked, to humor her.

"Good money," she said and gently tugged back the collar of my shirt. An arctic breeze from the fridge washed over my nipples. In a quick still-shot fantasy Danni stood before me, shirtless. Her bra would be made of heavy, reinforced fabric, enough to hold what Danni had. Imaginary thumbs rolled across her collarbone and loosened her shoulder straps. Sometimes just looking at her muscles weakened me.

"What's the haul?" I asked. "Boxes? Are you thinking about bringing boxes or something? DEA doesn't appreciate boxes of drugs spilling over the border. Boxes over la línea can mean twenty years in some states. How much, tell me, are you talking? Because I want to talk you out of it."

"Not how much," Danni said. "Who."

"People?" I yanked her hand down. "I'm no coyote, Danni. That's dangerous. And organized. Besides, haven't you been following the news? Someone is picking off ilegales out there."

"Probably another pissed-off rancher," she said.

"Some vigilante has been patrolling the border with a high-powered Remington and shooting immigrants as they cross over. The maniac is dropping them like pheasants."

"That doesn't involve us. Look, am I dangerous?"

"Getting shot in the desert, I'd say, contains elements of danger, yes." I tapped the cooler lid down.

"People are safer with me than with some scumbag pollero, and you know it. Polleros treat people like cattle, concerned only with money. Taking their money and then shoving them around."

"You want money," I said.

"I don't want my mom, anymore, to live off commodities. Besides, we've always wandered this land, and no government will tell me, them, who can come and go. If I make a little money doing it, okay, that's nice, plus my mom doesn't have to eat canned food. The sugar, all the sugar. Why do you think we have so much diabetes?"

"But it's dangerous. Out there, out there in the desert."

"It's in our nature. Who we are, as human beings, we move. I'm just helping people do it. Helping people be people."

"I don't know," I said.

Customs agents saw my light blue dented Honda a lot. The lifers at the Port of Entry were convinced that I traveled south for cheap massages and private cock tickle festivals. They thought I had a nasty habit because that's what I told them. I tossed them matchbooks printed with the logos of whorehouses along Calle Escondido. To subvert focus, I acted the part of a loudmouth, just another undersexed American man proud of my disgusting conquests. If the agents ever wanted to spot-check my glove compartment they'd be in for a surprise. Flick a lever and an extra, hidden window opened. Superglued to the inside paneling were dried mustard seeds and cured rabbit fur in the event agents decided to use the dogs. It was a precaution. I liked to keep careful. I ran a dozen or so bottles at a time—two dozen max. I didn't skim off the top and I kept business simple, honest.

Outside, a saguaro threw a flexed shadow across the hood of my car. Behind me Danni's footfalls raked the gravel sloppily and sounded to me like pouts. Two jets in formation streaked through the ashen sky, their contrails dividing the heavens into quadrants. One thing struck me as true: Danni had the view. Olive-green, chest-high brush rolled toward the horizon, and the only thing stopping it from running on forever was a distant swell of mountains, bubbling from the earth and smashing into a sky that outlined the ridges in blue.

I mopped a pile of thrift-store cassette tapes to the floor and set the Styrofoam cooler on the passenger seat. I belted it in. Danni inspected the child's car seat through the window, ogling it, but she refrained from commenting. When I started the car, Danni swung her boot onto the hood, throwing the pen into her mouth again. Her well-worn jeans were tattered and rode high.

"Just give the idea some thought," she said. "That's all I ask. You, me, we're good. I know you need money."

I rolled down my window. "You'll have better luck winning your pension off video poker," I said. "But listen, do me this favor. I'm on the hunt for Mexican scrip pads. Official médico forms. Doctor's pads. It'll save me money." I watched her lick the demolished pen. "And by the way, I keep asking myself," I said. "What year were you born? I've been trying to remember our age difference."

Danni laughed to herself. "You know better than that, soldier."

4   The café hummed with low chatter. Japanese lanterns dangled from exposed beams over our heads, and the teenage barista, a girl with pixie hair organized by blue barrettes, called my order number even though I was standing directly in front of her. She wrapped my chocolate-drizzled cookie in wax paper, slid it across the counter, and tossed change on top. As I set the mugs in front of Seymour Epstein, he said, "Such downy flesh. So unpuckered. Such untried shores."

The old man was busily watching two college-age kids play footsie on a wide, plush sofa. He appeared fascinated by the pair. He studied them through amber-tinted tortoiseshell glasses. His old-man prescription made his eyeballs appear enormous.

"Let's introduce ourselves," he whispered to me. He looked down at his mug. "You forgot the sugar."

A bowl of sugar was on the table, beside the sweeteners. I pointed at it.

"Ah, screw it," he said. "Stuff messes with my blood numbers anyway." The old man liked pretending he didn't have Type II adult-onset diabetes, that he didn't have any health issues, that his hands were as steady as a surgeon's, his heart as sturdy as a twenty-year-old's. I knew better. I kept Epstein's stat sheet in my grandfather's file cabinet. I had every client's stat sheet—everyone filled out a form. After my pharmacist told me about Mr. Garland Bills, I now kept informed about the health conditions I was helping to treat.

"Did you see your doctor about those headaches yet?" I asked him.

"That dickhead doesn't know a goddamn thing." Epstein swatted the air. "Man probably bought his diploma from one of those low-rent Caribbean schools," he went on.

"But you're having headaches?"

"Now? No. My eardrums buzz sometimes. I'm losing hearing," he said. "So what and who cares? I'm eighty-two years old, cryin' out loud. Forget it. I'm fine."

Epstein lifted his feet onto a chair, getting more comfortable in his old haunt. The clientele tonight was mostly students—kids burdened by classes, what to wear, whom to date. I'd tried talking him into going somewhere else because the Standard Bean was too close to the university, and I wasn't particularly fond of the street or its shops, which were eager to turn eighteen-year-olds into retro hippies. Epstein was a professor emeritus of mathematics, and I knew age had forced him into retirement. That, plus his colleagues had urged him. He'd finally given up at seventy-seven, he'd told me, when the equations on the chalkboard began resembling petroglyphs. Now in his twilight years, Epstein liked to act like the fraternity boys he once instructed, believing that his ninth decade was a chance to reclaim his second.

When the old man bit into a sugar-free cupcake, I saw a lifetime of dental work in his mouth. Wires connected two teeth in the back. Gold crowns capped molars.

"The knees of an innocent," Epstein whispered. "Did you see the way she tapped his neck with her finger?" Epstein tapped the air with his. "I should return to teaching," he said. "I should sharpen my chalk."

Epstein's big, magnified eyes worked pendulum-like behind his glasses. It looked like he was adding and subtracting the various body parts necessary for a sexual equation. Epstein was a regimented person, and despite his age he had the solid, compact body of an acrobat. He was completely bald except for two stripes of white hair on the sides of his head. Tonight he'd covered his liver-spotted dome with a houndstooth touring cap. He had the supple glow of someone who had applied lotion to the dry spots and trimmed back the overgrowth. I knew Epstein got plenty of play on campus, yet he preferred to go out on the town, in pursuit, on the hunt.

"I'm getting worried about Gwendolyn Wetherbee," I said, trying to budge his attention away from the coeds.

"Yeah, well, she's a migraine, all right," he said.

"I'm thinking of cutting off her supply. Bringing only the meds she needs."

"Ease her off slowly, though," he said. "She's had a tough few years with her husband's illness. That kind of nightmare should never happen to any-one. And let's not forget, she lives on my floor. We have enough midnight emergencies out of her. Gillian, across the hall, has started a transfer peti-tion. Gillian wants her moved."

"Moved out?"

Epstein nodded. I thought about it. A petition to relocate Ms. Wether-bee: to another floor, possibly another facility. And it hit me: no more Ms. Wetherbee! "We should at least introduce her to Narcotics Anonymous," I said. "Ten days off opiates and she'd normalize. Someone should get the old bird help. Each time I visit, it's just, the guilt."

"On the other hand," Epstein said, dipping cake into his coffee, "let her have fun. I'm sure the Shopping Channel is more palatable on drugs. And, you know, it *was* nice to see those dilated pupils in class. Their tender, con-tent faces. That boy with the falling eyelids, headphones wrapped snug around his neck. I had a student go down once from cardiac arrest."

"From drugs?"

"We'll never know," Epstein said. "It was the final class of the semester."

Gradually we fell into our typical café trance. The café was warm. We slumped in our chairs. We took time finishing our drinks, crumpling nap-kins into mugs. Our small white plates looked sufficiently smeared, which gave me a feeling of accomplishment.

I noticed Epstein get sidetracked when two brunettes traipsed loudly through the door. Both were tall and athletic and outfitted in red and blue university colors. T-shirts hung off trim torsos and above too tight work-out shorts. Epstein drew a breath.

But I could have cared less about them. I took out a pen and smoothed out a dollar bill on the table. I had a few bad habits. One was writing my ex-girlfriend's phone number on dollar bills and then giving these dollar bills to perfect strangers. It was juvenile, and irresponsible, but it made me like the world a little more, it made me think of things more evenly, and though I needed the dollar, though I needed this and every dollar, it was after all only a dollar, and it was worth it. I printed Juliet's number underneath IN GOD WE TRUST on the backside. I duplicated the digits on the front. As a final flourish I drew a wispy flame above the "1" in the upper right corner, turning the numeral into a candle.

"Ready to go?" I said.

"Already? Hot chicks in here tonight," Epstein said.

I dropped the marked-up dollar in the tip jar on the way out. The barista smiled, but I lingered too long, wanting to be congratulated or something, and her mouth went into a line. Epstein was already at the door, his hand on his lower back, as though touching some phantom pain. I noticed the old man's touring cap on the floor, and one of the athletic brunettes was bending to pick it up. The elastic of her shorts rode low, making visible the top portion of a purple G-string. Even with his heavy eyeglass prescription, I knew the old man could see her just fine. The girl was built. In her tight shorts she was a three-car pileup.

Traffic was light, the gutters strewn with the weekly newspaper, and in my rearview mirror some joker thought it would be hilarious to ride my draft. The truck was close, and nearing. So close it could have kissed my bumper.

"Just pass already," Epstein said, his palms pressed to the dash.

"If I brake, he'll roll right over us," I said.

I sped through another light but couldn't shake the truck. I changed lanes. So did the truck. I slowed, hoping the truck would shoot around me. Its headlights filled the car's interior. Apparently the truck was headed in the same direction, but after a bit it turned down a side street.

"Thank God," I said.

Our destination was a huge fitness outlet that abutted the train tracks downtown. I veered into an open slot along the curb, but when I opened my door the truck from moments before blew past and almost removed the door from its hinges. A warm rush of wind filled the car. The truck braked and shuddered to a stop. Its backup lights illuminated as it pulled beside us. I looked at Epstein. The old man blinked. Tinted windows obscured the driver. It was a big number, a white Ford F-150. Very quickly a man jumped out, ran around the truck, and laid the dirty end of his cowboy boot against my door, shutting me back inside. Epstein squeaked. The man stabbed his finger against the brim of his white Stetson, inching it up to reveal a grin. He gave us a wild-eyed staredown before retreating to his truck and revving the engine. Finally he drove off. We digested the event in silence, composing ourselves, expelling it with deep breaths.

"Well," Epstein said after several terrified moments, "we frightened him."

"Only a fool would have."

"He doesn't know who he's messing with."

"I've seen him," I said.

Epstein turned. "You know that jerk?"

"Saw him the other day," I said. "On campus."

"What does he want?"

"I don't know."

"Well, fucking find out."

Epstein slowly opened the door and limped toward the store's entrance, shaking his head. Tonight Epstein selected a new wall: Cardio Sculpt. The old man's tastes were refined by now. He had recently hired a neighbor's grandson to install shelving in his hallway closet. Now his DVD library was organized newest to oldest. The old man walked the aisle, thrumming his thumb against plastic spine cases. He tugged one out. The cover showed a young woman clad in a snug green bodysuit.

The women's-only fitness outlet carried every imaginable type of exercise equipment. Stability balls, kickboxing gear, and jump ropes with pink sparkly handles. A female mannequin dangled from a rubber swing, its legs folded into a position I never knew possible.

"So hard to choose," Epstein said to me. "It's a world of possibilities and the probabilities of disappointment are high. *Ten Target Toners Volume 2* was a gigantic letdown. And once you select one, it means you don't pick the other. This is a true zero-sum relationship." He snorted.

A blond woman was staring at us from down the aisle, projecting her embarrassment onto me with pursed lips, as though I was guilty of bringing a monkey into the store.

"They can take away my driver's license," Epstein said to her, "but they can't take away this." He held up a video with an attractive woman gripping two kettle bells. The lady cringed and walked away.

I left the old man to his fitness DVDs and browsed. On display inside the glass counter was an impressive array of pedometers. Muzak crackled from an overhead speaker system and the store smelled of plastic. For a moment I remembered with fondness my mother trying out various exercise regimes, and our house filling with the requisite equipment, and the accomplished sheen on her pretty forehead as she made dinner. All of that was such a long time ago.

When I went looking for him again, Epstein was already at the register, holding two bottles of deep-tissue sports massage lotion. Stacked on the counter were three Cardio Sculpt DVDs. The uppermost box showed a woman on her back, feet in the air, doing bicycles.

"That one is water-based," the cashier, a man with patchy facial hair, explained. "The other is synthetic."

"Water-based," Epstein said. He held the bottle to his face and tried reading the ingredients. "Or synthetic. Water, synthetic. Tell me. Which glides best?"

"Sir?" the cashier said.

"Bag it all," Epstein said. "I'll try both."

The streetlight illuminated a size 10 dent on my car door. What was worse, the man who had applied the dent was now parked down the block, hiding among shadows beneath a burned-out light. A tingle worked up my spine. The stranger must have circled the block. The last thing I was looking for was confrontation. I told Epstein about the truck and the old man squinted and spun his pink plastic bag into a makeshift weapon. It rustled in the breeze.

"Get in the car," I said.

"Don't need to tell me."

When we passed the F-150, the truck didn't follow us. I checked the rearview mirror, realizing after a mile that we were safe.

"You've *seen* that man?" Epstein asked me.

"Just the other day. Around campus."

"Did you do something to upset him?"

"I don't know."

"Oy vey."

The old man's date was waiting on the sidewalk outside the restaurant. Epstein's poor eyesight prevented him from seeing her. We were across the street, at the light. As far as I could tell, she looked to be at least two decades his junior. Red hair fanned out over her coat's fuzzy collar.

"She just waved at us," I said.

"Peg here already?" Epstein asked. "Isn't she beautiful? She's beautiful. Isn't she beautiful?"

Oh, there was plenty of Peg to keep a man warm. "A peach."

I eased to the curb and Epstein lowered the visor. He inspected his teeth in the mirror. "Aren't you forgetting something? My snacks?" he said.

I sighed, leaned over, opened the glove compartment, and flipped the special lever. The hidden window slid sideways. I double-checked the name on the bottle. Sildenafil citrate, 100-mil doses. Epstein ate them like candy. "All you need is half," I told him. "Fifty mils should do the trick."

"Well, let's pray for priapism," Epstein said and opened the door.

I grabbed his forearm. "What about me?"

"Still?" he said.

"Still," I said. Epstein took out his wallet and handed me a ten. It was the price he paid for me to cart him around.

The old man slammed the door. I watched him lift Peg's hand and kiss her, old-fashioned-like, on the knuckles. He was shorter than her by a foot. Behind the wheel, in the dark, I watched Epstein hold the door open, ladies first, a true gentleman. And as they disappeared inside, I saw the old man pinch Peg, to her giggling delight, on the ass.

FUNDAMENTAL TO LIFE at Paseo del Sol, unspoken amid the balanced meals, the outings to Biosphere 2, and the twice-a-week senior ballet class, was the community's true purpose: It was twenty acres of planned death.

Outside on the casita's patio, I punched numbers. I'd set my grandfather's old calculator on my papers. The white numerals had rubbed off its ancient buttons. A warm, dry breeze spread down from the north, and cicadas buzzed in the bushes.

Income equaled expenses flowing out. And the numbers, even more, didn't factor in the unexpected. The only way to improve business was to raise my fee, assume more border runs, more clients, and get more involved. But just thinking about that made me tired. Besides, I was getting out.

I saw Warsaw hovering behind the sliding glass door. My friend poked his head out. "Two more RBIs," Warsaw said. "Put those papers away. You're missing the game."

"San Francisco?"

"Los Angeles." He grinned. We had a twenty-dollar bill riding on the outcome. And Warsaw was up.

"Another minute," I told him.

Growing old was expensive. Money accumulated over the course of a life, sure. There were a lot of wrinkled fingers wrapped around wads of old bills. But old age was also the time in life when people spent the most to keep themselves alive.

In order to afford Paseo del Sol's entrance fee, my grandmother had liquidated her nest egg—eighty thousand dollars in stocks. And yet, each month, the corporation nailed us with a long list of operating costs. Footnoted in her contract, in six-point type, was a laundry list of extraneous fees. Wellness program fees, shuttle service fees, on-call nurse fees, on-site audiologist fees, water usage, recycling, security, off-campus recreation, and so on. My grandmother's contract was tiered. She occupied space according to her ability. Whatever happened health-wise, the facility would care for her needs. But wheelchairs, diapers, and supplemental dietary beverages were not included. She had an apartment in an assisted-living tower, three square meals, nine-to-five access to nursing staff, and all the social and spiritual activities offered. She received full red-carpet treatment as long as I kept up with the monthly fees.

But I had heard stories. I understood what could happen. Nana had an acquaintance, Dee Thompson, a friendly old bird with feathery blue hair and blouses as bright as lollipops. Months after moving into La Catalina, Dee Thompson had done a face-plant on her bathroom tile. Fractured her hip. Management had relocated her to a shared double room in the building at the end. She'd been there ever since, behind locked doors, and instead of recovering, as everyone had expected her to do, her health had declined.

The conversation that set everything rolling had been awkward, as usual. My mother now lived in Anchorage, embedded in a healthy but boring second marriage, and she hadn't been very interested in seeing to the affairs of her dead ex-husband's aging mother. The two women had always respected and tolerated each other, in that way business associates respect and tolerate each other, but after my dad's death their relationship tapered off.

So I assumed responsibility. It had taken me months to organize Nana's paperwork. The first thing to pique my interest was the skyrocketing cost of her *eleven* different medications. Pills were a major cash-suck. Pharmaceuticals alone were nibbling away at her diminishing bank account, even with insurance. So one afternoon I followed Danni Zepeda's advice and crossed the border to Nogales. That I could cross over and buy the same drugs for one-fifth the price sparked the idea. Nana, the good citizen, disapproved. She was a yearly voter, active in the local library, not a parking violation to her name. She disliked my plan. At one point she even surprised me by threatening to phone the authorities. But we needed money to cover bills. Plus, it saved us money. I began introducing myself to Nana's neighbors and friends, showing off my best smile. The business, born from necessity, grew.

I heard Warsaw yelping inside the casita. I pushed a button on the calculator and the display went to "0."

"A question," Warsaw said when I opened the door. With a raised finger he ordered me into the kitchen, where I watched him riffle through the utensil drawer. Warsaw then dropped to a knee and peered under the sink. He inspected the dirty tile under the oven. "Obviously you've got a problem in here," Warsaw said. He looked up from his knees, like he was praying. "What is that horrible smell?"

"Something crawled inside the wall to die," I said.

"Get rid of it," Warsaw said. "Your kitchen reeks of tainted meat and iodine. Disgusting. And it's hard to pay attention to the ball game."

"Are you ready for your first run?" I asked him, dragging him off topic.

Warsaw blinked. "Of course I'm ready."

"I need supplies from Agua Prieta."

I handed him a list, including a map, and the name and directions to the hole-in-the-wall Mexican pharmacy. Warsaw studied the med names on the sheet.

"So, that's it? Go down, drive back? It's that simple?"

"It's that simple," I said.

My grandmother's casita, a two-bedroom, one-bath affair, was in the Menlo Park district on Palomas Avenue. Afternoon shadows dropped from "A" Mountain and bathed the patio in blue light. Massive old saguaros rose off the hill, and from a distance the hillsides resembled pincushions. It was 1,130 square feet, with old-fangled pronghorn antelope wallpaper in the hallway. I liked the place. I had always liked the place. Bubba had set down red tile in the kitchen and hardwood floors throughout. There were laminate counters next to the stove, a non-working fireplace, and Mexican blanco fino marble in the bathroom. About the pronghorn wallpaper: I had considered removing it. Every time I headed down the hall for a piss I'd think I'd wandered into Wyoming. I slept in Nana's room but hadn't gotten too comfortable. I was fixing the place up for an eventual sale. We had shipped most of Nana's furniture to her apartment on the morning of her move. Since then, I'd filled in the gaps here and there with furnishings from Goodwill.

Warsaw reconvened in his usual position near the TV. On his back, knees up, using his George Greg book as a pillow. He turned the volume up. He was positioned to attempt a sit-up, but I knew better. He was too lazy for one. He looked like elongated bones assembled inside loose-fitting clothing. Even so, part-time highway labor had hardened my friend's arms.

"I drove out to the reservation today," I told Warsaw. "Turns out Danni has her hands in other things. Such as, such as. She asked if I was interested in running people over the border."

On TV the Giants were at bat. "What people?" he said.

"I don't know. People who'd rather live here than over there."

"Where?"

"They'd rather be here," I said. "Rather than over there, in Mexico."

"That's funny," Warsaw said. He tipped his head forward, sipping his beer. "I'd rather be over there."

"I'll never understand how you graduated from Yale."

I returned to the patio and shoved my papers inside folders, listening to the hiss from my neighbor's welding torch. A low pink adobe wall separated our conjoined yards. Through a small cubed window I saw flying sparks.

Alejandro was a sculptor, a man with a gray bush sprouting from his chin. It was my suspicion that he had a raging case of social anxiety disorder. He was so nervous whenever he talked—so nervous that his fingers shook. The man refused to look me in the eye. Our conversations always skipped across the surface, flat pebbles that hopped several times but ultimately sank. The weather. The heat. How the mountains change color. Oh the dramatic West, and so on. Installed in his front yard was a gang of galvanized steel gunslingers. Each sculpture was ten feet high, four eerie figures captured during a quick-draw, their nonexistent feet buried beneath a plane of round gray pebbles. It would be hugely hilarious if Alejandro weren't so serious about his art pieces. Little red price tags dangled from their pinkies. As if anyone was going to slam on the brakes and buy them.

When I went inside, Warsaw was not in the living room. The baseball game had been replaced by a Spanish-language telenovela, some hospital drama. I heard the sink whining behind the bathroom door. I walked down the hall. I tried the handle. Locked.

"Compadre?" I said.

"Go away," Warsaw said on the other side.

"I have to use."

"A minute, dickhead."

"I'm waiting."

After some time Warsaw knuckled open the door. A thick lather of shaving cream coated his left arm. For some reason his other arm was raw, and very red, and completely shaved from knuckles to shoulder. He was holding my razor. Hairs clogged the blades. I saw his book on the counter.

I was too afraid to ask. So I asked, "Who won?"

"It went to the Dodgers," Warsaw said. "You owe me an Andy Jackson."

WARSAW HARASSED ME until I relented and agreed to head out for a drink—*one drink*—to stare at women over the rims of pint glasses. It was one of the more masochistic things we liked to do.

On a huge television screen at the Green Onion was a muted round of golf, the professional players dressed like adult toddlers. The place smelled of French fries. We fielded stares from the regulars as we lingered near the entrance, especially Warsaw, who proudly held on to a book—his Book, The Book—as though he was about to preach from it.

We waited at a tall round table with high-backed stools, and the waitress, for some reason, was dressed in a bumblebee costume. Her black-and-yellow outfit had a foam stinger that bounced as she walked.

"Why do you insist on bringing that book?" I asked Warsaw.

My friend scratched a razor nick on his arm. "I feel close to him, to George Greg, is all. I never read a mind like his in college. Can't we leave it at that?"

"The TV called him some kind of cult leader." I glanced at my friend's shaved arm. "And I'm beginning to believe it."

"Nonsense."

"Take a look at the cover. The book doesn't even have a title."

"His face," Warsaw said. "Look at his face, how content. That's as good a title as any."

The cover did indeed show the man's face, with his name wedged beneath his chin. "How can a bald man's face be a book title?" I asked. "That's the stupidest thing I've ever heard. Just be careful. That book might touch your mind wrong."

"It touches my mind just fine."

"I don't trust any man with two first names," I said.

When the waitress returned with our beers, Warsaw set a generous tip on her oval serving tray and said to her, "*Bzzzz.*"

"Boss makes me wear it," she said. "I know, stupid. Either one of you know the name of a good lawyer?"

"*Bzzzz,*" Warsaw said again, watching the stinger bounce as she went to another table. "Nix the bee outfit and she's cute. What do you think?"

"Why are you such an asshole?"

"Hold on." Warsaw raised a finger. "Ladies over at the bar."

Mid-thirties, dressed for a night out, smoky eye shadow, smart-looking. Two of them, friends. The taller woman—strong calves, didn't slouch—looked to me like she took her daily multivitamins. Her companion, shorter, rounder in the hips, was what men with certain skills called an easy target. The two women won the attention of every beer-buzzed man in the place, collectively half a dozen. "There must be a better way to meet someone," I said.

"We're not friends with many women," Warsaw said. "We don't do yoga, the mall, church. We have fewer options. Our best bet? Sit tight and look like we're discussing property."

I drew off the icy beer, already preparing to leave. But Warsaw was getting comfortable on his stool. He liked being here. Bars bored me. Bars were once familiar treading ground, because bars were dependable. Spend enough time in them, you began to know the substances inside and the character types, the losers and powders and machismos and pills and friendly queers and the bad and funny and violent drunks. Most of all, the easy targets.

When I'd set out from Tucson at eighteen, I traveled around the country like a bird in flight. It had been hard to stay in any city for long because I never felt at rest. Whenever I stayed somewhere too long, psychic moss crept in. It was impossible to commit to any city, much less any relationship. To me that was akin to agreeing on the place where I'd be buried. Turns were happening now, at thirty-three, good, painful kinds of turns. I was emerging from a prolonged adolescent cocoon—that distinctly American bubble that falsely promised I'd never have to stop, never have to settle, never have to make a decision of any consequence.

These shifts in me started the day I met Juliet at an acquaintance's barbecue in Northampton. The two of us clicked, or perhaps, something in both of us snapped. Regardless, we were good together for several years. Juliet gave my life consistency. At the time that was what I needed. She was opinionated, and she belted out laughter as loud as a bullhorn. Her convictions were unmovable. She was also thriving in her career. Eventually I finished school and landed a teaching job, the first solid job of my life. Juliet had seen in me some kind of potential, and I milked those thoughts. She didn't put up with my bullshit. And somehow, I didn't run. I didn't leave. Instead, I moved in. Two years into the relationship Juliet carefully set an explosive squarely upon my chest, detonated it, and now I was back in Tucson, inside a sports bar, watching my old high school friend pick apart a soggy beer coaster.

"What about the woman who just walked in?" I asked Warsaw. "She's interesting enough."

"Right, right. She seems tricky and dangerous," he said. "In other words, my type." The young woman in question had tattoos all over her arms so that the world would know she had an opinion. We watched her pull up a stool beside a gentleman with more muscles than both of us. Warsaw shrugged.

Customers came in, had a drink, left. It was a slow night. Not much of a selection other than the original pair, and apparently we appeared as desperate as they did. Eventually they initiated eye contact, which was all the motivation Warsaw needed. He bucked and hopped off his stool. Then he won them over by ingratiating himself into their laughter.

"Annie, Bess, Sid," Warsaw said when he walked over with them.

We decided on a game of four-way pool, Men vs. Women. Bess had a cute nose, smelled of citrus, exciting hands, but her friend, Annie, the athletic one, seemed achingly bored. She was here, like me, as her friend's accessory.

"Let them win," Warsaw whispered when I dropped the seven into a corner pocket. Midway through the game—we were dismantling them, the women were terrible at pool—Bess leaned against her cue and fired the typical question at me. "What line of work you in?" she asked.

"Oh, he deals drugs," Warsaw said before I could answer.

"What he means to say is," I said, taking huge gulps of my beer, "I don't."

Warsaw sawed the cue over his knuckles. "Tell them. We're all friends here. Sid's a drug dealer." I looked at Warsaw, giving him wide, questioning eyes. "Oh, come off it," Warsaw said.

Bess was drawn in. She put a finger to her nostril, pushed in, and winked at me. "We could be friends," she said.

"And what about you?" Annie asked Warsaw.

"I do nothing," he said.

"You must do something."

"I like to scare the shit out of myself," he told her.

Annie's bottom lip squirmed, as though a fly had landed on it. The eight ball fell into a side pocket. Men won. Annie and Bess sequestered themselves in the corner by the jukebox. Decision made, they thanked us for the game and walked away. Soon they were engaged in conversation with a couple of beefy types at the bar. After a bit we watched Bess follow one guy out the side door.

"I'm quitting women anyway," Warsaw said. He rolled his cue across the table.

"Weld your mouth shut and we'd have a chance."

"George Greg's golden rule," he said, reminding me about his stupid new philosophy. "Scare yourself." Warsaw glanced at the mirrored clock over the bar. "Still drive around with that baseball bat in your car?"

It was early yet. We hit the liquor store, then the baseball field. The lights went off at night and hovered above us like steel cranes. The field smelled elemental, of dirt, of chalk, and it was lit only by the yellowy glow from a dim bulb inside the restroom.

Warsaw assumed the dark mound, set a bottle of gin at his feet, loaded balls in his pocket, and warmed up with a fast pitch. I was unable to see the ball until it was past me. In our younger days, when we had better knees, Warsaw and I played plenty of ball. Played on the same teams. High school, county league. Warsaw went All-State. He had been that good, and he still had an arm.

I stepped out, then back inside, the batter's box, feet apart, knees bent. Another ball smashed into the backstop.

"Take a swing," Warsaw said.

Darkness swallowed my friend, and for a moment I found myself in a perfectly comfortable, murky space, the breeze in my ears, calmed by starlight, content with the bat in my hands. In my mind's eye I took one perfect, solid swing, the meat connecting rightly to the ball, and I could almost sense the good, smart sting in my forearms, could almost hear the dwindling whistle of a well-hit ball hustling toward deep center.

The warm shadowy field carried me back to when I was sixteen. I remembered stepping to the plate during play-offs, the eyes of the crowd on my stance and on the tip of my swaying bat. Nana watched from the bleachers. I remembered the shit talk coming from behind the catcher's mask, from the husky kid with bad acne and fingers like sausages. The umpire squeezed up to the kid. Squaring off against the pitcher, sixty feet and six inches away, I was steeled for an honest fight. The opposing team was from Tempe, sonsabitches all. The players punched their gloves and chewed gum and spit sunflower seeds on the hard desert turf. When you were at bat, when you were on deck, you carried the weight of your team on your shoulders, you were a one-man team, nine against one, just you and your prehistoric weapon swinging for the right to be crowned King of First Base, King of Second Base, the proud warrior who punched through the defense with a line drive to that open spot of field. I remembered connecting bat to ball. I remembered the sweet taste of triumph followed soon after by the sting of wanting my parents to witness their son's victory.

"Are you ever, pussy, going to take a swing, pussy?" Warsaw yelled. Off in the shadows Warsaw had a ball in one hand and a bottle in the other.

I raised my bat. Allowed it to sway. Felt it whistle above my ear. Warsaw reared back. The ball rushed toward me. I swung. A dead pocket of air.

5   I always sped on the way down and followed all rules on the return. Mexico was sixty-three miles and an hour south of town. Monsoon rains had deepened the valleys and turned the desert a cammo-green color. During the drive Epstein remarked on a billboard advertisement for a restaurant in Two Guns, Arizona, called Forking Incredible. We drove over a flattened Sonoran sidewinder and watched the mirrors for dried puffs of dust in our wake.

"I quit my job," Warsaw said, from the back.

"You quit?" I asked him.

"Yesterday," he said.

"You never told me you were thinking of quitting."

"That highway roller was killing my lower back," he said.

Epstein sat shotgun, rubbing his knees in anticipation. He was dressed in a sport coat and smelled of woodsy aftershave. His touring cap was angled on his head. I felt Warsaw's long legs pushing against my seat. I'd been monitoring my friend in the rearview for most of the drive. Warsaw didn't know what to make of the child's car seat beside him, and, anyway, he was too self-involved to ask.

The border wall became visible on our approach to the southern gateway. It wormed up and down hillsides, dividing former neighborhoods. The thing put an ache in my throat whenever I saw it. Border Patrol vehicles idled alongside the fence, parked every hundred yards. Green grilles covered every inch of glass on the trucks as protection against rock throwers. There was so much enforcement that the area felt like it was under totalitarian rule. And the wall, just seeing it, ruined something basic in me: this shabby, sun-rusted catastrophe constructed from Vietnam-era landing strips and set down like a hatchet between the twin Nogaleses, separating two countries that shared a city with the same name. The wall may have seemed like a good idea in D.C., but around here it was a common joke. Anyone with a second-grade education knew that if you crawled a few miles in either direction, away from the cities, the wall ended, giving way to unlimited miles of harsh, sere flatpan. The Port of Entry was a different story. It was a circus of stadium lights, customs agents, and unmarked BP vehicles ready to chase cars that sped through the arched passageway, which wasn't unlikely, which I had seen happen on two occasions.

We were met with red brake lights. I maneuvered behind a car, queuing up, watching one man carry a heavy mirror down the middle of the road, desperately trying to sell it to waiting vehicles. As the vendor approached the car in front, which ferried a family, I saw the father's face harden in the mirror's reflection.

I scooted to Nogales several times a week. It was a larger, more daunting town than Agua Prieta, but I preferred Nogales for its proximity. I also adored my druggist here, a cuter, more fluent alternative to the fat-nosed thief in Agua Prieta.

Epstein said to Warsaw, as we waited, "Your nose is the color of a cayenne pepper."

"Too much working outdoors," Warsaw said. "That's why I quit."

"Those beet-red cheeks of yours remind me of someone," the old man said. "Mind passing along your mother's maiden name?"

"Jasinski," Warsaw said. "Why?"

"That's right," Epstein said, stroking his chin. "The Jasinski gal. Sweet Polish girl. You have the same face as your mother."

"Highly unlikely you know her, sir," Warsaw said.

"Brown hair, like yours. Same cylindrical mouth. Rugby shoulders. And tits like McIntosh apples."

In the mirror I saw Warsaw pass his knuckle over his lips, clearly displeased. Epstein had been harassing my friend for the better part of the drive. And Warsaw, apparently unsure how to read a man fifty years his senior, had cast himself into the role of deferential junior. "I don't appreciate that kind of joke," Warsaw said.

"No joke. I knew that Jasinski woman, your mother, quite well. You could say biblically."

Our Mexican border guard was a thin man with a disgruntled smirk. Oftentimes there weren't even guards when driving south, but there were today. And the man was clearly disinterested in three more gabachos pouring into his country. He was already eyeballing the next vehicle in line. He saw us all day, every day, Americanos traveling south to sightsee desperation and flirt with his chicas. The guard barely inspected my tags before waving my car through.

Wandering into border towns felt to me like veering off course. The shift was gentle but sudden, like passing from a cold to a warm patch in the sea. Signs morphed into another language. The streets trembled with unfamiliar sounds, and the colors were luminous, disorienting. The border was not Mexico. Nor was it the States. The border was its own beast, a place alive with false promises and implied terrors. Warsaw drew our attention to a pair of high-heeled shoes on the chipped esplanade. The shoes were pointing north, as though the woman in them had snapped her fingers and vanished.

We cruised off the keyed-up tourist grid, passing a man walking a mule spray-painted to resemble a zebra, and rolled toward Calle Escondido. My first stop was a miraculous dirt field carved from a streetscape comprising knickknack shops and strip club whorehouses. Neon signs hung off brick and stucco and adobe buildings with names like El Mustang and Lolita's, but the real magic happened across the street, where a recessed, hand-shoveled ballpark had sprung up despite its pornographic surroundings. The outfield perimeter walls had been cobbled together with old billboards. It was a damn fine place to watch a damn fine game of baseball, and a game was already under way. I saw one woman—dressed in a see-through blouse—loitering outside her establishment and watching the players on the dirt pitch. I watched her toke greedily on a cigarette stem, as though participating in a private race, blasting ropes of smoke through her nostrils.

I loved this place. The baseballers were college-age kids who never attended college and who played for the love of the game and local adoration. Americans in the know found their way here. Minor league scouts also knew this diamond hardpack as a famous spot for pickup games full of top-notch players. Word was that several Cubans, known for style and talent, sought out this special park. The field served as an ad hoc feeder system for the Southwest leagues. One lucky Mexicano, now on an escalator to the Red Sox, had been discovered on this very field. Because of its location, I knew the whores liked spending downtime wandering outside whenever they heard cracking bats. It was hard for me not to love the field for what it represented, the blind determination to play a game, no matter the obstacles.

"Give us an hour?" Epstein said, already outside the car. He looked eager to slam the door. I knew Epstein had been a ball fan since the Dodgers were in Brooklyn. A kid drove a ball into left field. "Make it two," Epstein said. "Appears to be a good bout."

Warsaw joined Epstein outside in the sun. My friend wanted to witness for himself the field that was gossiped about up and down the border, but now that he was here he seemed out of place to me, his fists in his pits, his eyes bouncing—a lone man waiting for a train in a distant, unfamiliar city.

"This is a business trip," I told them. "I'll be back when I get back. So stay right here, okay?"

"Three hours," Epstein said and slammed the car door.

I knew Nogales. I knew this wedge of Mexico. I knew the roads. I knew which ones never to turn down. There were shadows down certain alleys that you did not want to follow to their source. My antennae grew more attuned whenever I crossed over. The stale, exhaust-filled air sharpened, turned tangier, burning with each breath, as though chock-full of particulate.

A beat-up pickup pulled beside me at a stoplight. There was a pile of shrink-wrapped dolls in the truck's bed, bare-assed dolls with red, puckered mouths. The tiny bodies were swathed in plastic, airtight, and suffocated. Behind the wheel was an old man in farm-boy overalls. He smiled.

I knew the city. I knew to stay focused. The wealthy owned gated fortresses and lived on ranches outside town, while the poor huddled inside shacks cut into the hills, modern-day cliff dwellings made of warped plywood, strips of fiberglass, old paneling, and cinder blocks, whatever could be scrounged from the dump and carried away. Barrio scenery was a heartbreaking cobweb of wires—pirated electricity, shared, sold, and bartered. Car batteries fueled TVs that glowed inside makeshift huts. I watched the roads for discarded pieces of metal.

My pharmacist had a great smile and a long name. Amelia Guadalupe Santamaria Lopez's primera clase farmacia was perched on the summit of a flattened hill in Colonia Malverde. Her two-story building had south-facing views over a dusty barrio that surrounded several boxy, monolithic maquiladoras. Her small business attended to the needs of the poor warehouse workers, mostly young women who had traveled north in search of factory jobs. I'd found Amelia on Danni's suggestion. Amelia's drugs were far cheaper, of higher quality, than drugs sold in the farmacias in the turista zone.

When I drove up Amelia was already out front, and she was passing an envelope to a tall, gawky, storklike man in a basketball jersey. The man swiveled his long neck when he heard my car and quickly moved down the hill.

I got out. "Carrying on a little side business?" I asked Amelia.

"Follow me," she said rapidly and grabbed my elbow. "Quick." She shoved me around her building. Turning the corner she said, "These men. These men are here now."

"What men?"

"Los Toros," she said. The name put a hiccup in my gut. "They been around," Amelia said. "People afraid. Maybe is time for me and Hilario to move back to Puebla."

Amelia pushed me up a wobbly staircase in mid-construction to a screened-in porch. Her apartment was modest, glazed in heat, and with purple velvet pillows on a lime-green couch. I noticed a shrine inside a hollow kitchen cabinet with unlit votive candles below the usual suspects: Jesus, the Virgin of Guadalupe. But there was an additional picture in the mix, a magazine-gotten glossy of John McEnroe, from his younger days. In the photo his tight curls glistened. Amelia and her son, and her brother, were serious about tennis.

Amelia swiveled the wand on the window blinds, peering out. Her spooked-out expression began to make me worried.

"Mind telling me what's going on?" I said.

"They have too much time," she said.

"Who has too much time?"

"Los Toros," Amelia said. The heat blotched her smooth brown cheeks.

"Los Toros doesn't operate around here," I said, to remind her. "This isn't Juárez. You're talking crazy."

"I don't crazy, Sid." She returned to gazing out the window.

Oh, I knew about the group. I'd heard the name before. Everyone had. According to legend, the Mexican government had once assembled para-military units to fight Mexico's gnarly narcotraficante problem, but when the American-trained units went into the fields to begin cleaning up, the soldiers discovered that the narcocartels paid far better than their government sponsors. Now—the story went—Los Toros worked for the cartels, terrorizing for paychecks. But evidence of their existence in Sonora was scant. They lived on through gossip, reinforced by rumors, buttressed by disinformation. It was always talk, just scary talk.

"How do you know that guy was with Los Toros?"

"His shirt. The bull. He want money."

"He was wearing a Chicago Bulls jersey," I said. "I saw it."

"The same," she said, shaking her head. "The same."

When Amelia finally calmed down, we descended her heart-attack stairwell and she lifted the steel garage door of her pharmacy. It clacked upward along its tracks. Trying to budge the worry from her eyes, I asked about her son, Hilario.

"Oh, he good," she said. "His backswing is good." She smiled at me. Her smiles were soul-sweeping events. Straight bangs, thick as broom straw, hung over her huge almond eyes. Amelia was my finest contact South-of. Her brother was a podiatrist in town, and he had scrip pads. He wrote the scrips for the harder-to-get meds. He also charged me way too much for the service.

I unfolded today's long list, and Amelia's "tip" fell to the counter. She tucked the cash in her pocket. "More prescriptions than last," she said.

"That time of month, I guess."

"Is okay. I like more business."

My lists were detailed: drug, dose, manufacturer's name, and generic substitute. I'd designed spreadsheets on my computer at home. I didn't want folks accidentally dropping on my watch. I knew when customer supplies would run low. I kept my operation solid.

Amelia's pharmacy smelled of ointments and gauze and bolted to the walls were plastic bins stuffed with over-the-counter items. Farther back, behind the counter, was a closet-size vault that held the real treasures: opium derivatives, synthetic substitutes. MS-Contin, Dilaudid, Demerol, etc. Amelia kept her territory tight. She was square inside the barrio, within ear-range of desperation, and she protected her hole-in-the-wall with a sphincter-clenching sawed-off shotgun, which she'd shown me on several occasions.

Amelia whipped open the first paper bag and set her fingernail on two initials: M.A. An order for timolol, liquid glaucoma medicine. I never used customer names. Initials only.

I watched her move from vault to bins, filling orders, stooping under tubes of rebar poking from the wall. I was never quite sure what, exactly, she was constructing. Scaffolding hugged one side of her building. On the other side was a hand-painted mural of Hidalgo, stucco eroding from his face, revealing a concrete base. The other buildings on her street were perpetually being reassembled. A wall fell. A roof collapsed. Wind and sun wore things out, and I supposed it was like trying to keep windblown ocean-side shacks livable.

As Amelia counted pills, I studied a map of Mexico on her wall. The map had been folded, refolded, packed, and unpacked hundreds of times. Each of the thirty-one Mexican states was a different color. Between Mexico and the United States ran a blue line half an inch thick, from California to Texas, the Pacific to the Gulf, two thousand miles of borderland. For every mile there were thousands of ways to simply jog over.

"How much do you think those guides make helping people move across?" I asked her.

Amelia tugged the cap off a pen with her teeth. She scribbled on a bottle. "Why?"

"I don't know. Curious."

"You don't want to be curious. Beside," Amelia said, "the coyote job is unsafe. People with guns, people who rape, kill. That's no business for you."

"I'm not looking for a lecture."

"Fifteen hundred for every pollo," she said.

"American *dollars*?" I said. "Per *person*?" The amount surprised me and I quickly did the math. "Ten people equals fifteen thousand."

Amelia lifted an eyebrow. She was gauging my level of interest. "Sometime more. Sometime less. Depend."

"We are in the wrong business, amiga," I said. She clucked her tongue and shook her head. "Also," I said, remembering Ms. Wetherbee's request, feeling guilt tug at my throat. "Do you have transdermal opiate patches? It's for a client."

"Lo siento," Amelia said. "My brother need to write prescription. Beside, I don't have."

"That's a no?"

"Sí," she said.

"Okay, good. That's fine," I said. "That's good."

Later, Epstein was on the sidewalk, right where I had dumped him. But the old man was now sharing a cigarette with a prostituta from one of the bars. The woman's tight elastic shirt stretched over her humped belly, and by the way she fondled Epstein's elbow, she looked to me like she was trying to turn him into a trick. I rolled down the car window and overheard Epstein speaking Spanish. I didn't know the old man possessed this talent.

"No smoking," I said to Epstein. The old man tilted his head, noticed me idling in the early-evening shadows.

"You're no fun," Epstein said. He spouted off something in Spanish. The woman laughed and pinched his earlobe.

"Nicotine doesn't mix well with your heart meds," I reminded him.

The old man's smile fell. I was undermining his brief Mexico vacation.

Epstein's fingers scissored and I saw the Marlboro drop. His lady friend stomped on it with her plastic heel. "Where's Warsaw?" I asked.

Epstein jabbed a thumb over his shoulder. "He disappeared inside there."

I knew the establishment, Bar Honey, as the kind of joint where women cupped your sack for the price of a beer. It was the same dirty bar where I got the matchbooks I tossed at the border guards. "He went *inside*?" I asked. "You never go inside. You're supposed to be watching baseball."

"Game's over," Epstein said. He shrugged. "So he went inside. That friend of yours, I tell you. He's the real deal."

We killed time under the bar's humming neon sign. My irritation at bringing Warsaw only increased as night descended. Moths crashed into the neon tubes with quick, snapping sizzles. Epstein's friend studied me as she picked at her teeth with long, elaborate fingernails. Tiny black-and-white soccer balls decorated her thumbs. I wondered if this touch made her feel athletic.

"This is idiotic," I said. We'd been waiting for a while. "It's getting darker. This neighborhood isn't safe." A man suddenly cleared his throat behind me. I flinched. I turned to meet an American man holding a car key. The stranger was aiming the thing. Apparently he disapproved of my ass fraternizing with the hood of his car.

The second-floor lights of Bar Honey were dark, except one. When Warsaw didn't return, I took a breath and entered. Dust twirled in the air, and my shoes bonded to a wood floor scattered with bits of plaster. It made me think the ceiling was about to cave. Several defeated tomcats balanced their elbows on the bar while women half their age hovered around looking for opportunities. It was an almost sadder scene than the time I saw that woman without feet in Agua Prieta. Of all the danger-headed things Warsaw could do, disappearing inside a Mexicano whorehouse was one of the worst.

Upstairs was quiet. An electrical device buzzed behind one locked door. I hunted around and found Warsaw in another room. The door was open a bit and I saw Warsaw on a bed, in the corner, with a woman on his lap. And he was reading to her from his George Greg book. The pages were folded over, pieces of paper bookmarking important passages. Except for boxers, my friend was naked. What was more disturbing: his chest was shaved. Towels smeared with shaving cream were crumpled on the floor. Chest, legs, and armpits—he was a total whiteout.

"I was gone two hours," I said and pushed the door open. The woman pinched her shoulders up.

"Lupita, Sid. Sid, Lupita," Warsaw said. He tossed a razor blade into a bowl and water splashed the floor. "Lupita's an amazing person," Warsaw told me. "We're taking her with us."

"Oh, yeah? What about the Port of Entry?" I asked.

"What Port of Entry?"

"The border."

"What border?" Warsaw asked, quite serious.

"The international border that separates our countries, you asshole. I can't mosey across with a hairless clown and his Mexican friend in my backseat. How will that look? They'll search the Honda."

Warsaw stood and beat out his T-shirt. The nicks on his chest had pimpled into red dots. "That's not my concern," Warsaw said. "That's your problem."

I pressed my finger against his smooth chest. "It's our problem," I said. "This is no bueno. And I'm supposed to hand the business over to you?" I looked around, wondering about the rest of Warsaw's clothes. "Where are your jeans?"

"Raul took them."

"Who's Raul?"

"Better you not know," he said.

Warsaw couldn't find his shoes or socks either—he believed Raul had taken them—and said this was perfectly okay. "Not to worry, not a problem." Warsaw told me he'd left his passport in the car and didn't bring his wallet to Mexico. "Just cash," he said, as though he wanted me to congratulate him. When Warsaw put on his T-shirt, blood from his nicks absorbed into the cotton and spotted it. He wrapped his lower half in an apricot bedsheet, stained with God-knows-what misery, and before leaving he bent down to Lupita. He brushed back her hair and kissed her forehead. "You have my number," he said to her.

As we made our way into the downstairs bar, the clientele turned their attention on Warsaw, who was half covered by a bedsheet. Two men spat and laughed. Another big guy scowled and hopped off his barstool, but the moment his boots touched the floor he wobbled like a cheap punching dummy and quickly sat back down.

Epstein was on the sidewalk, smoking again. I snatched the Marlboro from his mouth and threw it into the street. Warsaw, hidden by the bar's door, poked his head around and looked to me for guidance.

"Here," I said and tossed the old man my keys, but it was dark, and the old man was blind, and the keys struck him on the chin. Epstein flung his head back and stared at me with humongous eyeballs. "You're driving," I told him.

"I don't have my license," Epstein said. "The State of Arizona confiscated it." He pointed at his tortoiseshell glasses. "They said it was my eyes."

"I don't care. You drive."

I watched Warsaw run from the doorway to the car. He jiggled the door handle. It was locked. "Hurry. Open the door. Hurry," he said to me, bouncing on his toes.

I took the passenger seat. Warsaw dove into the back.

Epstein didn't surprise me. The man drove exactly like an eighty-two-year-old. He flipped the turn signal miles before any stoplight. Our car inched at a snail's pace through the dark night streets. He turned onto Avenida Obregón, approaching the tourist ruckus, where we heard high school howls echo from all-night cantinas.

Epstein craned his neck, considering Warsaw, who was nearly naked in the back. "You haven't said much all night," Epstein said. "You're a curious one."

I saw Warsaw muss his hair.

"Tell me, what are you after?" Epstein asked him.

"What am I after?" Warsaw said. "What does that even *mean*?"

"What do you want? From life," Epstein said. "Or, I suppose, out of life."

"What is this?" I said. "A tea party? Pay attention to the road."

"I asked the boy a question," Epstein said.

Warsaw had not been a drama major. In college he'd majored in finance. He had been a Yalie Whiffenpoof with an interest in international stock markets. He'd received the student rate on the *Wall Street Journal*, so when Warsaw said to Epstein, "I have a big crush on nothing," his answer struck me as a tad melodramatic.

I instructed Epstein to turn off Avenida Obregón and onto a side street ruled by knickknack turista tiendas. The stores hawked crap to anyone interested in buying crap—los muertes skulls, sequined wrestling masks, fake Gucci purses. I jumped out when I saw the right store. I bought size large. White T, jeans, socks. I also threw down for a big, stupid, cheap sombrero and several colorful blankets, paying the vendor full price, no time to barter. The man dumped everything inside plastic Walmart bags. I scattered the blankets around the backseat and tossed Warsaw the clothes.

My friend fit into nothing. The jeans were too tight and the T-shirt hung off him like extra skin. But they were temporary. They would work.

"I can't button these," Warsaw said, lifting his hips.

"Too bad," I told him. "Let's go," I told Epstein. Epstein blinked huge inside his glasses.

I opened the glove compartment, slid the hidden door, and rummaged through the white bags. I stole a Xanax from Ms. Fesmire's stash.

Traffic heading into the States bottlenecked at the checkpoint. The northbound line was a long, slow-moving caterpillar. Dogs were sniffing luggage tossed on the pavement while mustached agents were searching car trunks, flipping ashtrays over, and inspecting VIN numbers with flashlights. On their knees the agents peered underneath cars.

"Here's the story we tell," I said to the old man. He listened.

It would be a long, excruciating wait. I swallowed the pill, praying that our agent wouldn't question two volunteers from Senior Dynamic Services who were escorting their eighty-two-year-old client to Mexico and back for his affordable, biannual dental appointment.

6   The telephone woke me. My mind rose through echo chambers. It was still dark.

On hands and knees I crawled across the hardwood floor toward the horrible, never-ending ringing. My phone was buried in a pile of socks.

"Sidney, you didn't," she said.

I said, lowly, "Juliet?"

"Sidney, how could you?"

It was Juliet. The sound of children trickled through the phone. Squeaky swings, laughter, high-pitched shouts. The numerals on my digital clock blazed like neon. "Jesus. It's five thirty in the morning," I told her. I listened for another moment. "Are you near children? Is that the sound of children?"

"I'm on our bench," Juliet said. "My arms are crossed, if you have to know. There's a phone against my ear. I am in our neighborhood park."

Our bench. Our neighborhood. Our park. Three thousand miles away my ex-girlfriend was sitting on a bench watching kids in our old neighborhood park. I knew the place well, and I imagined feet pounding against metallic slides, sand clenched in small pink fists. I lay back, contemplating a tiny hole in the bedroom wall, put there by a nail, thinking of it as a perforation that allowed the room to breathe. "What are you doing in the park? And what are you doing watching children? And what are you doing calling me? Aren't you supposed to be behind a fancy lawyer's desk?"

"There are phone calls coming from Arizona," she said. "I checked the area code. Said Arizona. Tucson. Who are these people calling? I use this phone for business."

"How should I know?" And then I asked, genuinely curious, "What do they say?"

"What? I don't know. One was a heavy breather. And yesterday I had a discussion with a woman about sesame noodle recipes. I fell into it."

"It's five thirty-three in the morning. And I don't know what you're jawing on about."

"If this is another passive-aggressive attempt to exact revenge."

"My eyes are closed. I'm sleeping."

"How's your grandma?" she said. I wanted to hang up, but didn't. I missed her, then didn't. "You there?" she said.

"Is it that easy to forget what you did? I wake up one morning, and voilà, greenish discharge. You gave me another man's sexually transmitted disease. Are you ever going to tell me his name?"

"He gave it to me too," she said, as if I needed that golden reminder.

"Yeah, and yeah, well, what's next on the menu?"

"Look, he's no longer around, and besides—"

I couldn't stand her mentioning him, couldn't stomach thinking about him. I tried to hang up, but I'd spilled spaghetti sauce on the END button and it didn't work. When I checked the connection, she was already gone. I collapsed in bed, pillow over my face, listening to the morning traffic on a nearby boulevard. I felt warm air seeping into my lungs, a sensation almost too much to bear.

Juliet would awake at five forty-five, precisely, every weekday morning. She'd nuzzle with the pillow for a while, nudging the sheets down to her toes as she acclimated to our cold bedroom. It was a slow, deliberate unwrapping. In the bathroom she'd tune the waterproof radio to a mid-tempo rock station. Then, like a mother testing baby's milk, she'd extend the backside of her wrist into the shower's stream, assessing temperature. Shampoo, conditioner, shampoo, conditioner. She'd end it all by meticulously scrubbing away dead skin with a loofah. Legs lathered, she'd shave, pop her birth control pill, followed by a flurry of bath towels and underwear segueing into stockings and usually a form-fitting skirt. Before leaving our brick duplex, she'd mist the air and traipse through a cloud of perfume. Every weekday morning.

There were things I'd learned from these years. Everyone had needs, desires, wants. You had to fight so yours didn't get shoved out of the way.

But you had to not eat up everyone else's wants with your own. Fairness, more or less—that was what it was about.

I considered the subject of needs often. What a man needed. What *I* needed. Connecting again with the sound of Juliet's voice made me miss her. Her damn sweet voice reminded me of everything I didn't have anymore, and I found myself focusing on the gauzy memory of her long toes, her lotioned feet, how she kept the nails trim and neat.

But a man had to live. A man had to move on, get on with life, live it and enjoy it before he woke up one morning rolling around in diapers. A man needed to stoke the coals to keep the fire from going dark.

MY GRANDMOTHER was at her glass dining table sipping a finger's worth of ten-dollar whiskey from a mug adorned with a saguaro. Light shot through the blinds and created rungs on the carpet. I knew alcohol interacted with several of her meds—nothing serious, other than drowsiness—but I rarely mentioned the side effects. I figured, at her age, she had earned the right to enjoy a noontime buzz.

"Yes, again, that is the correct date, Ms. Patterson," I said into the phone, attempting to untangle the very tangled telephone cord. I liked using my grandma's landline. It was such a nostalgic treat. I watched Nana pick up her needles, clicking them, the sound like scurrying crabs. A canvas tote on the floor overflowed with colored yarns. "Fine, yes, Ms. Patterson. Thank you, Ms. Patterson." I set the phone in its cradle. "That was Ms. Patterson," I told Nana.

"I would have never guessed."

"Sixteen people are coming to your birthday party."

"Oh, I don't know," Nana said. "I'd just rather not and say we did. Couldn't we maybe, instead, go to a movie?"

"I've reserved the community room. Eighty-nine is a lot of years. That's almost a century. You're a sequoia."

"Parties are a hassle," she said. "Who will clean up the mess?"

Nana had told me she didn't want a fuss. That she didn't want a party. But God forbid if I actually granted her that wish. She'd drop dead from disappointment. I knew her too well.

I grabbed an old rag off the counter. Today was cleaning day, and on my list were windows and surface areas and bathroom. Campus Admin offered optional cleaning services, but the price on their professionally printed brochures was an insult. When Nana had moved in, she'd told me she wanted the service. At her advanced age, she didn't want to be on her knees wearing yellow rubber gloves. But as the superintendent of her bank account, I'd made the call: absolutely no cleaning service!

I started on the sills and moved to the baseboards. Dust was everywhere. You couldn't get rid of it. It lodged in the teeth. It drifted into the eyes. The desert, just dust.

When I finished the windows, I tossed the dirty rags in a plastic bag and headed to the bedroom closet for reinforcements. My grandmother's apartment had deep closets. Five hundred square feet in total, yet she had mansion-sized closets. On the day of her move Warsaw and I had shoved Nana's antique eight-drawer Chippendale dresser inside the bedroom closet. And that's where my grandfather now lived, inside a drawer, inside a flat mahogany urn. My neck got hot whenever I neared the closet, trying to understand why people did what they did.

Bubba had been an old man before he was ever old. He just had that type of soul. "Serious since the age of eleven," Nana often said of him. Of course, he had enjoyed himself at times, I knew. Bubba had golfed, he'd loved golfing, and he'd thrown away his share of quarters on the casino slots. Bubba had retired from the Postal Service two years before congestive heart failure claimed him. Even now, I remembered the gentle way the man would kiss me on the cheek, unashamed, his teary eyes blazing with decency. At the time I hated the kisses. That another man kissed me. Thirteen years old, with another man kissing me, but what I wouldn't give now for a few more smacks.

The thought occurred to me from time to time, but I didn't like lingering on the fact that I was the next Dulaney man in line. I'd spent too long thinking about the blank spaces that opened when people vanished. My grandfather. My mother. And my father, dead at thirty-three, my age.

My grandmother stored her cable-knit sweaters in the top three drawers of the Chippendale dresser. Whenever she knit a new one, she'd wear it for several months before retiring it. Then there was the bottom drawer. It was full of boxes of unused thank-you cards, Christmas cards, birthday cards, get-well cards. It was a storefront of emergency-use greeting cards. Concealed beneath these was my grandfather's gun arsenal.

Over the years I'd returned to the guns out of curiosity. The firearms roused my feelings for the man. When I was younger, my grandfather had taught me how to shoot, just the basics, but even so, the guns were incongruous with the type of quiet, gentle man who had owned them. His collection included a Colt 1911 semi-automatic sidelock, a skinny-barreled Walther P38, and inside an oak case, sheathed in velvet, a five-pound double-action Smith Wessy, so heavy that it almost hurt when I lifted it from its case. I palmed the serrated grip, flicked the cylinder release, and tickled the cold steel trigger. The thing was ridiculously big. A gun in the open invited a sense of enchantment, of otherworldliness, of supernatural awe. The Smith Wessy demanded my reverence. I moved the gun to my other hand. It felt heavier in my weaker arm.

I heard my grandmother's footsteps approaching from the hall. "Sid? Are you rootin' through my guns again?"

I slipped the Smith Wessy under a sweater. I opened the drawer that housed my grandfather just as Nana came in. "What are you doing in my things?" she asked.

"Why do you store Bubba's ashes in here? It doesn't seem right," I said.

"Bubba was shy," she said.

"But you keep him in the closet. Inside a drawer, in a box."

"He liked his privacy."

"He's in a drawer. Doesn't that strike you as weird?"

"He's nearby," she said. "That's what matters. If I had him in the other room I wouldn't be able to move. I'd die of grief, looking at him in that box." She pulled a cord and the closet light went off. "Do you want to know what I think?" she asked me.

"Do I have a choice?"

"You're using me as an excuse not to get on with your life."

My left side, near my ribs, stung.

"You need to move on," she said. "I love you, but you need to stop pussyfooting. No job. No woman. You're stucker than a duck in mud."

"What?"

She cocked an eyebrow. Her swollen ankles looked like heavy socks melting down her leg. She pinched my shirt and inspected a recent tear in it. "I don't know why you do it."

"Do what?"

"The visiting, cleaning, coming to dinner. I don't need everything done for me. Stop doing everything. It's sucking up your best years. Stop hanging around us diminished folk. Get out there and live."

"Nana," I said.

"Don't Nana me. You have ten working fingers and a mouth and you know how to use them at the same time. Meet someone," she said. "And listen, trust me. When you do, trust me. Tell her you want to be with someone who could write an honest account of your life."

"Why would I say that?"

"That's how Bubba snatched my heart from Billy Thompson," she said and tightened a scarf around her neck.

"Who's Billy Thompson?"

"The man Bubba stole me from," she said. "I was with another man before your grandfather. But your granddad took care of that. *Ooooh.*" She smiled and balled her fists. "Thinking about all that now makes my lips tingle."

TWO BLACK GARBAGE BAGS were waiting for me by the door. "Going out," I called.

"Bring a coat," Nana said.

"It's a hundred and four outside."

"I feel a chill coming!" she hollered.

I hustled around outside of the tower and tossed the bags over a wooden fence. They landed in the Dumpster with a thud. I was pleasantly surprised to see the pretty Latina social worker across the quad. She was pushing a patient in a wheelchair in the direction of the lake.

Mesa Pathway sparkled. Colored shards of glass were mixed into the cement. No matter where I was on campus it was like walking on a dance floor.

I saw the social worker stop at a bench. She sat beside her patient, a woman with a fairly advanced condition. The old woman was seat-belted into a wheelchair to prevent her from tumbling out. Flapping on the back of her chair was a miniature Arizona license plate, which gave her name: Frittemeyer. I'd seen these license plates before. Stickers in the upper corners stated the patient's name and room number.

I slowly walked past them and took the next available bench. I was reluctant to acknowledge the woman's beauty, but it was impossible not to when she was measured against the patient at her side. The social worker had bronze skin and Indian in her bone structure and open, curious eyes. Stray hairs dangled over her nose.

We were not alone. Three teenage girls had taken refuge by the lake. I watched them lounge under the afternoon sun, which softened the blacktop and made the world smell of resin. The girls were trespassing, clearly, and out for some mildly criminal fun. They reclined on a square patch of grass and whispered among themselves, passing a cigarette around. When a duck crashed awkwardly into the water, one girl screamed.

Ms. von Bausch was outside too. The old woman walked briskly along the path and fluttered her fingers at me. She was doing her laps. She was always doing her laps. Ms. von Bausch, a lanky, slim woman, was the campus athlete. She had a red belt in Cane-Fu and had recently been spotlighted in Paseo del Sol's newspaper. I'd read that she'd qualified at the Phoenix Regionals and was now training for the National Senior Olympics in Palo Alto. I watched her moving along, fists balled, head down, hips punching with each stride.

The social worker caught me staring. She broke off eye contact. When her gaze returned to me, she held on a heartbeat longer. Shyness thawed with each successive glance. She patted the elderly woman's elbow, and her cute, sharp nose twitched. Then she touched her neckline, a gesture that I interpreted as an invitation. And then I noticed, off in the far distance, there was a man outside the wrought-iron fence, standing there behind the bars like a prisoner. The man had a camera to his face. He was snapping photos. He was taking his time, adjusting a large telescopic lens.

There was nothing interesting to photograph other than an old woman with her keeper, three teenagers, and me. When I stood up, I saw the man lower his camera. A white F-150 truck baked in the sun behind him. I knew that truck. From this distance, the man's close-cropped hair looked painted on, and as I rounded the lake, the various parts of his face fell into alignment. I recognized him. The same man who'd put a dent in my car door.

I walked faster.

The man casually set a white Stetson on his head, tapped it down, and crossed the street. I was at the fence when he jumped in the truck and revved the engine, as he'd done before. I noticed an airbrushed reproduction of a plane on the tailgate—an old-fashioned biplane breaking through cumulous cloudscape. The man's window slid down, and the polka beat of a norteño corrido came from inside, the same kind of annoying percussive accordion music the kids at my favorite taquería played. Just as I was considering hopping the fence, the truck rolled down the street. It disappeared around the corner.

In the late afternoon the sun was hot, bright, and working. I unclenched my fists from the fence, feeling sudden nauseating shame. It was ridiculous. Ridiculous. I did not know that man. That man didn't know me. He was just taking pictures. I told myself stories, trying to invent some logical explanation about why someone would be following me. I was glad I knew where to find a gun. The day was getting impossibly hotter.

IT WAS MY FIRST VISIT to the building at the end and, I hoped, my last. I stood on the far side of the dark-wood reception desk, watching the housekeeper untangle a power cord from an industrial vacuum the size of an outdoor air conditioner. The housekeeper was searching for an outlet, but unfortunately a woman in a wheelchair blocked the nearest one. Her body swayed to the left. She was in a fuzzy black cardigan that ended at her knees, revealing a set of gray, scaly shins.

Finally the lovely social worker returned from behind a swinging door and said to me, "Sorry, things get busy. Now what did you need help with?"

I stood quietly stunned, embarrassed by my astonishment. The woman's face was bright and honest and shiny as wet celery. I placed one hand, then the other, on the counter, watching her push a pin in and out of a cushion strapped to her wrist. Her name badge said MONA. She had a charming row of crooked upper teeth and a dimple on one side. Her toenails were purple. When she touched her neck the top of my mouth went dry.

"I'm wondering if I can reserve a nurse," I managed to say, though I didn't know what I was saying. "Uh, um, if that's possible?"

She pursed her lips, presumably tasting something she'd rather not. "I'm going to pretend I didn't hear that," she said. "*Reserve* who? What do you mean by *reserve*?"

"What I mean is . . . I misspoke," I said. "My grandmother lives across the quad and we're having a birthday party. And we need a nurse. Her friend lives in this building and she needs to be accompanied by a nurse. Someone told me those are the rules in the campus manual. I'm just trying to follow procedure."

Mona nodded. She opened a binder and clicked the end of a ballpoint pen. "Six o'clock," she said. "Request noted. Your name?"

"Sidney. Dulaney."

Her eyes darted left and right, then with playful suspicion settled on me. "So, you're him."

"Him?"

"*Him.* The guy. Our campus criminal." Mona's full lips were built for whispering in perfect enunciation.

"I'm studying for the professional knowledge exam," I said. "I'm a schoolteacher."

"Uh-huh," Mona said, smiling as though we were now in league.

"High school English," I said.

She quickly wrote my name in the binder. "Your *reservation* has been noted." Then she came around the desk, grabbed my hand, flattened my palm, and set a large wooden button on it. "Here, Butch Cassidy, hold this for one second," she said.

I watched as she bent beside the woman in the wheelchair. She snipped away extra thread on the old woman's cardigan, and when she asked for the button, I held out my hand, the button there, her smallest finger grazing my inner wrist—a peculiar voltage knocked against each rung of my spinal column. In eight skillful needle strokes Mona managed to reattach the button to the woman's cardigan, fastening it beneath the woman's wild gaze. "There, there," Mona said heroically before standing, whisking past me, and disappearing again through the swinging door. I wanted to follow but didn't.

The old lady in the wheelchair propelled herself forward, and now she blocked my exit. For a moment I tried to imagine how helpless the old woman must have felt, how outright dependent. Wheeling to opposite ends of the building must have been an excruciating trial of will and perseverance. The chair cut her body into thirds: torso, waist, dangling legs. And the miniature Arizona plate said her last name was Albright, room 32, age 91.

Ms. Albright reached out to clutch my pinkie. Her chapped hand was coarse, like fine-grade sandpaper. She gestured for me to stoop, and when I did, her breath hummed with penicillin. She pointed her bony finger at a ficus plant and asked me, "Is that your son?"

I blew open the door and left in a hurry. Paseo del Sol's residents—those who were well—were outside, relaxing in beach chairs, reading magazines, and lounging under umbrellas in the hot, snapping air. I saw people promenading from one building to another, around the lake, toward the independent town houses. A popular columnist from the newspaper, Ms. Carlie Arthur, passed out copies of the latest edition of *Sunspots*. I knew Ms. Arthur as a lover of gossip. She crushed hard over any new scuttlebutt, and she wielded much power on campus. Whenever she wanted to print rumor as fact, she'd float a boomerang, spreading the information far and wide and waiting until it got back to her, and as soon as it did, she printed it as truth. I kept my distance from Carlie Arthur, too afraid she'd someday print something about me.

In the center of the quad I saw Epstein laboring over a new gas grill. I walked over. A gust of wind whipped down and nearly blew off his Diamondbacks ball cap.

"I don't know how you can just traipse into that building," Epstein said to me. He poked at two raw burgers. Red oozed out. "The smell alone gives me nightmares. Dead skin and plaque mixed with laundered sheets. You'll need to anesthetize me to get me through those doors. Did you notice how wide the doors are, by the way?" he said, obsessed by the subject. "Wide enough to accommodate wheelchairs and gurneys."

"I met her," I told him. "I did it. I finally met her."

"I refuse to believe."

"Goes by Mona," I said.

"Congratulations," Epstein said. "You get a trophy when you bring me a pubic hair."

The wind sang down and Epstein's ball cap lifted from his head and rolled like a tumbleweed across the quad. It stopped by an elderly lady sitting on the ledge of a flower bed. Her hands were folded crisply in her lap and she was staring off into space. A shadow dropped from a tower and crawled across the woman's kneecap.

Over in the campus turnaround, I saw a group of night-trippers getting onto a bus courtesy of the Hoodoo Hotel and Casino. Then I watched one man step down and motion to others. Low murmurs rolled from one person to the next. Conversations died down, and now everyone was looking as Mr. Garland Bills casually walked across the quad. He was dressed in a clean blue tracksuit and white tennies. In passing he nodded politely at his fellow residents, bearing a sort of self-conscious pain. He swept a hand through his brown hair. It was unheard of. A man his age, late forties, perhaps early fifties, living in an apartment inside an elderly residential village. I watched him approach Ms. Haybroke and help adjust her sun umbrella. She considered him with awe, like someone encountering a celebrity. Finished, he walked the long way around the lake, toward the gated entrance, passed through it, and entered the outside world.

"Don't know much about him," Epstein said.

"Some men, I guess, enjoy being left alone."

Epstein swept the burgers onto paper plates. "Game is on," he said. "D-backs at San Diego. You coming?"

I looked at the woman sitting at the flower bed, curious about what was happening in her universe. "I need to take care of something," I told Epstein.

Blank stares around campus weren't uncommon. After hanging around this long, I often knew the main reason behind them. The woman was wearing a silk blouse and a chiffon scarf stitched with a green vine. She looked dressed for a springtime banquet, or a wedding. Even her makeup looked ready for opening night. I walked over, melting away the lines by her eyes, folding back the years, recoloring the gray in her hair, thinking that her pulse must have once been quick, her smile a bolt of lightning. I retrieved

Epstein's hat and took a seat beside her. I tried mimicking her impeccable posture, straightening my back, hands in my lap. The lights inside the dining commons cast a soft yellow glow over the diners. When I had given it enough time, I set my hand on the woman's frigid knuckles. She didn't move. We sat, breathing the thermal air, warm breezes on our cheeks.

"My sister," the woman said.

I squeezed her cold hand. "When?"

"I got the call yesterday," she told me. "She was in her backyard feeding a cat. A stray found a home in her bushes. She tumbled. That was it, they tell me. That's the word they used. *Tumbled*. As though she was playing games."

"Where did she live?"

"San Pedro, California," she said.

I told her that I'd never been.

"There's an old marina," the woman said.

The wind pushed down and snapped her scarf. I watched as she pursed her lips and closed her eyes and welcomed the rush. When her eyes opened, I noticed that one was filmy. An atmospheric cornea.

"Have you eaten?" I asked, gesturing at the commons.

"Not tonight. Tonight I can't find my appetite."

"I can take you somewhere. I know several places."

She shook her head.

"You have family in town, I hope."

"Three daughters."

I patted her hand. "Good. That's good." Lending her my arm, I escorted her to her apartment in La Santa Rita, level E. The woman's grip was light, so light it was as though I walked alone, but when I looked down she was there. Her milky eye rose to meet mine.

"I wonder who will care for the cat," the woman said. Her question got me wondering too.

"Cats find ways," I said. "They're resourceful. That cat found your sister."

The woman attempted an uninspired smile, as though she was afraid to smile, unsure if it was okay to smile anymore.

"I'm glad she had that cat," she said.

I pulled a card from my wallet. My cell phone number was printed in raised black lettering. A snake was wrapped around the Bowl of Hygeia in the upper corner. I took her hand and set my card in it. "Call if you need anything," I told her. "I help people around here. I help my grandma's friends."

7   Several nights later, Danni Zepeda bounced away from the hotel bar double-fisting two mojitos. Pulverized mint floated amid the ice. I watched her hips—hips squeezed into worn, tight-fitting blue jeans. Her biceps spoke of money spent on personal training. And I liked women who knew how to wear jeans.

I'd tried buying the drinks, but Danni, being Danni, provided for others. She set the glasses on the table next to a wandering jew, its deep green leaves a lavender color on the bottom. She fell into a chair and fanned herself dramatically with a brochure she'd snagged from the lobby. Even at night, the temperature had yet to drop.

"I thought we were due for a cool spell," Danni said. "It's hotter than this time last year. This is July misery."

"That's the reason my clients moved," I said. "Mild winters and blistering summers. Desert is good on the bones."

She tucked a cocktail straw behind an ear, and together we watched a blond woman with a pulled-back face descend into the outdoor pool. Around the pool were similar women: toned, golden, fake-lipped, and hidden behind glossy magazines. It was so hot only bikinis were necessary. There was a medical convention at the hotel, Danni informed me. "Varicose veins," she said. "The experts in varicose veins have gathered." She tossed the brochure on the table. The words "Endo Venous Laser Treatment" overlaid a picture of tight, firm buttocks.

"So, these are the doctors' wives," I said.

"No, these are the doctors." She sipped her drink. "But that's not why you're here."

Yesterday I woke up to see an F-150 parked on the street outside the casita. A white F-150 truck. That's the reason I was here. I must have stared out the window for hours. Finished three cups of coffee, anxiously read the newspaper, tromped up and down the antelope-papered hallway. Finally I went out and knocked on the truck's tinted window. There was no one inside. I felt the hood for heat. It was cold. It was the same truck as before, with the same stupid airbrushed biplane on the tailgate. Worrying about Nana—and the business—was enough for me to handle. I was not interested in adding more worry. But an F-150 parked outside the casita did worry me. And what Amelia told me about Los Toros in Nogales worried me. And the panic button really went off whenever I perused the latest news out of Mexico. Mexico always seemed to be on the verge of economic turnaround or full-scale war. That madness could easily spill over the border and monkey-wrench my only source of income.

"Jesus, I need to get away from this job," I said. "And now this character, this guy in the truck. I'm in trouble."

"Here we go," Danni said. "You said the same thing three months ago. You thought police had sniffed you out. You're overly cautious. Paranoid."

"Police did stop me. I got a ticket, didn't I?" I said.

"Faulty brake light," she said and crushed ice between her molars. "Relax, soldier. Nobody pays attention to pharmaceuticals. We move a different class of drug."

"You also mentioned people."

"People, sometimes, sure. Depends on pay. I don't move anyone. If I'm going to assume that risk, I need a sizable paycheck."

"How large is that paycheck?"

"Why? You interested?"

"I do have bills." I sipped my drink, scanning the bar for men wearing white Stetsons. A column of feathery smoke rose from an ashtray on an outdoor table. Wind dispersed it. I didn't like talking about the business because talking about the business made me think about the downsides. Police, men driving white trucks, et cetera. I braced myself and eagerly waited for the impact of the gin. "I'm being watched," I said. "Someone is following me. A man put a dent in my car door. Took pictures of me. Now he's parking outside the casita."

"Like I told you," Danni said, "I placed a phone call. My journalist friend knows about these border *things*. Sip your drink. Like I said, relax."

A stranger in a double-breasted suit strolled into the lounge, pulled out a stool, spun, and stretched his arms out on the bar. He eyeballed the pool area, the veranda, and the lounge. I could tell he was a man of fast opinions. Danni glanced sidelong at the guy, measuring him in the way of a skilled woman. The man put a finger in his tie, loosening the knot. My cell phone vibrated in my pocket. It was Juliet, in Northampton, ten forty-five on the East Coast. She would be under the covers by midnight. "Do you have a dollar bill?" I asked Danni.

Danni watched as I carefully printed Juliet's phone number in three different places. I set my empty glass atop the bill, leaving a tip.

"The ex?" she asked.

I nodded.

"Are you ever going to stop that?"

I shrugged. "You told me to relax."

Danni returned to the bar, and I watched her toss her hair in the businessman's direction, leaning on the points of her elbows, her ass, hard as a boulder, jutting out. The man locked his eyes. His movements were overly conspicuous. He leaned over his drink, stirring a tiny straw, elbows on the bar, wrist bent, head cocked, smiling. He had the toothy smirk of a sales rep and a perfect helmet of stockbroker hair. Even from across the lounge I could make out thick, greasy comb marks.

Danni bought another round, plus two pours of Blue Label. She threw the whiskey back without wincing and pinged my glass. A big blue vein throbbed on her forehead and her eyes turned opaque. Danni surprised me by pulling out a hotel keycard. "It's a long, dark drive back to the reservation, soldier," she said. "And look, I've been drinking."

"You got a room."

"Indeed. There's an excellent view of the Santa Catalinas. Big bed too."

"This drink and I'm on my way," I told her. "The gentleman at the bar looks interested, though. He removed his expensive jacket."

"What if I like teachers?" she said. "What if I like to be taught?"

"You're forgetting. We already tried this."

"Only one date," she said. "You never gave me a chance."

"You were my babysitter. It's too weird. Isn't that weird?"

"I thought it might have been one of your fantasies," she said.

Oh, Danni—she knew me. She ran the keycard along her chin, considering me. "Look, let's start over." She pulled the straw from her ear and chewed on the end. A dirty, dirty habit. "You like playing with me," she said. "You always did enjoy playing games."

"Monopoly," I said.

"Okay, how's this for a game?" she said, and from her canvas tote bag she carefully extracted an official médico pad. It was new. Untouched. Danni set it squarely on her thigh, caressing it with a stubby, gnawed fingernail. With one pad I could order hundreds of prescriptions, circumventing Amelia's brother, and save cash. Danni disappointed me by scribbling on the uppermost scrip, wasting it. She placed the scrip facedown on the table.

Out of the corner of my eye I could feel the businessman heating up my neck. The man was watching, waiting. I picked up the scrip and read it.

"You want to try once?" I asked.

"You got it, soldier," she said. "Plus, I didn't thank you for the wandering jew. It's my favorite perennial."

My thoughts went to the Latina social worker, her purple toenails, her shiny hair and semi-crooked teeth, and I felt an urge. Danni smiled and clenched her teeth on the straw. I smiled back.

The gentleman at the bar swiveled on his stool as I followed Danni toward a bank of gleaming elevators.

8 Sunlight filtered through a cleft in the hotel drapes, strafing my eyes. I awoke with severe discomfort in my thigh. I tugged the sheets back, and there, in my quad, was a sewing needle. It was embedded a quarter of an inch. I blinked. It didn't register. I touched the end and pain rippled down my leg. I couldn't believe it. Black thread was still attached to the end. I carefully extracted the needle, quietly rose from bed, and deposited the needle in the trash. Danni was still asleep, the sheets coiled like snakes around her arms. During the night she had shot for all the bases, but now she looked content, spent, without worry. The DO NOT DISTURB sign swayed from room 512's door handle as I eased the door shut.

I had errands. First on my list was the pawnshop to unload Ms. Wetherbee's watch. I was in the car when my phone rang. My ex-girlfriend called at the strangest times.

"People keep phoning this number," Juliet said. Impatience registered in her voice. There was static on the line, clicks, a vibrant whine, and then she was back, saying, "I know you're behind this."

I threw the phone to my other ear. "I'm shifting from first to second," I told her calmly. "The light just turned green. I'm trying not to speed."

"You're also writing my phone number on bathroom walls," Juliet said. "Is that it? Above urinals? When are you going to grow up?"

"I'm doing no such thing."

"Then why do people keep calling me from Arizona?" she asked.

"I'm moving on. I'm taking the necessary steps to distance myself from our relationship."

"What's that mean?"

"I just had a date," I told her. I heard silence. Then I heard deep breathing and I imagined a crack quietly working through a crystal wineglass. I imagined Juliet's mind turning like a slide show carousel as she tried to conjure up Danni's face. A woman, blond? A woman, nice smile? A woman, not her! "With a very nice woman," I told Juliet.

"You met someone?" Her voice sounded sentimental and dangerous.

"This may be the one," I said, not believing it. "I like her a lot. I may have finally found the one."

The line spat dead air, a vacuum. I pushed the END button, for emphasis. I wanted to wound her, as she'd wounded me. A scenario projected itself across the windshield, the same as before, the same as always. I extracted discomfort and the tiniest bit of sick pleasure from the scene. It was night. Juliet and her man-affair were in his apartment. The lights were dim. A fire crackled. A bottle of beer sweated in Juliet's hand. She was in a warm, playful mood. She perused his bookcase. She pulled out a book. They'd both read it and began a heated discussion. They disagreed. She took one side. He took the opposing. They argued, mildly. Juliet grazed his chest with her bottle. He reached for it. She hurried away, tripped on his rug, bending in mock desperation. He drove the argument home.

I often wondered how it was even possible to dislike someone I missed so much. I wrote Juliet's number on dollar bills so that she would call me, so that contact wouldn't be lost forever.

I dialed her back, and naturally she refused to answer. Her voice mail beeped. "Remember that dawn when we woke up and drove to the lake? Remember how calm it was, and how quiet?"

STANDING AT THE PAWNSHOP'S COUNTER was a teenage girl who tapped a key against the glass. Guitars were strung like meat slabs behind her. The store had radios, amps, and old saddles for sale, each affixed with red DISCOUNT tags, and it smelled of mothballs. Each old castoff looked sad and forgotten. I never enjoyed visiting Lucky Lou's.

I set my postal bag on the counter. Along with Ms. Wetherbee's antique watch, I also fished out a plastic sandwich baggie with three gold molars. Ms. Haybroke's pension check was late, so as payment she handed me three gold teeth. I didn't know why I put up with it.

"Lou around?" I asked the girl.

"When Lou's out he lets me do the buying," the girl told me.

Her hair was rigged into a tight bun, and her face looked like porcelain, and she was quite pretty.

"You're a teenager," I said. She was fourteen, maybe fifteen years old.

"So? I can spot a cubic zirconia faster than anyone," she said convincingly.

The girl began with Ms. Wetherbee's watch, inspecting it under a bright lamp, examining the markings, the scratches, rolling the band through her small fingers, testing its weight, watching how the links flowed. Then, to my amazement, she placed the watch to her ear, eyes wandering to the ceiling, and listened to the gears tick. Following her big cabaret, she scrutinized the teeny diamonds with jeweler's glasses.

"M color," she whispered to me. "Fine cut. That's good."

I didn't know what to make of young extraterrestrials like her. I welcomed the occasional daydream about having kids, but past the age of twelve they had the ability to become unpredictable, and scary, and better than you in every conceivable way. This young girl was already a budding diamond expert.

When the girl finished she crossed her thin arms and informed me that store policy was fifteen percent.

"I know that part. Fifteen percent of what?"

"One thousand and that's final," she said. "And fifteen percent of market value for the gold teeth."

I thought about it. Fifteen points on one thou was one hundred and fifty. It wasn't great. Not much for the gold either. Ms. Wetherbee owed me more than the watch would bring. "One thousand is the best you can do?" I asked her.

She nodded.

"Fine," I told the little specialist. "Let's roll out the paperwork."

MY NEIGHBORHOOD FoodMax sat a quarter mile off Speedway Boulevard. It was surrounded on all sides by acres of hot, sunbaked parking lot.

The city was a congregation of parking lots. People loved parking lots. I was from Tucson. I was from Arizona, and Arizona was just dust and sun and mountains and parking lots. People loved the convenience of parking close to the source. People hauled themselves out in toe-curling heat, and this was where they met, their backs sticky, their flesh ripped from sizzling leather seats, their faces sun-blotted. Tides converged in parking lots. I was amazed and stunned and enlivened in parking lots. Arrows directed the flow of traffic. Uni-directional byways divided efficiency from chaos. People laid claim to temporary rectangles of pavement like ecstatic homesteaders—the closer to the entrance the luckier. If they failed, they justified the long hike as beneficial to their health. Keys out, sunshields stuffed in windshields, deep breath, go. Mothers clung desperately to children, as though they were hunted, as though they would be snatched, run over, flattened. Couples held hands. Couples argued. Couples lugged paper bags, hurrying away like robbers with loot. It was the smell of burnt rubber and melted tires and oil ponds on searing blacktop. Reverse lights signaled salvation. There was a pedestrian sense of entitlement the nearer one got to the entrance. Shepherds in fluorescent orange vests tended to flocks of runaway carts; there were always some missing, poached, stolen to become members of another herd across the boulevard. People wandered around lost, as though struck with delirium. People called out for each other, heads just above the car line. People were as anxious and stupefied and dumb-founded in parking lots as they were about death. I couldn't even see the store entrance. It was just parking grids, trucks, cars, reflections, and light poles with numbers.

At the FoodMax, there were thousands of parking spaces.

Inside, there was order. Grids. Air-con. Safety.

I strolled through the cereals, coaxing a cart with a tricky wheel. In the bakery the balloons on Nana's cake looked lopsided and deflated. So I sent the cake back with retrofitting instructions—scrape the balloons and reapply.

I checked my list. Chips, salsa, bread and cheese for finger sandwiches, paper plates, napkins, avocados for guacamole—skip the beer. Skip the candy and cookies. A half sheet of chocolate raspberry cake was sufficient. There would be too many diabetes cases at the party, Epstein included.

I was in the canned soup aisle when an empty shopping cart sailed down the wide lane and slammed into mine. I flung my hands off the handle, and there, down the aisle, framed by warring potato chip displays, stood the man with the white Stetson.

I felt my cheek spasm. I felt my chest tighten. The man was wearing a long-sleeve button-up and black cowboy boots. A chaotic bush of black hair sprouted from his unbuttoned shirt. The man looked to be around my age, give or take, but that just depended on the quality of water coming from his faucet. Judging by his stance, knees bent, arms at the ready, he was anticipating my next move, because the next move was mine. I was holding a coupon. I considered hauling ass to frozen foods, but instead, wanting to brush the guy back, I plucked a sixteen-ounce can of minestrone soup off the shelf. The man watched with interest. He looked around for materials. He snatched a bag of sea salt chips from the display rack and palmed it like a football.

I rolled the soup can in my hand. Liquid shifted as I approached him. Adrenaline made the nerves in my teeth tingle.

"You're taking pictures," I said to the stranger.

"I like taking pictures, is all," the man said. "It's a hobby." When he smiled, I noticed gold trim between his two front teeth. The man had plugged his diastema with a shot of dental gold, as though that might pretty up his smile. A wide brown leather belt reined in his minor beer belly. Dead center, I noticed, was a buckle with an onyx bull bordered by a line of diamonds. Real diamonds.

"You're the one driving the truck," I said.

"Bought and paid for."

"I don't appreciate being followed. I don't like you around my life."

"That's the thing."

"What's the thing?"

"Your life," he said.

I squeezed the soup can. "Mind telling me why you're parking at my house?"

The man poked up the brim of his hat. "We're interested in you," he said. His gold ring had a bull set in bas-relief. "I've been watching you work."

"So that's it. You want me to stop working? Stop bringing people medicine?"

"No, no. We like that you're earning."

"We?"

He brought his ring to his lips and kissed it.

I said, "A man can do damage with a heavy soup can, you know."

The stranger shook his head and tugged up his pant leg. Strapped to his ankle was a black nylon gun holster with a Velcro strap. The holster was empty. "That's the last time you'll threaten me with soup," he said. "Understand?"

I ran fast inventory on the shelves, looking for an item with more heft. The minestrone was my surest bet. "So what do you want?"

"Every time you cross the border, you give me a teddy bear. Easy."

"A teddy bear? What are you talking about?"

The man scanned the empty aisle. "You give me a present."

"What present?"

He rolled his eyes and tensed his shoulders. "Money," he said. "Payment. A cut. You can even slide it under my pillow, if you like."

"That's extortion," I said.

"It's how we do business," he said. "You may have heard about the man in Culiacán. Well, I work for his son. But we all work for the man in Culiacán. Consider it a friendly tax. And what the tax-man wants, the tax-man gets."

"Forget it. I'm just a courier," I said.

"What couriers do is legal. What you do is illegal. And what you do happens in Mexico. According to the man in Culiacán, it requires a tax."

I felt my cheek twitch again. I was unsure how to proceed. So I did the first thing that occurred to me. I turned and walked away from this wannabe vaquero Mafioso. The man's boots clapped against the linoleum as he followed. His hand landed on my shoulder.

"You and me," the man said. Tilting his head, trying to get chummy. "We'll be friends. My name is Diego."

"Estas loco, Diego," I said.

"That's the second time," he said. "You get two passes, and that's it."

Diego tossed the chips into his empty cart and moved down the aisle. I watched his boots clap against the linoleum until he rounded the corner, and then he was gone.

The parking lot was flooded with cars trawling for spaces near the entrance. It was hotter than when I'd arrived. Reflections flickered off other reflections, and my eyes went teary. I ducked between two SUVs, in section N-18, and sat on a kidney-shaped atoll shielded by three young palms. I felt my heart pounding. I briefly considered heading back inside, summoning the manager, and asking for copies of the security tapes. Then marching the tapes to the police. A man inside the store had threatened me. A man had rammed my cart. But the scene I envisioned was cartoonish: standing in front of the store manager (a thin man with oval eyeglasses, I imagined) with my head necked-back and my shoulders to my ears in a stupefied, palsied sort of way.

In the land South-of corruption was rampant. When policía put down the bite, you paid. La mordida was Mexico's national pastime. But the government that operated in the shadows was an entirely different creature. They didn't take you to jail. They didn't question you. They cut down your life, maybe applied some light torture. And the man in the Stetson was part of that world. And now that world had drifted into mine.

I jumped up and scanned the lot. I didn't see the white F-150. I crouched down. I had an unbelievable urge to cry. There was no sign of an airbrushed biplane or the guy's golden smile anywhere.

A shadow suddenly crawled across the pavement between the two cars. Standing over me, with a grocery bag on her hip, was the pretty social worker from the building at the end.

"Here you are again," she said. "In the FoodMax parking lot. Are you hoping to reserve a parking space or something?"

"Mona," I said. She squinted at me. "Your name badge. You were wearing a name badge," I said. "Your name is Mona."

"So this is how you play. And your name is Sid. And you're the campus criminal. And you like to reserve people. How am I doing?"

"It's not like that," I said.

Mona was in frayed mauve sandals. A small buckle connected across the top. One of her toenails was chipped. She glanced at her watch. "Well, I have a work appointment," she said. "Some people have real jobs. If you'll excuse me." She brushed past me, heading for a breach, close enough that I could smell her hair—lemons.

"Wait," I said.

Mona stopped. She balanced the bag on her other hip.

"I'm not what you might think. I'm not a bad person."

She looked at me strangely, kindly. "I never said you were," she said.

9 I spent Sunday morning working on the casita, isolating future repairs and fixing what was broken. A real estate agent had stopped by for a preliminary walk-through. She'd made lists of improvements for me. The most pressing issue was the pronghorn wall-paper. "Absolutely one hundred percent undoubtedly has to go," she'd said.

Several silver-dollar-sized holes decorated the wall in Nana's room. Time had deepened what were once picture mountings. For each, I cut out gyp-sum board, taped it up, troweled down joint compound, and sanded out the high edges. I touched them up with slaps of paint.

My grandparents had kept the spare bedroom in stasis for the past three decades. Long ago it had been my father's room, later my room. Over time the items in the room began to vanish or were carted off to Goodwill: bed, night table, basketball trophies. Now it was empty, except for several holes in the door, a chip in the window, and newly primed walls. I taped the moldings and laid down a plastic drop cloth. By the time I finished painting it, the room began to put me at ease.

An idea occurred to me. I grabbed my baseball bat and some spare balls from the car and arranged everything in the corner. Still, it wasn't enough. The room looked too barren. So I rooted around the closet in the other bed-room for Bubba's Red Sox cap. I hooked it around the bat. I peeled the drop cloth off the floor, and in a mason jar went old house keys: a makeshift rattle. I rummaged around the backyard shed and found several warped old children's books. I rolled the foldable cot into the room, accidentally scratching the hardwood. Soon the room filled in the right way, as it had once been, with the right items, and it resembled, when I finished, a kid's room.

I spent too much time wondering if it was in my nature to raise a child. I would like to believe there was a man in me, if the time came, who would push forward and assume the brave responsibility of fatherhood. When I was with Juliet, I'd wanted that.

As a final touch, I lugged Bubba's handcrafted rocking horse from the shed. I carried it between my knees. I wiped off the dust with my forearm and set it in the corner. Baseball bat, baseballs, rocking horse. The scene threw out hope, and for a moment I imagined setting my boy down on the horse's flat back. I pictured the horse creaking as my boy rocked back and forth, back and forth, on the hardwood floor.

SPEAKING TO MY MOTHER had become a special event. My mother had a demanding schedule, always hard to reach—didn't like to take personal calls in public, thought it was rude—and she often forgot to call me back. But every other Sunday, like clockwork, she called.

I waited in the living room, leaning against the wall, staring at a picture frame that resembled a painter's easel. I liked this photo of her best. It helped me visualize her whenever we talked. The photo showed my mom and dad when they were younger—before I entered the world—weekending in some park, happily married, a pair. Their shadows melded into a single block behind them. Late twenties and wearing a green T-shirt, my mother was young then, with squinty eyes under desert sun and a big-gum smile and carefree brown hair blowing over her head from a wind. And then there was my dad, standing odd as a Joshua tree, one arm awkwardly perched on his hip, but handsome in his way, in a sleeveless shirt with a garish tie that looked like a purple fish. His eyes betrayed concern, mouth not quite torqued in a smile, shoulders riding to his ears. Sometimes it frightened me whenever I closed my eyes at night and couldn't remember what they looked like. But at least I had my mother's voice to hold, and I did when she called after her Sunday brunch.

"Between your stepsister and her father and the office and the annual folk festival, oh dear, I barely have a minute, but it's good to hear your voice," she told me right away, from far away. "When are you coming to visit?"

My mother's do-over, second family distressed me. My stepfather was pleasant enough. And I had a friendly relationship with my stepsister. We all knew each other but didn't really know what to do with each other.

"Did I tell you Stephanie has developed into quite the scientist?" my mother asked me.

"You did."

"Out there on the deck right now making black powder or I don't know what. So pretty outside today. I tell her she needs to take advantage of these long sunny days while she can."

"Tell her not to blow out the window like last time," I said. "Tell her that I say to leave the experiments for the classroom. For everyone's safety."

My mom went on about Stephanie, and I asked the obligatory questions, recalling my brief visits to Anchorage over the years. Flew in, flew out, like surgical strikes; dinners around the old oak table in the muted dining room; lumpy guest bed; the shower window scummy with soap residue. That reality dueled with the fantasy that always emerged the moment I departed. Without me around, I imagined block parties and neighborhood festivals and Mom mothering Stephanie with a kind of precise fury. I knew my mother. When she did pay attention to you in person, she paid attention with her entire being, never asking permission before nailing you with unexpected hugs. And I missed that. Listening to her now, I envisioned her substitute family under dazzling new light: this happy trio living harmoniously inside a house with a polished doorknob, green mountains up high, gray water down below, pretty wet parking lots all around, a moose bumper sticker on the car, and each night handing out trophies to one another.

From outside, I heard the high whine of Alejandro's saw burrowing through the walls. The sound made my fingernails ache.

"I need your advice," I said. My mom was now a Realtor, the person to ask. "I don't really understand this property disclosure statement form the agent gave me. Something's rotting in the kitchen wall. Do I mark that down on the form?"

"What's rotting in the kitchen wall?" she asked. I heard true concern in her voice.

"A thing. Something died. I don't know."

"What died?"

"Another question. Do you know if Nana ever had problems with scorpions?"

"Last week, I put some books in the mail about home improvement and staging kits," she said. "They should already be there. Paint the walls, buff the floors. Also, when you show the place, put tiny soap in a wicker basket inside the bathroom. People go crazy over that kind of nonsense."

In the background over the phone thousands of miles away I heard a loud pop, followed by what sounded like my mother clapping.

"Stephanie did it!" she exclaimed. "Made gunpowder. I can't believe."

"Mom," I said. I looked at my mother's photo. I wondered how she might have changed since I'd seen her last. There was a muffled noise over the phone, followed by a clunk as I imagined the receiver falling to the chair, another as it dropped onto the floor. "Mom? Hello?" I said, listening to footsteps. "Mom?"

I MADE my deliveries on Sunday night because I knew folks would be in.

When Ms. Bunny Vallance swept back her apartment door she was wearing a tight-fitting yellow silk blouse, and judging by the outline, she was not wearing any support. She smiled at me and her forehead refused to wrinkle.

"Your total comes to five dollars," I said. She snatched the bottle from my hand, shook it like a maraca, and pulled me inside.

"I'm watching the window," she said and sat me down on a counter chair. "The monsoon clouds are rolling. Can I interest you in a cocktail?"

"Whatever you're having, Ms. Vallance," I said.

"Bunny. How many times have I told you? *Bunny*."

Ms. Vallance's taste in furniture courted the eccentric: twin bean-shaped pewter tables and, atop one, a suspiciously phallic baguette sculpture. I heard African drums on her stereo. Her comfy bachelorette pad had sea-green walls with beige trim, the corners lit with soft lamps. Flickering around her apartment were vanilla-scented candles in large glass candelabra. I also heard water running in the bathtub.

Ms. Vallance parked a second glass on the counter, poured too much whiskey, and opened a chrome case, winking at me as she extracted two long brown cigarettes. She flicked her gold lighter and pretended to blaze the ends. We shared conspiratorial glances as we pretended to smoke. I heard the faucet in the bathtub stop.

"It's months away, I know, I know, I know, but I was just arranging everything on my bed," she told me. She drew the infinity sign on my wrist with her fingernail. "I was wondering how many swimsuits to bring this year. You really should come along."

"I might if I had your bank statement," I said.

"Oh, kid. You could come along for a week," she said.

"Wish I could."

I knew in the late fall Ms. Vallance would be departing to spend another winter aboard a cruise liner. This winter her destination was South America.

The rooms on the ship, she'd told me, were small but well equipped, she got three meals, company her age, plus nights full of music and nightcaps and dancing. For someone her age, it was the life.

"I hope you're coming to my grandmother's party," I said.

She smiled. "Now, aren't you a decent creature. Don't worry. Already picked out my dress. Lagerfeld."

I leaned back, watching her draw hard off her unlit cigarette. Ms. Vallance set the example. She was the standard-bearer, what others her age should strive for. She had once confessed to me that it had taken half the century to get to the best part of her life. She was forty-three years older than me and she was a world-class optimist. All emergency signage in her apartment had been removed.

"I'm so glad you stop by and see me," Ms. Vallance said, rolling her cheek into her hand. She placed her fingers around my mouth and forced me to smile. "What I wouldn't give," she said, hurrying her finger down my cheek.

Our playdate was interrupted by three loud knocks. Seymour Epstein was at the door, dressed in a blue cotton robe, open at the neck, showing off heaps of white chest hair. His magnified eyeballs bore comparison to something from the gag store. "That you, Sidney?" the old man said to me.

"Seymour, you're early," Ms. Vallance said. "I said eight o'clock. *Eight* o'clock." She looked at me. "He's having headaches," she said and led Epstein by the elbow toward a sleek Scandinavian couch.

"You're still having headaches?" I asked the old man.

"Nothing a temple rub won't cure," he responded.

Ms. Vallance plopped the cigarette into her glass. "We have an appointment to rework Seymour's temples," she explained. "I've been reading up on pressure points. The body is an amazing work of art."

I surveyed her apartment once more. Warm bath, steam curling from behind the door. Light African drums on the stereo. Vanilla-scented candles. Ms. Vallance was in a tight blouse, braless, while Epstein was in a robe.

I snatched the envelope with my five dollars and headed for the door.

Ms. Vallance said, "Sidney, please stay. Where are you—"

Watching senior citizens seduce each other was not my idea of a good time.

Epstein shouted, as I was closing the door, "Don't forget tomorrow! We have errands. Things! We have things! Remember, the café!"

THE NEXT DAY I got an exasperated phone call from Warsaw. He was across town, he said, in the emergency room, behind blue drapes, his pants around his ankles. I could barely hear my friend's garbled voice over the hospital ruckus in the background.

"You got me into this, stupid prick," Warsaw said over the phone. "So guess who gets to pick me up?"

"What happened?"

"Some guy blew through a stoplight and rammed me on the drive back from Mexico. I was attacked." Warsaw's voice fragmented; the line beeped, static crashed, and then he was gone.

Epstein and I had just arrived at the Standard Bean. The old man was surveying the café for coeds. "We need to-go cups," I told him.

We parked in the neatly manicured lot at Pima County General. The campus consisted of modern glass structures built around an old-style adobe building, and a limousine golf cart drove by us on our way toward the hospital entrance.

In the ER, I waited beside Epstein in a garden-patterned chair. Epstein casually thumbed through *Muscle and Fitness* magazine, considering a picture of a woman in mid pull-up, but me, I was unfamiliar with hospital culture, with how one behaved. The white coats unnerved me as much as the laminated wall posters: blueberries were good; fiber in the morning; and don't forget to shrink-wrap that penis!

"Should I ask the desk again?" I asked Epstein.

"They'll bring him when he's ready," Epstein said.

Across from me was a man with a horrific case of meth mouth. He was tapping his knees with his fingers as though playing bongos. The man's front teeth were on permanent vacation from his smile, and every now and then his wild eyes leaped over at me, his tongue appearing in the gummy slot, like some gray monster from within.

Finally a nurse escorted Warsaw down the hall. My friend was wobbly and had to hold her hand. I half expected him to be dressed in hospital pajamas, or to be in a wheelchair, but he was walking and wearing work pants spattered with dried blood.

I noticed a remarkable mound on Warsaw's forehead, so large that it appeared staged. Around his neck was an inflatable neck brace. Strangely, his eyebrows were completely shaved.

"I hope the doctors did that," I said.

"Don't take this personally, Sid, you stupid asshole, but I quit," Warsaw said.

"You can't quit."

"I just did." He nodded at the nurse and then at Epstein. "I have witnesses."

"But I'm giving the business to you."

"I don't want it. That maniac on the road changed my mind."

My friend was dazed. It was the bump. The bump had to be behind his raving, which didn't let up as we escorted him to the parking lot. In between pained, labored breaths, Warsaw related his story, pausing for dramatic effect to throw hard glances at me. The accident had happened just outside town. The two vehicles sat smoking and mangled in the intersection. From behind the wheel Warsaw had watched the other driver open the door of his crushed SUV, feel the air for stability, vomit onto his knees, and unholster a sizable gun. He began waving the weapon at the clouds. The guy, according to Warsaw, his voice hurried, was a mean-looking sonsabitch with a handlebar mustache and a purple Tejana hat on his fat head. Following the guy's big song and dance, he jumped in his SUV, and in the parlance of the police officer, "pulled an expert hit-and-run."

"So let's make it clear," Warsaw said. "I don't enjoy getting rammed midway through a four-way intersection at noon on a Monday. Okay, Sid? I quit." He blinked rapidly. "I left my job with the highway department for this nonsense. And have you *seen* Mount Kilimanjaro on my forehead?"

"Your accident is unrelated. It was just that. An accident."

In the car Warsaw tugged on the seat belt, making sure it was secure.

As usual, I overshot The Pony Express trailer park. Sunlight had bleached the name off the road sign and the hidden driveway was easy to miss.

This section of town was full of heart-wrenching, poorly paved encampments. Aluminum sheds next to aluminum homes sizzled under the sun. There were no trees in Warsaw's murdery neighborhood, which apparently didn't faze Warsaw's nearest neighbor, who was outside on her porch, absorbing the heat, looking out over her fenced-in yard, a twelve-by-twelve square of electric-green concrete. I saw an oxygen canister beside her. Tubes ran off it, which cinched around her hollowed-out face.

Warsaw lived at the end, no surrounding shade, not even a bush. And it was off-yellow. That was about the nicest thing I could say about his trailer. Epstein surveyed the scene and told us he wanted to wait in the car.

Warsaw's place was a beat-up mess, holes in the linoleum, and cheap blond wood paneling. Like some kind of porno set. In the bedroom there was a mattress next to a banker's box brimming with Mexican gore tabloids. Four dishes were stacked on a mini fridge. The most notable thing about his place was that there was nothing in it: no TV, no stereo, not even a wall clock. His home struck me, I said, as a place a serial killer might find comforting.

"At least I don't have a dead animal in my kitchen wall," he said and shed his work boots. More and more Warsaw was beginning to look like someone else, like someone I didn't know. I wanted to ask about my friend's eyebrows, about what he was doing with his body hair, about what he was doing with his life.

I carefully sidestepped a used Band-Aid on the floor. "Your lifestyle choice is really pissing me off."

"George Greg lives simply too," Warsaw said. "Says so in his book."

Not long ago, I'd asked Warsaw what his father thought about him moving back to town, not using his Ivy League degree, throwing his potential at lesser things, and living in a trailer park. Hurt had lit up in my friend's eyes, a special kind of hurt I'd never seen before, and Warsaw had said, picking lint from his tongue, that his father had told him, "As long as your cock gets hard, I'm a proud man."

Warsaw eased himself to the mattress and draped a damp green washcloth over his contusion. More George Greg books were scattered across the floor.

"Look at how you live," I said.

"Too much comfort can disable you," Warsaw responded. "And I've had a lot of comfort. So much that I never had an opportunity to feel terrified. Scaring yourself can feel wonderful. I'm telling you."

"By that logic, you can't quit. This business scares me every day."

"Indeed, indeed. But sitting there in the hospital, with the doctor's flashlight in my eyeballs, something happened," he told me. "As he was looking inside me, I realized my limits. When you're frightening yourself, you have control. But when you're sideswiped by some crazy hombre, the world is scaring you."

EPSTEIN PINCHED HIS KEY into the door and kicked it open. His eyes were tired and his hair was bristled up. I followed him in.

A light went on when the old man shuffled inside. His apartment was bachelor spartan, but unlike my friend's trailer, the old man's spread had the air of a guest condo, a place lent to friends visiting from out of town. Epstein had a nautical theme going. Fishing nets on the wall. Three model ships inside glass jars. Against the wall in the living area was a complicated entertainment system, thousands of dollars' worth of equipment.

But you couldn't escape the picture frames. The mantel above the just-for-show fireplace was loaded with them. This was his temple, his source, his supply of past faces. The pictures of his wife, Effie, showed her lounging on a lawn, sitting in a chair, and posing by a tree. There were also snapshots from the old man's deep-sea fishing excursions and numerous photos of his daughters, the twins, Sarah and Miriam, who both lived in New York and harassed the old man's cell phone constantly. I looked closer at them. Sarah and Miriam were an exquisitely dressed team, attractive in their youth, with urban hairstyles and wide, accomplished smiles. Epstein rarely mentioned Effie to me. From what I had pieced together, he'd sold their house after she died, gotten rid of everything in it, and tried to press RESTART.

Epstein fell to the couch and dipped his hand into a beach cooler. He extracted a cold longneck and held it out for me. Epstein couldn't have beer—his meds didn't mix—but he liked having cool ones around for guests. I watched him dig around the ice until he found a vanilla nutritional supplement for himself.

He killed his beverage in four heroic gulps. Then he set the can on the table and leaned on his knees. "Let me ask you something," he said. "What are you looking for? Are you going to run drugs for the rest of your life?"

"Why?" I said.

"We're concerned people," Epstein said. "It's good to have concerned people in your life." He rubbed his hands together. "So. Let's have it. What do you want?"

After dealing with Warsaw and the hospital, I was too tired for questions like this.

"I'm asking you," Epstein said.

"You're my friend because you don't ask those questions."

"I'm your friend because I do."

"All right," I said. "Someday I'd like to catch a game at Fenway, for starters."

"Let's not play that game," Epstein said.

"What kind of answer are you looking for?"

"A true answer. What you want. Out of life."

"First, my grandma."

"What do you want?"

"Now you," I said. "Are they serving something funny for dinner around here?"

"I'll keep asking," Epstein said.

The beer was cold, just how I liked it. "I want a family," I finally said. "Like yours on the mantel. I want a boring, comfortable life with people that I love in it. Is that good enough?"

The old man spread his arms across the couch, drawing a heavy, tactical breath. He didn't say anything more. The tired old man. His tired old eyes. I knew he was not used to this late hour. Epstein never talked about the other men in his family. And it occurred to me now and then that many of those men occupied the past tense. Epstein had mentioned a brother once, in passing, but he'd never mentioned him again. I began to wonder about living to his age, about Warsaw, not having him around to annoy me. I saw my hair receding, my skin loosening, my friend growing old alongside me until only one of us remained. I felt pulverized by the daydream.

When Epstein began to nod off, I lifted him from the couch and guided him down the hall. The old man gripped my elbow. I took my time untying his arch-support shoes, rolling down his thick, sweaty tube socks. He grabbed my arm and eased into bed. Above his headboard was a buoy with his wife's name painted on it.

The old man didn't thank me, didn't need to, as I turned off the lights in the apartment, locked the door, and quietly let myself out.

I SPOTTED HER FROM A DISTANCE. Mona was outside in the dusky parking lot, trying to cram a large black case into the backseat of a small yellow car. A lamp radiated an oval glow over her struggle. She was hunched like a linebacker, her shoulder straining against the case. I approached from behind. "Need help?"

Mona's arms jumped at her sides. She turned. "You scared me."

"Empty lots do that," I said.

"Man materializes from the shadows."

"It's only the campus criminal," I said.

She was still leaning against the case, preventing it from falling. "So are you going to help or not?"

I carefully led the case in from the other side. Mona pushed, but when I told her to hold, she didn't, and my hand got stuck. "Okay, pull it back a little," I said. Mona shoved the case harder. "Pull back! Mona, my hand." Mona leaned with her shoulder once more, bullying the case inside, pinching my hand against the door.

"Voilà!" she said. She swiped her hands as she rounded the car. "Funny we meet again in a parking lot."

I massaged the pinch from my knuckles. "It's the hot new place," I said. "That's a big case. Must be an impressive instrument."

Mona looked absentmindedly toward the building at the end. "Sometimes when I'm not at my desk I play cello for the residents. Only four people showed up tonight. People tire of hearing Bach. A cabulance arrived in the middle. Someone fell. And of course, everyone wants to watch that show."

A shadow broke apart the light from a distant lamp. Near the building at the end we saw Mr. Garland Bills walking on a path and dressed in a tuxedo. His hair was combed and as shiny as a black widow's belly. It was the only time I'd seen him without a tracksuit. Garland Bills saw us and maneuvered sideways defensively, disappearing behind a desert willow.

"A strange man," Mona said.

"Not as strange as some," I said.

"You know of others?"

"I have a friend."

Mona shifted, and I heard her sandals tap elegantly on the cement. I liked the idea of her playing cello in sandals. And I liked her lissome arms, her lanky disposition. She held herself in a hug. I pulled a photocopied invite from my postal bag.

"My grandma's birthday party is coming up," I told her.

"I remember."

"Look, I have one invitation left," I said. "It's going to be the season's hottest event. Scalpers can't even get their paws on these. Please tell me you'll be there."

10 Ajo Cemetery's office was inside a humorless white cinderblock building, and everyone in the place had large, sad, watery eyes, as though they were continually crying or being cried at. The secretary marked my payment down in her binder and handed me a receipt.

"So, that's it?" I said.

"Congratulations," the woman said. "Proud owner of a grave."

I got dizzy thinking too much about them, the gravestones, and the heat made me even dizzier. Outside, the sun over-accentuated each one. Each was a person, a reminder. I wandered through the cemetery, the burnt grass smelling of hay, wondering about the dead underneath my feet, the slushy bones inside airtight boxes, the mud everyone eventually became. Cemeteries offered little consolation to those left behind. Replace a person with a stone and it was still just a goddamn stone.

The sun needled my neck, and I wondered, when the time came, where would I lie?

I read the names, lives bookended by numbers. 1919–, 1910–, 1987–. Beloved wife. Brother. Father of. Husband to. Loving twins died at birth.

My father went into that good night by way of a cottonwood tree branch outside my boyhood window. From memory, from what I remembered: he awoke in the middle of the night, carefully arranged twelve eggs inside a Pyrex bowl, placed the bowl in the middle of our dining room table, and then went to the garage in search of load-bearing vinyl rope. All sensory information from the next morning, after we discovered his body ten feet from the dirt, after the police, the coroner, remains blank. A psychologist later called my fuzzy dream state "disassociation."

Frederick Dulaney, Certified Public Accountant. Sometimes I wondered what his former clients would have thought if they'd known their accountant had died with barely enough in his estate to cover his debts. My mother buried him with his gold wedding ring.

My dad had once given me a baseball signed by Mickey Mantle, but the man had never really understood the emotional mechanics that make for a good father. He didn't believe in translating emotion into sentences. I don't quite remember him ever saying *I love you, I'm proud, good job.* It was my childhood job to divine affection out of grunts and mumbles. There must have been decent moments between us, but I was young, and memory was tricky. It was like going to the basement and briefly toggling on the light and then trying to remember the placement of everything in that room years later.

And indeed it crushed me, after my father died, the way my mother began looking at me as she once did him, as though I was charged with apologizing for his fatal flaw. I disliked that she saw relics of him in me, commenting on how I had his same nose, his jaw, his eyes, etc. Early on I began to understand how my father's decision to end his life disturbed my mother. She began sleeping too much and then not sleeping at all. She broke down in line at the stationery store. She went skydiving. She set the goldfish free in a mud puddle. Eventually she declared that we needed to move, but by then Nana had made a warm nest of a bedroom for me in her house, where I often slept whenever my mother was crazed. When she finally departed on a plane for Alaska, she told me she'd return for me when she felt better. She never did.

I sat on the grass beside a headstone engraved with the dates 1961–1968. The name on it said Jessica Delilah Payne. In her seven years the girl barely had time to open her mouth and stick out her tongue and taste the air before she closed her eyes and went to sleep forever.

THE STRANGER ACROSS THE STREET from us fingered the rim of a ten-gallon cowboy hat with a turquoise band. As he waited at the crosswalk, he put his thumbs in his waistband and lifted and let his blue jeans fall. I noticed a black bandanna wrapped tightly around his wrist. The light turned green. He walked big and awkward in a knees-out sort of duck waddle.

"That's your trusty newspaperman?" I asked Danni.

"He knows what he's talking about," she said.

"He looks more like a goat rancher."

Introductions were brief. The man declined my offer for a cup of coffee as we picked a table in the back of the café. The man crashed into a chair. He was a typical borderlander, all tendon and grit.

"What's going on down there is the Sinaloa cartel butting foreheads with Juárez," the man explained to me, fiddling with his bolo tie, and as a professional snoop, I supposed, the man ought to know the details of such things. Danni unscrewed the top on a thermos and drew a deep sip.

"These Mexican cartels own different sections along the border," he went on, "what's called plazas. And now that their northern neighbor is cinching up routes in the east and west, the cartels are vying for midpoint control. It's hard to move product near El Paso these days. And forget about California. *Pfft.* The Americans shut down Tijuana with that border wall. Sinaloa and Juárez both want the wide-open middle. Sonora. The theater. If you control the theater, you control the conveyor belt to the north."

The middle-aged man referred to the borderland as a theater, as the grounds of operation, using war terms. He had a torqued nose that looked once-broken. Old acne scars stippled his cheeks. As he talked to me—and he could talk, he was blessed with the gift—white foamy spittle gathered at the corners of his mouth. I concentrated on the man's scars. Scars lent him credibility. They were physical testimony of endured humiliations. As I understood it, the man wrote birdcage journalism for the local weekly paper and, according to Danni, he kept his finger on the pulse. She turned to him to dispel rumors, to get confirmation. The man apparently watched the wires hourly. He talked to the people: cops, coyotes, pollos, BORSTAR agents, politicians, even the teenage migrant glue sniffer with a good view of border events from an abandoned railway freight car. The man kept talking, laying background, telling me stories. He had seen a lot. Too much. His general outlook was apocalyptic. He thought of the border as a new kind of hell. A year ago, he told me, a Mexican colleague of his in Nuevo

Laredo named too many names. Journalists South-of were never supposed to speculate, offer opinions or possible motives, and they avoided naming names. Careful editing of lead stories could mean the difference between life and death. His colleague—a woman—dug deep. She'd spied on off-limits stash houses. She poked around wealthier neighborhoods. When she hit on some precious information, she published an article. Days later, when she was out on a morning jog, she disappeared. *Poof.* Like that. Into the desert. "She became a number, a statistic. One of them. Los Desaparecidos."

"So about Danni and me," I said. "How do we figure in?"

The reporter wiped his mouth with his forearm. "Danni distributes medications to the people of her nation," he said. "The O'odham have witnessed flare-ups in the past. It's a busy route. After all, her nation is a sawhorse that touches both sides. As for you." He smiled weakly, and I sensed derision in his eyes. "You handle an elderly community in Tucson. There's no connection between you and the cartels, and there's no reason to connect you and the cartels. The money you collect, pardon, it's pitiful. It's not even a dinner tip to these people. You're bush league. You might as well be a gnat wandering onto their air traffic control screens as they watch 757s touch down on desert airfields."

I inhaled, leaning back. The espresso machine in the café blew out pressurized air. "What about the vaquero in the white F-150?" I asked.

"An opportunist, I'm sure," the reporter said. His eyes narrowed as he flattened his hands on the table. "Listen, this guy speaks perfecto English, and with no trace of an accent? And he knows his way around town? I'm sure he's bi-national. Father was an American, his mother a Mexican, or vice versa. He comes. He goes. He's got an American passport and Mexican loyalties. I'm sure he's fishing for kickbacks. Somehow he found out about you, about what you do, and he wants a fraction. This cabrón looks at you, pardon, and sees easy money."

At the café counter, a young boy squirmed and tried to free himself from his mother's grasp. I watched him lean back with his full weight, his body slackened in protest. The boy's feet, his elbows, his nose—he was so small, so pure of heart, still free from life's burdens. For a moment I saw myself with this child—throwing a ball, wrestling with a dog—and a shot of jealousy mainlined through me, then exited with a shiver. Finished with the father fantasy, I said to the reporter, "Tell me what you know for certain."

"I *never* use the word 'certain,'" he said. "That word is not in my vocabulary. But this is what I do know. Border politics shift overnight. Money changes hands. Allegiances form and disintegrate. Appointments are missed and chaos ensues. This is what's certain. If the man following you associates with the cartels, keep your distance."

"He wore a ring with a black bull," Danni said. "Sid told me about a belt buckle too. With a bull on it."

"So you mentioned," the man said. He squirmed, crossed his legs, and laid a hand on his knee. "That's a problem. A bull means one thing. Los Toros."

"I thought Los Toros wasn't around here," I said.

"Let me make it clear to you. If this man is involved with for-hire, ex-military mercenaries, you do not want to be near him or know him." He paused before adding, "Exclamation point."

"He wants a percentage," I said. "A tax."

"What figure?"

"Never said."

"Look, he may not come back," the man said. "You've spoken with him. Threatening someone on American soil is a crime. It doesn't play well in court. He approached you. You declined. He thought he could frighten you. He may be a petty thief, a man looking for an easy meal. Lay low. Hope he goes away."

"Tell me what we're really talking about here," I said. "Brass tacks."

"Brass tacks?" he said with a snicker. "Now you're talking brass tacks?" He threw a yellow-toothed smile at Danni. "This guy says to me 'brass tacks.' Brass fucking tacks. I haven't heard those words in years. Danni, I don't know where you dig up these characters." He locked his eyes on me. "Okay, for argument's sake, let's say this guy associates with Los Toros. To be safe?" he said. "Do you have access to a firearm?"

11 Late-afternoon light flickered through the kitchen window, playing across my friend's hairless body. The freckles on his shoulders looked enhanced and touched by sun. Warsaw was leaning on the cool stovetop burners, palms down, shirtless, sockless, wearing boxer shorts decorated with different cat breeds. I set my bag on the counter.

"So you broke in again," I said.

"I took your key, made a duplicate, slid it back on your key ring," Warsaw said. "That's called stealth."

"That's called stealing. I come home and find you in my kitchen. What are you even doing here?"

Warsaw pointed at a garment bag hanging on the door. "Your grandma's party. I needed a shower. Mine's broken. And as your oldest friend," he said, pressing his palms together, "I'm asking you to do something about the smell in here. It's not funny anymore."

My friend was right. The smell of active decomposition now blanketed the kitchen. "It's on my list," I said.

"Shove it to the top," Warsaw said and lifted a razor blade from the counter. He slid open the patio door and stepped outside onto the brick. "Come on, I need you to shave my back."

I looked at him. The mound on his forehead had retreated. In its place was a yellow, haloed bruise.

"Come on, please. I can't reach," he said.

I ignored him. I counted the white paper bags, double-checking pill counts, matching initials with names, making sure everything was as it should be. I heard my friend scooting patio chairs around, which irritated me. Finally Warsaw's insistence won out.

I applied shaving cream to my friend's shoulders, down his back, and spread the meringue around evenly.

"That girl down in Nogales did a bang-up job the first time," Warsaw said. "Just need a touch-up."

I reluctantly took the razor blade from him and carved a straight line down his back. My neighbor's porch door unexpectedly opened, and Alejandro stepped out. He shifted his weight awkwardly from one foot to the other and attempted to retreat back inside, but we had already seen each other. He had seen me shaving my friend.

"Alejandro, hi," I called to him. I wagged the razor. "I heard you again last night. Working a lot out there. Are you building the O.K. Corral or something?"

Alejandro didn't respond. I watched him lower his welder's mask and step down off the porch. His helmet hovered toward his shed.

"I'm thinking of retiring," Warsaw said. "Dedicating my time to George Greg's vision."

"Don't be ridiculous. Retire from what? You don't even have a job. Besides, I fired you."

"You didn't fire me," he said. "I quit."

"Anyway, don't be stupid. You can't retire. You have an MBA, for Christ's sake. You could do something useful with that."

"I don't want to do anything useful," he said. "All I want to do is see how far I can take this."

I STARED at the balloons, speechless.

They were the same color that I'd selected at the store, a bouquet of floating cherries, but now altered by a felt marker. It was an awful way to start Nana's party, but the delivery kid was an effeminate type with gentle, sleepy eyes and a sad, wet smile, and he told me, in earnest, that the shop didn't stock balloons printed with HAPPY 89TH." "Only 'Happy 8th.' They don't go up that high," he said before hurrying toward the exit.

I arranged food on fold-out tables. A vegetable mélange watched over a bowl of purple fruit punch and sandwiches, crackers and cheeses. Paseo del Sol's community room was multi-use, utilized for lectures, travel slide shows, bingo, and events like ours.

Plopped in a chair by herself, with a purple cone on her head, my grandmother watched me assemble her birthday spread with an expression that told me everything I needed to know. Tinsel rose from the cone like silvery magma. "This is not very enjoyable," Nana said. "I'm an independent, mature woman. Not a child."

"The party hasn't started yet. Relax."

"You're treating me like a four-year-old. I should be gussied up. Wearing makeup, with my hair done."

"You're wearing a nice dress."

"Oh, stop it. You know what I mean. I need glamour. Where's the band to go with the stage? How many birthday parties do I have left? This looks suspiciously like some little boy's party."

"Wait until you open my present," I said. I set the purple envelope on the table. "You just wait." I had spent a lot on a gift certificate for a massage at a fancy spa on the hill. Sixty minutes of hands-on work, plus thirty minutes in a tub. I knew my grandmother would love it. There: That was glamorous. I'd even added a pedicure to the ticket.

Our first guests bore hurrahs and good wishes. They kissed Nana's cheek and gathered at the buffet for inspection. Soon Epstein arrived with Ms. Vallance on his arm. The old man had transformed himself into a prepster. A yellow sweater draped over his shoulders, arms tied at the front, like some magazine advertisement. Bunny had enlisted a body-hugging cocktail dress so form-fitting that I felt blood rush to my cheeks. Both greeted

Nana, who was still in a chair, and then they wandered to a corner and spiked the punch in their plastic cups from Ms. Vallance's flask.

Ms. O'Neill wore fat, dangling pearls, and she was followed by Ms. Haybroke, who for some reason was in a light blue waitress uniform, the white collar perfectly starched. Ms. Parker, a recent transplant from New York, talked loudly and chomped on her gum and emphasized her sentences by flailing her hands. Our beloved athlete, Ms. von Bausch, arrived next, done up like an Olympian, in red, white, and blue tracksuit.

The conversations were polite but expectant, as though people were hoping I might put on a fireworks show.

Eventually Warsaw walked in wearing an expensive black suit, with crisp lines, an ideal fit at the shoulders. He was really something. I thought he'd actually look decent if he hadn't already completed the package. My friend's head was now as bald as a mannequin's. Warsaw saw me glaring and shot his cuffs.

The party picked up when Ms. O'Neill rolled an ancient slot machine out of a storage closet. It was an old standard, with chrome lever and reels stamped with fruit. Like some relic salvaged from a sixties Vegas film. Ms. Vallance rooted through her cocktail purse and shoved quarters in my hand. When it was my turn, I stepped up. The machine blinked: one credit. The lever pulled easy, ripped into place, and three wheels spun inside the glass. One blueberry, one slice of peach. The contraption hit big—lights and noise—and then the slot emitted a muffled, dying ding and shit fifteen quarters into the tin tray. Ms. Vallance smiled tightly and clapped like a proud mother.

Talkative clusters formed. I overheard Warsaw speaking with Ms. Haybroke about old-timey diners on Route 66. When she accidentally dropped her plastic spork, I watched him hunt down a napkin, wipe the spork clean, and hand it to her with a smile. My grandmother still refused to get up from her chair, sitting there like some queen, twirling a finger through her gray hair, smiling meekly at her friends, clearly embarrassed that people had come to celebrate her.

Warsaw walked over as I was putting the candles on the cake. My friend's bald, shiny head lit the way.

"You look like you contracted a disease," I said.

"George Greg," Warsaw said.

"If I ever hear that man's name again . . ."

"You should really read his book." Warsaw sipped his punch, looking more self-assured than I'd seen him in some time. My friend scanned the room, considering the old women, the old men. "And this is undoubtedly the scariest shit of all time," he said. "It's unbelievable. Why have you been hiding this?"

"I haven't been hiding anything. I'm here all the time."

"Sure, but you're so close you can't see it."

"See what?"

"That they're still in the game. Amazing, at their age, to be in the game. It may be bottom ninth, but they're in it. And now that I'm here, watching it all for myself . . ." He shook his head. "This is incredible. This is the best scare yet."

One person definitely in the game was Mona. I watched her walk in, and I felt a punch in my chest.

"So, that's your chica," Warsaw said.

"She's not anyone's chica."

Following closely behind her was Ms. Gwendolyn Wetherbee, who staggered in and leaned against a wall for support. The old woman was out of breath. I was surprised she was here. I hadn't invited her. She was too much of a disaster. I intercepted her and noticed that her lipstick had wandered outside the lines. There was a bulge in her lip. It was a warm night, yet she was in a fur coat and slippers shaped like elephants. A brown banana peel poked from her furry pocket. "What's that in your lip?" I asked. Ms. Wetherbee swallowed and winced. With a finger I folded down her lip. "You're chewing tobacco?"

She reached for a half-empty cup on a nearby table and spat a long, brown, ropey gob into it.

"Why are you here?" I asked.

"I thought it was disco night," she said, slurring her words. "These feet feel like dancing."

Her pupils were tiny black dots melted into clover-green irises. The old woman was blasted. To think she had family in town, sons who refused to help her.

"You need to get off the pills," I said. "You're a mess."

She brushed the pocket with the banana peel and it made a familiar sound.

"I heard that," I said. "You holding?"

"No."

Across the room I saw Mona talking with Bunny Vallance. "Give me one."

"Never," she said.

"Then you're cut off."

"I'll find someone else," she said.

"I'm counting to ten."

Ms. Wetherbee dug out the bottle before I reached six. I dumped a pill and halved it with my fingernail. I chewed on it to obliterate its time-released shell.

After a bit, I walked over to Mona. "Thanks for coming."

Ms. Vallance put a finger on my lips. "Mona and I were just talking about how easy it is for men to hunt for women in these old-folks' homes," she said. "The odds are certainly in your favor." And then, to end the discussion, she said, "Mona here looks to me like a pretty good target."

"Well," Mona said. Her neck went red. Very quickly she seized Ms. Vallance's arm and propelled her toward the slot machine, passing Warsaw, who was guiding one of Nana's friends to a chair.

A nasal drip, hard as a marble, rolled down my throat, sank in my stomach, wandered through my intestines, which I squeezed out in the cold-tiled bathroom. I washed my face and spit mouthfuls of chlorinated water into the basin. Thanks to the pill, my features began to ripple in the mirror. Tonight, tonight, I would ask Mona, tonight, for her phone number.

When I came out of the bathroom, I saw the man hovering over Ms. Wetherbee as though it were a perfectly natural thing for him to do. I stopped, and stared. He was across the room swaying on his boot heels. Ms. Wetherbee appeared to be asleep in the chair. Stetson, cowboy boots, buttoned shirt—it was him. Not only that, the man had a piece of Nana's chocolate raspberry cake in his hand. We hadn't even started the song. The gun was in my Honda, wrapped in a cheap Mexican blanket, and I still hadn't purchased bullets. The man had even swapped his white Stetson for a black number. I stayed close to the wall, feeling slightly numb, watching Ms. Vallance spike Epstein's drink again, watching Ms. Parker and her expressive hands, watching the man. When he set his plate on the floor, leaning over Ms. Wetherbee and shaking her birdlike shoulders, I rushed across the room.

"What are you doing to her?" I asked.

"We were talking," the man said. "She just fell asleep or something."

"Ms. Wetherbee," I said softly, leaning down. "Gwendolyn," I said. She was slumped. Up close, her cheeks were the color of ash. She was barely breathing. I touched her face. Cold. I lifted an eyelid. Her eyeball had wandered to the back of her skull.

"Dial the paramedics," I told the stranger.

The man's hand stiffened.

"Now!" I yelled. My voice echoed around the room. Everyone turned. Warsaw quickly appeared, holding a clean spork. My friend had a phone to his ear before anyone. Warsaw dictated orders, bristling with coordinates, evolving again into the friend from before, the friend I once knew, full of bravura. Paseo del Sol, Warsaw said into the phone. He said, the community building, elderly woman down, an elderly woman down, and *hurry*.

"What do we do?" the man asked me.

"I don't know," I said.

Nana and her guests caught wind of the emergency. Soon a claustrophobic circle formed. Ms. Vallance clutched Epstein's hand. Nana rose from her chair to walk over. Her birthday cone was crooked. I leaned closer. Ms. Wetherbee's willowy breath touched my face.

"What happened?" Mona asked.

"She passed out. I don't know. She just went to sleep."

Mona grabbed Ms. Wetherbee's wrist and searched for a pulse.

"What's her pulse tell you?" I asked Mona.

"I don't know. I'm a social worker," she said.

"Ms. Wetherbee?" I pinched the old woman's cheeks. Her lips puffed out.

"Help her!" Ms. O'Neill cried. "Save her!"

"Stay calm," Warsaw said, stiff-armed, acting like a barrier. He had a happy, terrified smile on his face.

Ms. Vallance pushed forward and threw grape punch in Ms. Wetherbee's hair. It didn't rouse her. Then Epstein did the same, dousing me in the process. Ms. Parker shoved three more sticks of gum in her mouth, and then the crowd parted, and from out of nowhere Mr. Garland Bills appeared in a red tracksuit and clean white tennies. Chest puffed, arm cocked in front, he shoved people aside.

"Let's back it up," he said forcefully. He ordered everyone around, and we all obeyed. He told Warsaw to fetch paperbacks from the bookshelf in the corner. The stranger went along to help. They returned with armfuls, and together they spread thick romance novels across the floor, creating a sort of bed. They lowered Ms. Wetherbee down onto it, her head tilting to the side.

"Clammy skin, shallow breathing. To the point of apnea," Mr. Bills said. "This isn't good." He pressed two fingers into her neck. He listened to her breathing. "Unresponsive," he said. His eyes blazed like two lighthouses. "She could fall into a coma. Do you have any Narcan?" He was staring at me. "Didn't think so."

Sirens sang in the distance, then the song died, and I knew the cabulance was through the gate. Mr. Black Stetson, whatever his name, watched with big, wet, frightened eyes while Warsaw paced a figure eight, his suit jacket now on the floor, his fists shoved in his armpits.

"She's stable," Mr. Bills said. "But she needs to get to the hospital immediately."

Two paramedics, both women, both in blue bodysuits, scrambled through the door. One lugged a medical tackle box, the other a foldable stretcher.

"How long?" one paramedic asked.

"She's been out a few minutes," I said. "Maybe ten."

"Please save her," Mr. Stetson said.

"Her name?" the medic asked.

"Gwendolyn Wetherbee," I said.

"Age?"

"Seventy-five."

"History of this type of thing?"

"I don't know," I said.

"Medications?"

"Painkillers," Mr. Garland Bills said. He was staring at me. "A lot of painkillers. Opiates." The medic shook her head, and I thought—how could I not?—what had I done?

"She needs Narcan," Mr. Bills said. "Narcan will pull her out."

One medic bent to her knee and pressed her cheek against Ms. Wetherbee's lips. She directed a pinprick beam of light at the old woman's eyelids, and suddenly her eyes opened, sparkling like sequins.

"Goodness!" Ms. Parker shouted.

Ms. Wetherbee took a long moment to look around, as though she was counting us. She mussed her hair, cricked her neck, and surveyed the ad hoc bed made from romance novels.

"Alhambra," Ms. Wetherbee said. Her green eyes rose to meet mine. "That was a nice ride. I've always wanted to visit Alhambra, Sidney. That was the nicest ride yet."

WE WALKED IN A PROCESSION, following the paramedics as they escorted Ms. Wetherbee to the waiting cabulance. Had it been someone else, anyone else, I wouldn't have been dragging around such massive guilt. My client, my fault. I was her supplier. Ms. Wetherbee's near-overdose canceled out my minor buzz. And tonight was the last time, I told myself, that I would take a recreational pill. Outside, in the warm night, as the cabulance lights reflected in the lake, I had half a mind to assume full responsibility for Ms. Wetherbee's care, but at the last moment Warsaw pushed forward and bumped my shoulder and lied to the paramedics. In front of everyone he told them he was Ms. Wetherbee's grandson—all 170 bald pounds of him—and even more, he was coming with them. Warsaw jumped in the back of the cabulance with a paramedic and grabbed Ms. Wetherbee's hand. The paramedic closed the door.

It was only half past eight and the partiers had decided to call it a night. Mona left before I could get her phone number. Oddly, Nana hugged me.

"Thank you, thank you," she said. She said we'd hit it out of the ball-park. Said it was more excitement than she was expecting. What an ending! What surprise! She was filled with such joy over the main event that she wouldn't let my arm go, telling me how thankful she was for me, for this party, for her birthday present. She hoped to draw a real hunk for her upcoming birthday massage, she said.

"IT'S DIEGO," the man reminded me. I sipped from a plastic cup and nodded. Man's name was Diego. Diego with the different-colored cowboy hats, gold in his smile, and the shitty habit of flaring up my stomach by following me around.

"You picked an interesting night to visit," I said.

"We need to talk," he said. A lamp in the shape of a swan's neck overhung his F-150 truck in the parking lot, illuminating huge boxes in the truck's bed: dishwasher, TV, stereo system. I leaned against the pole and watched Diego tie rope around a cleat. "These boxes," he explained, "belong to El Bebé." Diego blinked spastically when he said the name. "One of my chores is moving the necessary supplies south."

"Gigantic TVs qualify as necessary?"

"El Bebé likes telenovelas," he said. "Also, El Bebé would like to meet you."

"Well, I don't want to meet him."

Diego snickered. Without his Stetson, his hair bunched to the sides and looked like uncircumcised foreskin. "I'm looking at your face," I said as Diego pulled the rope taut. "I'm reading the lines by your eyes. Trying to guess your age."

"Why would a man want to do that to another man?"

"We all have hobbies. Let's say that's one of mine."

"Three-seven," Diego said.

Three-seven. Diego had several years on Warsaw and me, but thirty-seven was a good age, an age when a man knew how to fasten rope to a truck bed, among other things.

When he finished securing the load, Diego followed me to my Honda, where I lifted the hatch, unfolded a blanket, and grabbed Bubba's gargantuan Smith Wessy. I stood there with it, barrel pointed at the pavement, trying to mask the shake of my hand by clenching the grip. Diego stepped back and his eyes grew wide. Wider, in fact, than during the Wetherbee ordeal. A gun made more of an impression on him than a sixteen-ounce soup can.

"Belonged to my granddad," I told him. I aimed it toward the lake. "When I was a boy, he liked to drive me out into the desert. We'd find old mining encampments. Abandoned buildings. Shoot out the windows. We used this monster, if you can believe." I didn't handle weapons often, but as an American I was familiar with the basics. It was unloaded, safety on. "This model takes .45 cartridges. Have you seen the size of the .45 cartridge? An inch long, that cartridge. So you can imagine the size of the bullet."

"That's a big gun," Diego said.

"You could take it apart and build a bicycle."

"Why do you have a gun?"

"For the next time you show your face," I said. "This is where my grandma lives. It's her home."

"But we could make money," Diego said. He gestured at the boxes in the back of the truck. "I hate driving up here. Wastes my time. Do *this*, Diego. Do *that*, Diego. El Bebé shoves me around like a little brother. You drive south anyway, and I thought, it could save me the trouble, you know?"

For a moment I considered what he was getting at—pick up goods, drive them south, and pick up meds: double loads in both directions.

"How did you even find out about me?" I asked. "No one knows me. I'm as anonymous as they come."

"My cousin, Luisa," he said. "She washes sheets in that building over there. Everyone knows what you do, compadre. White boy running drugs for his grandma's friends. We have jokes about you. You're a real laugh."

"You have jokes? Tell me one," I said.

"They're in Spanish." Diego put a hand in his hair. "The humor gets lost in translation."

12

"Our curtains, do you remember our curtains? You wanted the navy blue. I told you, come winter, the sunlight wouldn't get through. We had routines, and arguments, sure, we had our arguments, but we had a life. We could still have one. I never wanted you to leave."

Juliet's voice mail surprised me, made me miss her again. It made me feel plugged in to some distant electrical source. This was the first time she'd ever said she hadn't wanted me to leave, that maybe she still wanted a life . . .

I listened to her message again. I checked the time. She'd left it in the middle of the night. I was already annoyed that I had to head to Nogales, and in this vicious heat, without air-con. I could have lived without any more messages. And I could have lived the rest of my life happy if I never had to visit Nogales again.

I LIKED TO BUY MIXED TAPES, worth a dime, from the Goodwill store in my neighborhood. My Honda was old, and the stereo only took cassettes. I made a pit stop before boarding the highway, searching through the picked-over pile for old tapes with handwritten titles on the labels. The dusty store smelled of that peculiar, lifeless, older-generation fabric that always disturbed me.

I went through the cassettes. FOR MAYA one label said. Another said FIRST ANNIVERSARY. Another: SISTERS. I liked these old cassette tapes. They brought happiness and surprise to a dull drive. Each had a story. Who had made these? And for whom? And what were their lives like now?

"Anything else?" the cashier said when I put EVE OF BIG DAY on the counter.

During the week I moved. I drove. So far on the odometer: 168,236 miles. I was a man earning money. Mexico was an hour's drive and my car was a sauna. Windows down was the way to go, which turned the car into a wind tunnel, drying my eyes and palpitating my eardrums. The highway was brown-on-brown and decorated with yellow highway signs and roadside memorials that commemorated crash sites.

Drugs helped when the body needed assistance, when defenses broke down, when something crawled inside and grew and wreaked havoc. Pills dissolved in the stomach and absorbed into the bloodstream, filtering impurities, reducing swelling, blocking receptors. Drugs aided when organs deteriorated, when the center fell out, when the only thing left in the fight was old, tired cells preparing to surrender with that final breath.

There wasn't a Mexican border agent this afternoon, and I passed through, no problema. Today Amelia had crossed the line in the opposite direction with her brother. She was fortunate. She owned a home, a business, enough to earn her a multiple-entry visa. In her absence, her son manned the farmacia's counter. Hilario had lighter skin than his mother and wore a gold crucifix, had scabby knees and, that afternoon, a glittering unicorn on his T-shirt, which he pinched away from his chest when I walked in.

"My serve has improved," Hilario told me. The kid's English was crisp. "Mom says that if we lived in Arizona, I'd be nationally ranked."

"She mentioned that."

I pulled out the day's scrip list. "Eight," I told Hilario.

Hilario cracked a knuckle, and while he went to work I stepped outside. A wall across the street was marked with graffiti. It was full of figures running across a vacuous desertscape. The entire neighborhood, in fact, was loaded with public art. EL DIABLO spray-painted on street signs. Weatherproof LA LLORONA bumper stickers. A culture replete with mythos. I knew photojournalists loved to snap pictures of this type of street, pictures that always showed two or three boys kicking around a pathetic deflated soccer ball, as though that was supposed to illustrate Third World downluckness.

The queue at the northbound port ate away the rest of my afternoon. An hour's wait. I listened to the new cassette, slow-dance numbers interspersed with rock 'n' roll, a wedding mix with no big surprises. My border agent was obviously more interested in his female trainee than me, and I slipped through undetected. North of Tubac I saw a secondary checkpoint under an overpass. Vehicles were directed to line up between orange highway pylons. I saw uniformed officers lumbering around, screened by baseball hats and sunglasses. Dogs trained to sniff human sweat paced alongside passenger vans. I began to get nervous. The rubes that were pulled from the line were forced to wait in the shade under a tent while agents inspected their cars. One officer bent at my window. His questions were pointed. On American soil, with Arizona tags, the questions moved fast.

"From?"

"Tucson."

"Travel south?"

"Yes."

"Buy anything?"

"A blanket."

At home, I had dozens of blankets, all sizes, shapes, and colors.

The officer pointed down the highway and I passed the exam for the thousandth time. The peaked Tucson Mountains enlarged as I drew closer, their sharp tips like upturned anvils.

South of town, my phone rang. I leaned over and retrieved it from my bag. I was expecting to hear from Epstein, to schedule our next game night, but it wasn't the old man's number. I recognized the first three digits. Only numbers originating from Paseo del Sol had the prefix. The woman identified herself by last name, Rodriguez, the on-call desk nurse.

"It's your grandmother," she said. "She was taken to the hospital."

I nearly swerved into the ditch. I said nothing. I couldn't even speak.

"I'm so sorry," the woman said. I was silent. I heard nothing but my heart, and all at once the car filled with particles, dust stirred up by the air vents, each one bright and blinking, each touched by sunlight. A fleck floated in the air, in front of my nose, disappearing when I breathed in.

"We're not sure what happened," the woman went on. "Your grandmother was found unresponsive. We called a cabulance. This is a serious emergency."

AT PIMA COUNTY GENERAL, I sat in a cold, hard, plastic chair, examining dime-sized acne craters scored into the doctor's neck. Under glaring lights his neck resembled magnified cake. I sat slumped, surrounded by whiteness, and I could not feel my hands.

"Looks like deep vein thrombosis," the doctor explained. "She had a clot. Any history of hypercoagulability, cancer, pain, heart problems, edema? The clot was set loose and looks like a cerebral vascular accident." His scars, his scars. His scars mesmerized me. "In other words," he said, "your grandmother now has a lesion in her left hemisphere. We don't know how much her motor speech or muscles will be affected. Nerves are contralateral and control opposite sides of the body. She may lose vision in her eye. And she's partially paralyzed on her right side."

Light dimmed. I couldn't feel my hands. "So what's this mean?"

"Prognosis? There's such a thing as spontaneous recovery. But we need to wait. We need to wait and watch and see."

I ground my shoulder blades into the chair. Deep vein thrombosis, cerebral vascular accident—how could anyone acclimate to such terrifying names? Interpreting this information was a job meant for a more equipped person, a responsible person: a woman. I rubbed my hands, but I still couldn't feel them.

The doctor's news was blinding, even more blinding than the intensive care unit, with its white walls, serious faces, and doors marked DO NOT ENTER. The news was made infinitely worse by all the white. So much white! I watched a nurse float by carrying a tray with metallic instruments. I wondered if her gloved hands had touched my grandmother.

The doctor's face tilted sideways for a moment. "You okay?" he said, grabbing my shoulder. He brought me upright. "We have a chaplain at the hospital, if you need her. These are always difficult times."

His scars looked beautiful to me—deeply, wondrously beautiful. I saw him waiting for my next question—there were so many, which to ask?—as I squirmed in the cold, hard, plastic chair, wrestling with this difficult truth: I didn't care if I owned the best grave plot. I didn't want Nana, or anyone I knew, to have anything to do with it. Nana would live. She had to live. I had no one else.

I clutched my throat. "Water? I need—"

The doctor pointed me to an alcove, and I thanked Holy God Almighty that I'd stolen several pills from Ms. Haybroke's order. I washed down three anti-anxiety pills under the doctor's gaze. The man came over and put a heavy hand on my shoulder. I shrugged it off. "She'll live," the doctor told me. "That's good news. But every indication points to twenty-four-hour care."

"Twenty-four-hour care," I said.

"She'll need a twenty-four-hour attendant," the doctor said. "Most families opt for round-the-clock nursing home."

Round-the-clock nursing home care was expensive. It wasn't the time to think about quality of life as measured by money. But I did. "I need to see her," I said.

"Not yet," the doctor said. "You can't visit her yet. We need to wait and watch and see."

"I'll wait." I would wait until *yet* became *now*. A cool dry breeze slid down my throat, and I was desperately thirsty again, and I still could not feel my hands.

I called Epstein. I got his machine. I dialed Warsaw—no answer. I was alone. I was alone inside a hospital. I turned from the doctor and trekked through the white halls, just another lost face among so much wreckage. A pretty black woman was sitting in a glass-enclosed room and weeping into a gardening magazine. In another room, a family clung tightly to one another, as though bracing for a shipwreck. This wasn't a hospital. This was an experiment in high-pitched grief. I wandered, from disappointment to self-doubt to the second floor, room to room, directionless.

In an empty room I pulled the drapes and called my mother. My step-father told me she was out doing errands. I thanked him and hung up. I considered looking up Mona in the phone directory, but I didn't know her last name.

Danni Zepeda answered after one ring, but she was preoccupied, and it sounded to me like she was inside some sort of echo-filled tunnel. A man's staccato laugh pervaded the background. "Not now, soldier," Danni said to me.

"But, Danni," I said.

"Who's got the biggest corncob?" the man said.

"Ring me tomorrow," she said. "In the morning."

With illness there was no justice. Illness was not a punishment. Illness wasn't sad: illness was. It just *was*. People were composed of different parts, organic engines with parts that sometimes failed. Something was bound to turn—if not one thing, then another. And how long until I saw Nana?

I stared dumbly at the clock in the entranceway, its wide arms holding fast to huge roman numerals. It was quarter past midnight in Northampton, Massachusetts. I considered phoning Juliet. She was built for emergencies. Juliet could talk me through. Calm me down. She was the last person to hold congress over my feelings. She was someone I once trusted with everything. Ms. Haybroke's pills turned me into a shadow of myself. I was built from clouds. My kneecaps melted. My femur ground into my tibia. I was a mass of jumbled, confused limbs. I didn't know how to walk. And yes, Juliet could, if she were here with me, get me through.

I sat on a sofa. Five rings segued into Juliet's rehearsed voice mail message. Sometimes I just wanted to hear her voice. I held the phone close. Sometimes sentiment was not necessarily a terrible thing.

The line beeped. I didn't know what to say. "I'm thinking about the forks we bought that summer. Remember, that summer, the antique store in Vermont? The forks with the tigers stamped on the handles? We liked those forks. Anyway, hi. My grandmother had a stroke."

I hung up.

I called Warsaw—still no answer, despite nineteen rings. My friend was probably out shaving a dog and inducting it into his cult.

The streets were empty and washed clean from a monsoon dump as I drove away from the hospital. The air was crisp and rusty. Bushes and trees in my headlights looked stylized. The chill behind my eyeballs began to thaw after a few miles.

The sweet, acrid odor made me recoil when I opened the casita's front door. The smell was overpowering, insulting, gag-inducing, unbearable, and unwelcome in my chosen lifestyle. I had not been paying attention. The dead creature in the wall had finally dissolved. In death it had won. The stink reached out from beyond the wall and touched everything. The smell glued itself to my sinuses. I pulled my collar over my nose and crouched at the kitchen baseboards. On hands and knees I sniffed along the wall, locating an especially disgusting area. It was so bad that my eyes filled with tears.

The vibrations started in my fingers, coursed up my arms, and sang through my spine. Painful pricks flowed into my fingers. My grandmother was still in the game, even though it was a game no one ever won. She was still in it. The brutal second half of life was filled with blind reckoning, when the body failed, the mind went, and everyone vanished. Holes in space opened and absorbed everyone. With birth, as labor set in, there was quickening toward light. Where there was light there was also its counterpart, a global, progressive deterioration into utter blackness. We would all ride that chariot.

Blood poured into my fingers.

I kicked the wall and hit a support stud. My shin ached, but the pain galvanized me. I grabbed the baseball bat from the spare room and returned to the kitchen. The wall was a large, unmovable target. Knees bent, I took my stance and imagined the meanest, hardest, motherfuckingest pitch. The wall was as thin as rice paper. I didn't even remember swinging, as I extracted the bat, amazed by the destruction. Sheetrock broke away erratically in my hands. I peeled away layers, tearing out sheets of insulation, scattering everything onto the floor. A highway of wires ran up and down the wall's interior. The hole grew wide enough to fit my arm inside. Still, I couldn't locate it.

I recalculated. I twirled the bat. Tapped it on my heel. I took position, summoning the ghost of Hank Aaron, and swung open another huge hole. And again, and another. I tore away plaster, digging inside, slicing my hand on an exposed nail. I tossed bits of wall onto the tile. At last I entered up to my shoulder, and I found it. Viscous, molasses-like fluid coated my hand and intermingled with my blood. I brought the thing out reverently. The dead rat was as big as an overfed cat. It had a severe, aslant face and its tail had turned black. It felt like a water-filled sponge.

I stared into its black, beady, open eyes. I needed more of Ms. Haybroke's fast-acting pills. I needed silence. Money. Drugs. Love. A hug. There were saintly demons in my blood. Everything that I'd worked toward was unraveling. My grandmother was in the hospital, behind doors marked UNAUTHORIZED. And the knots in my chest felt like they would never loosen.

I rooted around the kitchen for an appropriate container. I searched the cabinets. My grandmother had kept stashes of food in the spare-room closet. It was a cemetery of old food. I considered dumping out spaghetti sauce, shoving the rat down, when I located a lidless oatmeal container. I rolled the heavy, dead rat inside.

I slid back the door and carried the rat to the patio. Flashes from Alejandro's television lit up his bedroom window, and I heard tinny, obnoxious laugh tracks. I searched around for proper burial grounds. It was too dark outside. I returned to the house for a flashlight. There was a neat cluster of prickly pear on the side of the casita, and that was where I dug, underneath a spiny paddle, clawing at the freshly soaked dirt. Thankfully the wet dirt gave. When the hole opened, when the hole grew deep, I dropped the container. Before covering it with dirt, before sending it back to where it had come from, I bent over and inspected the rat's stony eyes. The moon filled them, one last time, with light.

SUNLAND

Part Two

13

The vine grew long and withered. People entered and exited as though on conveyor belts. A line got marked in the sand the moment we were born. And nothing, nothing, nothing could prepare us for growing old.

Each day bones strained, bodies accumulated moss, and blood, constantly in need of cleansing, was filthy with pollutants.

My nights had been plagued by dangerous, memorable, extravagant dreams.

I sat in an air-conditioned office, sucking in my thirty-three-year-old gut and listening to Grady Masters, Paseo del Sol's Housing Coordinator, who wore a name badge in the shape of a saguaro, like every employee in this amusement park did.

Grady yammered on and on, his elbow propped on his chair's armrest, tapping the air faintly, as though touching each of his words as they emerged from his mouth. "And during the transition period, it's best to keep all parties informed of her progress," he told me. "We're planning on relocating your grandmother once she's released to our care. Per doctor's orders, she'll have another go-round of physical therapy at the rehab clinic, and when the doctor decides she's reached her plateau, we'll gladly welcome her back. Arrangements are being made as we speak."

Everything about our conversation was slo-mo, tinny, Xanax-flavored, and I began to think Grady—with his small soft hands and parted hair and bird-boned shoulders and gee-golly nature—must have been lonely at home. A gauzy plane of light cut across the room from a recessed skylight. Specks of dust floated through the light like planets. "You must have questions," Grady said, and I gripped my chair.

I did. I was a month into it. The days had been fiery and stale and full of question marks. My grandmother had gone from sipping whiskey in the afternoon while tinkering with knitting needles to looking sad, terrified, thin, and incomplete in a wheelchair. Now she had trouble finding words. Now the look on her face annihilated me. She'd already been through a battery of physical therapy, if it was even legal to call her limited movements therapy.

Lift your arm, Nana.

Squeeze the blue ball, Nana.

Smile now, Nana.

The stroke had blinded her right eye. She was weak on that side and couldn't walk. Her physical abilities had been whittled down and destroyed. When I was with her, it was impossible for me not to draw comparisons—she, in a chair; and me, standing. My chest clenched whenever we hugged. I'd found some relief in pills and from brief, violent crying jags in the hospital parking lot.

"Let me get this—let me get this straight," I said. "You want to move her from her apartment and into the building with the balloons."

"The building with the balloons?" Grady asked.

"The building at the end," I said.

"Yes but—I don't follow. What balloons?"

"I've seen volunteers toss balloons at residents."

"Oh! You must mean the afternoon exercise class," Grady said. "Yes, they sometimes do use balloons."

I'd seen for myself balloons carom off the foreheads of confused residents. I'd visited the building several times now, scouting it out. In the mornings the hallways smelled of baby powder concealing lengthy shits. And those people: those crazed, impaired, *non compos mentis* people. Eyeballs floated seemingly unattached inside eye sockets. Confused appendages hung from gelatinous bodies—bodies molded as if by heat into wheelchairs. I'd seen folks staring at nothing in particular; in those eyes were black holes. The place was scarier than prison. And Grady wanted to relocate my grandmother there. "I don't want her moving into that madhouse," I said.

"Believe me, I understand," Grady said. "This decision is hardest on family members, but your grandmother will come to accept it. It's an intimate home. Think of it as an alternative family. Trust me. She'll receive the best care. It's a community of friends, especially our elders in that building."

"What a beautiful advertisement," I said and shifted in the chair. Grady's smile disappeared. "Isn't there another alternative?"

"Sorry," Grady said. He handed me a shiny tri-fold brochure.

I scanned it. Among the building's amenities were a full-time chef, twenty-four-hour security, herb gardens, and twice daily "cultural activities," including wheelchair yoga. Grady opened my grandmother's file and I watched him peruse her original contract. Then he casually informed me that my grandmother's monthly bill would nearly double. Somehow I didn't suffer my own stroke when he said that. I stared at Grady's softened silhouette. Xanax always chiseled my thoughts into useless scraps. I stood and put out my hand.

Outside, the heat was combustive and the campus was abuzz. I kicked a stone on the path, struggling to hold in tears. Residents were out basking in the heat, people in sweaters, people in parkas, people wearing mittens. Ms. von Bausch was humping around a six-foot-long javelin.

I crossed the quad toward the building at the end, which was shaded by desert willows, and peeked inside, momentarily calmed by how clean, modern, and adequate everything looked. Smells were to be expected. Other than Mona's mouthwatering face, the building's staff looked mostly asexual, but the nurses were supposedly competent, licensed, experienced— and according to the AutumnYears.com nursing home guide, the building had scored a respectable 9.3 orange leaves out of 10.

On the other side of the window I saw an old codger sipping from a can of non alcoholic beer. The man couldn't see me. He had a bud in his ear, the wire connected to a handheld radio. I watched him take a slow, thoughtful sip while staring at the blue pastel wall, staring at nothing. This was going to bleed me.

KATIE-ANNE, from District Admin, was brusque over the phone. She informed me that both my urine and my fingerprint tests had cleared. Katie-Anne talked fast and didn't answer my questions, and I sensed irritation in her voice. I'd never called, never used her cell phone number, never asked her out. She was all business. "Today you have middle school," she told me. "We've got a teacher out with strep throat."

"What's the subject?" I asked.

"Does it matter?" Katie-Anne said. "It's middle school. It's all the same."

The drive took me ten minutes through morning traffic. It was an inner-city school: cracked asphalt, utilitarian buildings, and modular overflow units. In the amber-lit hallways I was reminded of my former students in Northampton. I belonged inside a public school. It had once been important work to me. The kids shuffled past me in herds, armed with books and self-doubts and smart-ass remarks. Sandals slapped linoleum. Vague casserole smells came from the cafeteria. I overheard chatter about upcoming assignments, comparisons of grades. Here, all around me, were healthy school-age kids, overloaded with hormones, eye gunk, and gum tucked into soft cheeks. It was wondrous.

Students filed into my classroom and collapsed into desks carved thickly with profanities. It was the dawn of a new school year, and I was expecting more enthusiasm, but instead I was met with a dozen pink throats in full, collective yawn.

I wrote my name on the chalkboard and tried to project an air of easygoing confidence. I took roll call. But the boys, stooped like hunch-backs over their bags, glared at me, as though they'd been tricked. One girl, pretty and gnome-sized, had such stunning emerald eyes that I had to force myself to look away.

"So," I said and sat on the desk. "What are we learning this week?"

The kids stared.

It became apparent to me that this wasn't the best class, and these weren't the school's best students. I glanced at the top of the roll call sheet, where it said, "Developmentally Delayed." Classes were fifty minutes long, an impossible amount of time for me to inspire curiosity, and during first period, at the thirty-minute mark, bored whispers swept through the room. The classroom filled with the smells of sweated-out hair gel and cheap perfume. Kids fidgeted and passed notes. I was losing control. So I bounded to the school library and borrowed a movie and played for them a documentary about the Pleistocene period. It was a Government class and the kids didn't know what to make of the film. Still, I thought the movie wasn't half-bad. I decided to play it for my five other classes.

I ate lunch alone on a boulder with views of the school's split, sunbaked tennis courts. Weeds bloomed through fault lines in the pavement. It was exactly how I remembered middle school. Lonely, heartbreaking, and dull.

During sixth period, I helped avert a crisis. One boy with expensive basketball shoes pushed another boy with wavy blond hair, and I threw elbows between them. The instigator told me stories, saying the brouhaha had been heating up all day. But I was unprepared to act as negotiator.

One girl seemed impressed by my apparent authority. Despite the temperature in the room, she wore a jean jacket festooned in sequins, and she slid her desk alongside mine during the movie. Periodically she won my attention by blinking her big bowls. In the semi-dark I was preoccupied with my own concerns, navigating a developing plan. At one point the girl tipped her head and ran a finger along her unlined face and gestured at the pooled splashes on my roll call sheet.

"Today's my birthday," I told her.

The troublemaker lunged at the blond boy again, tipping his desk over. I ordered the kid to assume a push-up position, hands flat on the floor, arms straight, and elbows locked. When the last bell rang, the kid collapsed onto his chest, heaving.

My first full workday in ten months brought in one Benny Franklin, minus state and federal taxes. I made more money bringing just five residents their medication.

I FOLDED BACK Paseo del Sol's contract. It was sixty-three pages long and bound by an industrial staple. The "Resident-in-Transition" clause stated that I had seven days, after the last paid month, to remove my grandmother's belongings from her apartment. Later, after dinner with Warsaw at our favorite taquería, I started by peeling off the Post-it notes in my grandmother's apartment. She had written my name on every one.

I wrapped dishes in newspaper. The dishes went in boxes. The boxes went on a flat rolling cart, and as I was pushing another load to my car in the lot, I noticed something odd. Mr. Garland Bills was on a bench by the lake, alone, as always, just sitting there, listening to croaking frogs. A lamp cast a soft glow over him. I watched his hand rise to his mouth. Whenever a car turned onto the distant boulevard, headlights illuminated the reflector strips on Garland's tracksuit. Campus was quiet.

Mr. Bills didn't hear me approaching from behind. "Warm night," I said.

Mr. Bills's shoulder jerked. He turned. "Don't ever do that again," he said and popped a domino-sized block of cheese into his mouth. "I have issues with my ticker." He tapped his chest. Moonlight shone in his blue irises.

"What issues with your ticker?" I said. "I don't bring you heart meds."

"You think you know everything."

"Do I?"

"You bring someone medication and you think you have insight," Mr. Bills said. "You don't know as much as you like to think."

I sat on the bench and invited a long stare. For the first time I noticed, really noticed, Mr. Bills's thinning hairline. Moonlight clarified forthcoming balding patches. Mr. Bills was not as young as I'd always thought. The man was just younger than the others. He had a medium build, sideburns down to his earlobes, with full lips that hid teeth spaced apart like a picket fence. Mr. Bills scooted to the end of the bench and removed another piece of cheese from its plastic wrapping. I watched him take a substantial bite. Silence hummed between us as we looked over the lake. The shiny water was black as obsidian. Hints of algae rose from the banks. The moon made the tiny waves look metallic.

"I come out here when everyone heads indoors," Mr. Bills said, pinching the back of his neck. "I like to listen to the water."

"All by yourself," I said.

"I like the dark."

"Like a vampire."

"No, jerk. Like me." He gnawed off another plug of cheese. "I saw my son tonight," Mr. Bills said, surprising me. "He's visiting from Mali. That's

Africa. I could point it out on a map, if someone forced me. Jim's something. Living in the middle of nowhere. Huts, that kind of thing. Not even a nearby phone. Anyway, we went to dinner, took a walk, chatted. We're taking another walk tomorrow. A long one."

"I didn't know you had a son."

"Why would you?"

"I'd know these things if you didn't keep yourself closed off."

"A man my age gets to know how things work." Mr. Bills swallowed grandly. "A man gets to know people's prejudices, the way people respond to certain *facts*. I've reached that age," he said. "I know when to taper off unnecessary friendships."

"But people like you," I said. "People enjoy your company. Ms. Patterson told me you helped find an heirloom earring she lost in the dining commons."

"A diamond."

"You help people but you don't let anyone in."

"Paseo del Sol is good for someone like me. It's been a comfortable place to land after the divorce. All-inclusive. Very little cleaning. They fold my socks. Did you know that? I pay a small fee and they fold my socks. Used to roll them into a ball. Not anymore. Paseo del Sol takes care of everything."

"How old is Jim?" I asked.

Through the darkness Mr. Bills studied my face. "About your age," he said. "He wants to save the world. Kind of like you."

"I don't want to save the world."

"Oh, yes you do. You remind me of him. Regardless, we've always gotten on well. But that mother of his? Not anymore. She doesn't mention my name. She doesn't approve, especially after she found out. We were married twenty-eight good years. A fine lady."

"Gay," I said.

He took another bite of cheese. "The temperature in this town for that sort of thing can be chilly. Especially around men my age."

"You could always move elsewhere."

"Can't."

"Because you're ill," I said.

Mr. Bills flipped up the collar on his tracksuit. "You think you know everything, but you don't. Roger has the bug. Has had it for eighteen years. I get medication for him. He's sick, doesn't really leave his house, and, well, he also happens to be the love of my life. Exactly the reason my son's mother won't speak to me. I tried to be a good father. And when he can get away from saving the world from itself, he visits. He's the stronger man now." Mr. Bills tipped his head. "You have kids?"

Rolling a rock under my tennie, I felt its sharp edge against the sole of my foot. "Not yet."

"You want them."

I nodded.

"Well, be sure to keep up," Mr. Bills said. "Pay attention, and listen. Hang around, even when it gets boring, especially when it gets boring. That's the best sort of boredom a person suffers."

"And tell them they're good," I said. I kicked the rock into the lake and the frogs went momentarily quiet.

"That too," Mr. Bills said. "That too."

14
Early morning at the casita, I spread the morning paper across the counter, leaned on my elbows, and went shivery from the headline. Just when I'd convinced myself that Los Toros was a myth, or a gang composed of clowns like Diego, here was this morning's juicy news item.

As it turned out, a Border Patrol agent had been wounded during a one-sided firefight in the outlying desert. The paper laid out details. The paper stated known facts. The agent had been patrolling a lonely swath of drag, Tucson Sector, when his vehicle had come under fire. According to the paper, these weren't amateur pop shots. These were 7.62 mm rounds from link-fed automatic weapons. The agent had spotted "military" trucks escorting a "convoy" with the "lights out." The agent had seen men in "helmets" before "tracers" lit up the dark night and bullets rained down a few terrifying minutes of hell. Before rescue helicopters arrived, the "vehicles vanished." The only criminal activity the authorities had found during their sweep was two cowboys camping on private ranchland. The men had been "roasting weenies" over an open pit and half-lit on "mescal."

The southern border, delicate as a spit bubble. I knew anything could puncture it. Sealing two thousand miles of sand and sagebrush and skunkweed may as well have been a delusion. BP tried to keep everything lid-tight with their symbolic walls, stadium lights, and agents parked on mesas, but I knew it was all just improvisational artifice. I never knew what to make of the agents, though. My opinion shifted weekly. One day, agents were saving migrant skins from certain death. The next day, they were caught clubbing people. They were criticized for turning the border into a police state and then criticized for not stemming the flow. My all-time-favorite story, which I told whenever I'd had more than one beer, was about the agent who'd been caught pants-down in his big white-and-green SUV by an AP reporter. The agent had been parked in the desert, roasting like a green chile and pulling his meat to *Hustler*, when the reporter had wandered up and tapped off a few prime photos. The job of the Border Patrol was a tough one, because everyone knew the borderland was the autobahn.

Warsaw stumbled into the kitchen with gunk in his eyes, unsure of his footing, and grabbed my shoulder for support. My friend was in boxers again, little ponies this time. Apparently he enjoyed parading his hairlessness around. Even the backs of his hands were bald. Warsaw, more and more, resembled the author on his stupid cult book.

"Big day?" I asked him.

Warsaw rubbed an eye. "Escorting Ms. Johnson to dialysis."

I stared at him, long and thoughtful and full of judgment.

"What? You have a problem with that?" Warsaw asked me.

"As a matter of fact, yes."

"What do you care?"

"I care because I know you. You'll do this for a while, make people depend on you, and then you'll quit. Like always."

"Maybe I'm turning over a new leaf."

"Cut it out," I said.

"George Greg says remember that first moment, as a child, when you truly felt awe, and hold it. Around old people, I was terrified and reverential."

Lately I had been seeing my friend on campus strutting around like a proud peacock, as though he owned the place, with a bright yellow VOLUNTEER badge dangling from his neck. It infuriated me. As if Warsaw was actually interested in hearing about the special features on Ms. Haybroke's sewing machine; as if he was enthralled by Ms. Carpenter's long-winded tales about life on the Nebraska farm. I'd seen Warsaw tipping back margaritas with Ms. Vallance in the gazebo. I'd even seen him fixing walkers, adjusting bar heights. My friend wheeled patients to and from the building at the end with a smile as wide as Texas, and I wanted him to knock off his act.

Warsaw pulled one of his Mexican gore magazines from a utensil drawer, took one look inside, and put his hands on his head. I looked away, but not before seeing a severed leg.

"I'm tired of it," I said. "A bonfire. I'm going to find every one of those magazines and burn them."

"Maybe you're right," Warsaw said. "This is fucked-up shit, Sid," he said, pointing at the photo, pointing. "George Greg says scare yourself. I get that part. But this is really scary fucked-up shit. Maybe I should pull back a little. Wow. I mean, look at that leg. Wow. Have you ever seen such scary fucked-up shit?"

I looked at my friend. Bald head, bald arms, bald hands—bald everything. "Sure, I've seen scary fucked-up shit."

"I THOUGHT I could rearrange my life. Now I'm back where I began. Remember the neighbor's dog. Pepper? Remember how much we liked Pepper? I've been thinking about her. Thinking we should have had a puppy. Anyway, thanks for the birthday card. Warsaw took me out for tacos. He forgot his wallet and I had to pay. Mom left a voice mail. I don't know. I'm just calling to say thanks, I guess."

I watched each digital second die. Then folded the phone shut.

MY GRANDMOTHER'S TRANSFER from the rehab clinic happened as planned, in early afternoon, with paramedics and a gurney. When the muscular buzz-cut medic strapped her down for the ride, her eyes turned bright with fear, but I was there, on a fold-down seat, holding her hand and calming her down.

I watched Nana struggle to speak, and in a burst she said, "It's not clean."

"Nana? What was that? Say that again." But she didn't.

The Housing Coordinator met us at the front doors with a clipboard pressed to his chest. "Welcome, Ms. Dulaney," Grady Masters said and plopped his hand on my grandmother's gurney. Swinging his arms merrily, he showed us the way. "We already have your room prepared," Grady told my grandmother. "The nurses have been alerted about our newest addition."

Grady held the door open, and I stepped inside, but either the heat or my sadness or some combination-of stopped me. I clutched a gleaming handrail, going momentarily dizzy. A medic grabbed my arm. "This is not us," I told him. "Everything happens too fast."

Grady patted my cheek twice. "You'll learn."

He escorted us down a long hallway to my grandmother's new room, where the medics carefully eased her from the gurney and tucked her into a wheelchair. I noticed a bouquet of carnations on an end table. Grady pointed at a miniature license plate on Nana's new chair: last name, age, and room number. Tacked to the wall was a banner: WELCOME HOME! The family packet had informed me that 120 residents lived in the building at the end.

My grandmother's new home was on Agave Trail, room 45, on the left. Her window looked out onto a manicured path with a partial lake view. Every day she would get morning sun, which now opened the room in heat and light. Out the window, I saw Ms. von Bausch completing her daily laps with a water bottle in her hand. My grandmother had clean views of tan foothills that enlarged to the north into the jagged, olive-colored Catalinas. It was a hospital room, more or less, but carpeted. I disliked it.

Grady explained the carpet to me in detail. Carpets were important. Should my grandmother have an "accident," the carpet consisted of inter- changeable, antimicrobial, high-density tiles. "And you should know," Grady told me before he left, "carpet tiles are not included, so in the event of an accident, you'll be billed."

I didn't see a nick or scratch on the walls. The room was devoid of char- acter: twelve by twelve, nearly empty, and too, too, too white. A mechani- cal hospital bed was against the window near my grandmother's boxes. I'd thoroughly dismantled her apartment and the goal was to partially reenact the scene here.

The plastic mattress covering on the bed crinkled when I sat. "It's clean," I said.

My grandmother, in the middle of the room, in her chair, hands in her lap, looked pumped full of drugs. Something registered in her eyes, though, and she blinked. Guilt passed through me, the guilt of the witness, and I felt my chest tighten, and I looked away.

Throughout the afternoon a procession of Latina Nursing Assistants trick- led in and told us their names. Here was Ida, Rosa, and Mercedes. I shook their lotioned hands. They wore pea-green scrubs and had warmhearted smiles. They asked my grandmother questions. They touched her. The Nurs- ing Assistants fussed over her hair, which for a moment she appeared to enjoy, though I'd never seen her enjoy this type of treatment before.

With my car key I ripped into Nana's boxes. I aligned her collection of tiny hotel lotions in the bathroom cabinet. I mounted her chile pepper ris- tra, making sure to scuff the wall several times with my tennie. The place was entirely too white.

Her doctor had outlined the facts for me. Her first stroke had been followed by a series of smaller infarctions, a line of bursting rosaries inside her brain, leaving her with a slur and a hand frozen into a claw. Since the final punch, her talking had slowed, and it was nearly impossible for me to stare at the right side of her face, how it drooped. Her right eye was heavy-lidded and useless. She had trouble with language. She needed foods pureed and thin liquids thickened.

Without knocking, a charge nurse entered the room, folded back my grandmother's sleeve, and slipped on a blood pressure cuff.

"What are you doing?" I asked the woman.

"Procedure," she said.

She moved efficiently, her blue uniform scraping her inner thighs. She was pear shaped, with close-set eyes, tight curls, and I disliked her too. I disliked all of it. Each contraction of the blood pressure ball made me swallow a breath. I watched her scratch results into a binder. Her silence gnawed on me. I wanted to be informed. I wanted to be kept abreast of everything: to be updated on every single piece of information.

At last the nurse showed me her idea of a smile. "185 over 105," she said. "Primary hypertension," she went on. "Your grandmother needs to control her blood pressure and gain weight. How has she been functioning? Tell me more about her stroke. Was it hemorrhagic or vascular?"

I returned a massive look. "Her right side is partially paralyzed, so you tell me," I said. "Isn't the answer in your binder?"

"It is," she said, trying to smile. "I've been instructed to improve my bedside manner. My boss says to make agreeable conversation. Am I making agreeable conversation?"

After talking for weeks about my grandmother with doctors, nurses, and physical therapists, I was unsteady with my role as decision maker. Every small word out of my mouth felt like a large betrayal. And I distrusted anyone who talked *at me* as though discussing busted pistons, and not my grandmother, my dear nana.

"Look, she's weak," I said. "She's been in the hospital and through therapy. The doctor said she needs full-time nursing care. That's everything I know."

"I can assure you," the nurse said, holding my grandmother's wrist and looking at her watch. "We'll do everything to give her the finest care."

I watched the woman handle Nana like a doll, and I knew then, on this day, at this hour, that I could not watch this kind of soft, necessary, clinical abuse. I needed to leave before something else got damaged.

"I'm taking a walk," I said. My grandmother's eyes slid toward me, and I interpreted her red stare as unimpressed.

I wandered. I peeked into open doors. Many of the other residents were buttoned up in pajamas, draped in bathrobes, and dressed for bed. I thought that whoever had designed the building must have had an airport in mind. Six long halls fanned out from a central nursing station, and I imagined, when death visited, an invisible helicopter docking outside a room, loading its passenger, and lifting off.

And the rooms, the rooms. Each was converted into a miniature version of home: family pictures on the walls; knickknacks on the shelves; favorite armchairs. I slunk around, surrounded by strange creatures, distanced from their plight by the safety of my age. To my surprise I found Mona in an alcove, at a round table, hunched over papers.

"I know that confused look," Mona said to me. "Your first day."

"I've never been more pleased to see anyone in my life."

"You haven't been around," she said.

"Back and forth, the rehab clinic."

She nodded. She was in a pair of threadbare running shoes. She rubbed the worn toe of her shoe against her instep. "Sorry to hear about your grandmother," she said. "We'll take care of her."

"What a month."

An old man suddenly rounded the corner in a wheelchair, really moving, pressing hard, his head down, working the wheels, and he bumped into Mona's shin. "Ouch," she said.

The man smiled big and I whiffed a faint peppermint aroma easing off him. Strapped to the man's padded armrest was a leather holster with a plastic toy gun, trigger-ready. The hammer was cocked. The thing appeared realistic. His license plate said GORDON.

"Where's your shoe, Paul?" Mona asked the crazy old man.

"Huh?" he said loudly.

"Your shoe," she said. "Your left shoe. Where is it?"

He stared at the gray sock on his foot. "Lost it in the trenches," he said. He wheeled 180 degrees until he aligned with the hall. Then propelled back down it.

"It happens," Mona said and shrugged. "It's not lost on me, you know," she said. "Usually daughters get saddled with this role. Yet here you are. One of the few men here."

"Not including the gunslinger."

"I should admit that I've been looking around for you," Mona said abruptly. "Because I have these tickets. A friend gave them to me. It's for this thing." She paused, as though reconsidering, before leaning forward. "So if you're not busy, I'd like to *reserve* you."

"Are you asking me on a date?"

"I can't decide."

Her long brown hair, her brown eyes. The way her shoulder slumped forward lazily. Her skin, smile, crooked teeth. Her toes, her toes.

IT WAS OBVIOUS TO ME that there was a philosophy included in the price tag. Management had grand, important, invigorating ideas for the building at the end. (Mohandas Gandhi and Buddha were quoted in my brochure.)

By midafternoon the building began humming as though someone had activated a secret engine room. People gathered. Wheelchair traffic formed in the halls. Folks resurrected themselves from after-lunch naps. Not everyone remained in bed, down for the count. I saw many rooms reserved for many activities. One served as the multipurpose spirituality room. I read the schedule taped on the door. According to the times, out came the Torah on Friday nights. On Sunday morning, here came the Baptists at nine, Catholics at eleven, and Lutherans got the rest of the day. The building exceeded my expectations. It was nice, clean, well staffed, efficiently run, and gut-wrenchingly expensive.

This much was clear to me: the Activity Director was responsible for making the place lively. She was also the source of a lot of noise. I encountered her in the main hallway. She nearly traumatized me by the way she moved the air around, and with such confident disregard for self-respect. She shimmied before me and shouted and hopped around as though on fire. She clapped her hands three times while directing residents into the music room. I saw notes painted on the walls. It always surprised me when I saw someone fit into a job so well. And this lady—jug ears, frizzed hair, ecstatic banjo eyes—fit. Her neon-green blouse could have been spotted from a distance of ten miles. And it was clear that she loved her job. "Georgia, Georgia, how's my Georgia today?" the Activity Director asked an elderly woman in singsong. She bent and scratched the old woman's chin.

Behind another door I saw a class in progress. The sign said MULTISENSORY STIMULATION, and this afternoon's meaty topic was "Automobile." On tiptoes I peeked through a rectangular window braided with chicken wire. Inside, elderly women clutched plastic steering wheels in the 10 and 2 positions. I took note of the wheelchairs. All had license plates.

The women faced a movie screen. The movie looked like it had been filmed by strapping cameras to a car's fender: country roads, red and yellow trees, New England in the fall, and I was nearly convinced that I recognized a crumbling stone wall near Northampton. The film approached a curve in the road, and the women carefully, in unison, turned their steering wheels. A volunteer went corner-to-corner spritzing the air. A plastic-y new-car smell wafted under the door.

I pushed through the wide doors and walked outside and into the light—safe, finally safe. People were draining the last dregs of pleasure from the warm day. Joy and gladness shone on the faces. It was as if they were silently celebrating. They were not in wheelchairs. They did not live inside the building at the end. These were the lucky ones. My clients, my friends, were well. Finished with her workout, Ms. von Bausch waved her towel at me. Across the lake I saw a family huddled around a barbecue grill. Visitors sat with family members on lakeside benches.

Ms. Vallance cupped her hand and rotated it like a beauty contestant, and I waved back. Behind her I noticed a white F-150 truck rolling through campus, abiding by the fifteen-mile-per-hour limit. The truck stopped in the visitors' parking lot. I felt a sting enter my knee. I couldn't believe Diego would show his face in the middle of the day. And show his face now that my grandmother was in the nursing unit. I couldn't figure out how he had even entered Paseo del Sol without the required window decal. I thought I'd teach him a lesson.

I went to my car. Wrapped in an old dishrag was the Smith Wessy. In my hand the gun felt heavy and important.

Diego's truck hogged two spaces in the lot. I disliked people who took two spaces.

I crept between an suv and a four-door and approached from the rear, the gun at my hip, staying low. I advanced on the airbrushed tailgate, keeping just out of mirror-sight. At last I yanked open the passenger door and caught Diego by surprise. He reared back like a horse and dropped a magazine in his lap. His eyes narrowed when he saw me aiming the gun at his stomach.

"I have a gun," I said.

"I can see that," Diego said. He tried to disarm me with a smile. The gold between his teeth absorbed the cab's light.

"I don't think you understand. I'm pointing a gun at you. I bought bullets. It's loaded. I have a gun. I'm pointing a gun at you."

Slowly he closed his magazine. "And I'm frightened," Diego said.

"You don't look very frightened. I can read fright on a person's face. It's not registering. I'm not seeing fear. Show me fear. Tremble a little at least, for my sake."

Diego glanced at the gun again. He rolled his eyes and held out his hand, shaking it in the air overdramatically.

"Oh, forget this," I said. "It's pointless." I stepped on the runner and hopped in the truck and hitched the gun into the cup holder. I yanked the seat belt tight and fastened it. "Not even a gun helps," I said. "Not even a gun." The magazine on Diego's lap was something called *Aviation Monthly*. "Every day. Every day you follow me."

"I do."

"Okay, fine. I'll do it. I'll meet this El Bebé guy. Set it up."

"Why now?"

"I'm considering that other option."

"People?" Diego said.

I was silent.

"Okay, but when El Bebé says he'll meet, you run. Understand? Can you run?"

I directed the air-con vent at my face. It felt *good*. "What's your fascination with airplanes?" I asked Diego. "Biplane on your tailgate, and now I find you reading aviator magazines. Airplanes give you some kind of nut tingle?"

"My wife wants to visit Chicago. She wants to fly. I've never flown."

"You're married?"

"The idea terrifies me," Diego said. "It's unnatural. My body, up in the sky, but I want to try. She wants our son to meet his cousins."

"You have a *son*?"

"I'm working my way up to doing it this time," Diego said.

I leaned back into the cool leather seat. Then I lifted the Smith Wessy and pointed it at him again. "Start the truck."

"Please put that down," Diego said.

"Do it."

"Are you going to shoot me?"

"I haven't decided. Act scared. Act more scared."

"Where are you taking me?" he asked, clearly not scared.

"You're driving me back to the rehab clinic. I left my Honda in the parking lot."

Diego keyed the ignition, shoved the truck in gear, and asked over the gun's barrel, "Do you think we can be friends now?"

15

Our bill showed up in the mailbox, the corporation's loud, obnoxious, cactus logo bleeding across the envelope. I stared at the amount due, stunned, insulted. Prior to pegging the bill to the fridge, I dropped it on the kitchen floor and scuffed it on the tiles.

Hours later Danni Zepeda showed up at my door. She was right on time. "I'm sorry about your grandmother," she said.

"Thanks for leaving the food baskets."

"Least I could," she said. "How is she?"

"In a chair. In the nursing unit. Bad, wouldn't you say?"

We got in my car. It was beginning to get dark. Danni wanted to show me her special spot. As I drove, she rubbed lotion into her bulging forearms, but I noticed a trace of fruity perfume in the air, and I began to suspect Danni had ulterior designs.

"We shouldn't be doing this," I said.

"We shouldn't do a lot of things," she said.

"It just doesn't feel right."

"I know something that might feel right." She turned and I felt her eyes on me.

According to a faded brown sign, the town of Sells, Arizona, had 2,800 residents. From the capital of the O'odham nation, I drove south on Indian Route 19, detouring off-road at San Miguel, a remote village on the western margins of the Baboquivari Mountains.

My Honda jangled on the dirt road. Danni knew the route, and she itemized for me the obstacles and dangers, summing everything up in terrifying detail. Camera towers could often spot vehicles driving in the desert. There were also drag roads, flattened daily, and if you walked across these, trackers could see foot impressions in the drag and run you down. Some crossers strapped bits of mattress to their feet to sponge out tracks, she said. And of course there were natural hazards: rattlesnakes, mountain lions, bark scorpions, and barbed cholla. The wild jaguar, she also told me, was making a comeback in the region. The car bounced, the headlights leaped, my knuckles ached. Rain had carved the dirt road into a washboard. A jackrabbit raced into the car's lights and nearly gave me a heart attack.

"And there may be other groups out here, criminal elements, humping parcels of marijuana or worse," Danni said, sucking on her pinkie.

"Worse?"

"Let's just find a group to move and get this done. My sister just bought a new truck. Extended cab." She exhaled loudly. "She can't afford it, which means I'll eventually be taking over her payments."

Night was the time to drive. The dirt cooled and the air chilled and the stars flashed down sad, dead light. Night was also a good time for me to imagine into the darkness, and my thoughts careened to the psycho with the rifle. The paper had mentioned the heartless madman again, who stopped along secluded dirt roads, just like this one, exactly like this one, and took aim at people shuffling toward better lives. He was out here. And he hadn't been caught.

The road ended. Danni directed me through breaches in the scrub, where the road picked up on the other side. Not much farther, we reached the spot. I stopped the car. It was incredible because it wasn't. I saw a broken fence. And open desert. I realized I'd never seen a darker, more nowhere place. The sky was a black sheet pinpricked with bright holes.

Danni pulled an old Mexican blanket from my hatch and swept it like a matador around her shoulders. She turned on her flashlight. "The group will start from here and walk north to the waiting vehicle," she told me. Her boots crunched as she wandered into the shadows. Fixed above us was a three-quarter moon.

"Take a look at that hole. We could drive right through. This thing would only take an hour."

"Border Patrol would stop us *in flagrante*," she said. "Migra are all over this land. Can't see them now, but they're here. This is my route. Usually I travel at night. Problem is, the Border Patrol likes night. When I'm stopped, I flash my tribal ID. They usually let me pass. Walking is our only option. It's silent, nearly untraceable." Danni approached the fence and passed into Mexico. She snapped a twig from a bush and threw it in her mouth. "The group will depart at midnight. The walk takes seven, eight hours, depending."

"Walking?"

"My cousin and I did this with ten Panamanians. They moved fast and took four pee breaks."

"We never discussed walking."

"It's how we do this. And you will accompany them, as guide," she said. "I'll pick you up twenty miles north at the prearranged spot. Someone needs to show them the way. You."

"And if Border Patrol happens along while we're walking?"

Danni was silent.

"I'm not doing this alone," I said.

"This isn't a game," she said. "This isn't passing pills to old farts. These people will be counting on us. We're talking about other people's lives. If you can't handle this, you need to tell me now."

I tried not to think about what forced people to relocate countries, what specific pressures and horrors shoveled them toward the borderland. But I was broke. Danni knew it. Everyone knew it. She tossed the flashlight's beam into my eyes and then to the ground, from one pile of trash to the next. Water bottles, underwear, toilet paper. Half buried in the dirt was a discarded backpack.

"We're not the only people who know about this entrance," she said. "It's a popular spot." She meandered onto United States soil again and arranged the blanket across the car's hood. I watched her ass wiggle onto it. She hooked her boots on the fender and her knees fell open. "I've been think-ing," she said and extended her fingers through her hair. "We never really gave us a shot after that night."

"So? We tried. That was it. Just once, remember?"

"But we fit. Two puzzle pieces," she said. "It would be a shame. I think we make sense. Don't you?" I heard her voice catch. Her words were brief, tight, and honest. I could tell she was uncomfortable opening the door.

For a moment I attempted to wrap the idea of "us" into a neat, attractive package, but her offer felt more like a business proposition. Still, there was no doubting how drawn I was to any woman offering a relationship.

A crisp breeze bit my cheek. It was an amazing, clear, moon-rippled night. It hurt my chest and head thinking on it, about us, our placement in the grand order. Everything was just stars and dust. Danni turned the flashlight off. We were surrounded by blackness. I watched her lean back on her elbows, legs parted, barely there, nearly invisible.

Twin headlights soon appeared in the distance. They approached from the south, from Mexico. We were in the middle of nowhere, and we were not alone. The lights jumped around the darkness. It was a large vehicle. A truck. Perhaps, judging by its gauzy outline, it may have been military.

Danni hopped down from the car. "We need to go," she said.

16

Epstein's door was wide open. From inside I overheard a woman's voice carrying on, ordering the old man around, which was a new, unexpected occurrence in Epstein's apartment. I knocked on the doorjamb. No one answered.

"You have to eat more than waffles and peanut butter," the woman's voice said.

"Yes, dear," Epstein responded. I detected a low, depressed modulation in his usually spunky cadence.

"Did you hear me?"

"Fine, dear. Okay, dear. I heard you, dear. Whatever you say, dear."

Standing in the kitchenette, surrounded by flung-open cabinets, the woman set her hands on her hips when I walked in. "And who are you?" she asked me. "I suppose you just march into any old apartment?"

"That's my friend Sidney," Epstein said, shuffling toward the couch. "I forgot to tell him you were coming."

"Well, if he's your friend, maybe he should help clean up around here. It's a regular pigsty." I recognized her eyes from the photos on Epstein's mantel.

"You're from New York," I said.

"Ding ding. We have a winner."

"You have a twin."

"A genius, too," she said.

Sarah whirled through the kitchenette like a tornado, flinging boxes of crackers and old spaghetti and dried apricots onto the floor. "Two years, Daddy, past the expiration date," Sarah said, reading the label on a jar. "Two *years*." I watched her kink her neck, like an athlete, like this was her sport. I kept out of her way. She'd brought along from New York her stress-filled eyes and glamorous shoes and worked-out calves and fast-talking bossiness. I noticed the same forehead as the old man, yet she'd outgrown the doughy teenage cheeks from the photos. Her hair was professionally streaked and she was wearing a tailored blue suit with open-toe heels that showed off a pedicure. She was beautiful. Epstein had told me he'd had children in his forties, which put Sarah within striking range, but the idea was out of the question. Epstein hit me with that don't-think-about-it glare. The old man had been stuffed into a new tie and a freshly laundered sport coat. The tips of his black shoes shone. And his glasses, usually smudged, had been wiped clean.

"So," Sarah said and handed me a broom. "You're the friend Daddy tells me about."

"We have baseball in common."

"More than just baseball," Epstein said from the couch.

"I thought you'd be older," Sarah said. "Sweep that spot, over there. As in fifty years older."

Sarah told me to make sure to get beneath the cabinets too. "Have you been to the dentist recently?" she asked her father.

"Still need to make that appointment," he said.

"What about your yearly physical?"

"Nope."

"Daddy!" she yelled. Sarah caught me by the elbow, locked her eyes, and I was surprised by her partial smile. She whispered, "Miriam gives him the hugs. I put everything in order. Don't get in my way and we'll get along fine. Okay?" She winked at me and, in one swoop, she brushed everything on the counter into the trash. I watched her delectable hips sway as she retreated to the bedroom, where I heard drawers opening and closing.

"I should have warned you," Epstein said to me. "I almost forgot myself." I opened the old man's closet, expecting to find his insane DVD fitness collection, but the shelves were empty. A dust ball was on the lowest shelf. "Sarah called from the airport," Epstein said. "I panicked. Called Bunny. She rushed over with her laundry basket."

"Ms. Vallance is stashing your collection?"

"Bunny has a very understanding soul," he said.

"Where's your other twin?" I asked. "I had the idea that they came as a package."

"Miriam is in Geneva. Business."

"Sarah's cute."

"Sure, cute. So cute that she thinks she, and only she, can take care of me."

"I guess this means the café is off."

Epstein shrugged. "Family trumps café."

"But it's game night," I said.

I watched the old man think about it. "Sarah made dinner reservations. She's here for a few days, but please, for the love of Jehovah, *please* pick me up at the restaurant. I've been looking forward to this game. And I can only endure so much of her love."

Sarah flew into the room and bumped my shoulder. A brown padded envelope was between her fingers. "What is 'Women's Only Enterprises'?" she asked her father.

I watched Epstein remove his glasses and blow on the lenses. "They sell geriatric supplies. Nighttime bed pads. In case I leak. Want to know more?"

"Oh," she said. "Daddy, you need to pick up after yourself. You know I can't always be around to look after you."

THE SKY WAS PURPLING by the time I drove into Warsaw's trailer park. My friend was sitting on his rickety steps, his ripped T-shirt clinging wetly to his shoulders. He creased a page in his book—that ridiculous book—and tossed his laundry bag in the back. "You're an hour late, asshole," he said.

"How is it possible that you own nothing but have so many clothes?"

"I like clothes. So what?"

I didn't drive to the casita. Instead I took another route. And I noticed Warsaw squinching his eyes at the unexpected street signs. "Where are you taking me?"

I knew Ajo Cemetery's wrought-iron gates were open at all hours, and I stopped the car near a familiar section of lawn, removed my socks, my tennies, and got out. I walked over the still-warm, brittle grass.

The cemetery was quiet.

Eventually Warsaw opened the door, got out, and leaned against the hood. "So you bring me out here to bury me," he said. "You bring me to the cemetery to beat me, rob me, and bury me," he went on. "Is that it?"

"You've been staring at those magazines too much."

"I thought I was doing laundry at your house."

I counted the number of steps, measuring the square footage of the plot. A thin stratum of smog had settled over the valley. The moon above was a yellowed bruise.

"I could always sell it," I told my friend. "The Family Services Officer said that I was fortunate. I entered the market at the right time. There's a waiting list for this section of lawn now. One family died in a car crash and claimed the surrounding plots." I watched my friend count the freshly dug graves in the deepening shadows. Small dirt mounds had yet to level off. "I could always sell it," I said again. "Selling the plot would give me room."

Warsaw set a hand on his smooth head. "Jesus. What are we doing here?"

I sat cross-legged on my grandmother's future grave, running sharp, dry grass through my fingers. Each blade felt important, owned, mine. Warsaw ambled over, sat, and draped his long, cleanly shaved arms over his knees.

"No one ever tells you about the feet," I said to Warsaw. "Feet matter. Beautiful feet are a great thing. There's a connection, you know, between your feet and your health. Have you ever looked at an old person's feet? The first to go. Negligent foot care is the first sign. Imagine not being able to bend over and wash them. The nails grow thick and hard. You need to call in the troops with special tools in order to cut them. You need to keep them at the proper room temperature. In-grown nails, corns, calluses. Not to mention poor circulation and pressure ulcers. I tell my clients, keep your feet dry. Take care of your feet or you'll get mycotic nails. Nobody understands that it begins with the feet. You need to scrape them with pumice. Dead nails, fungus, dry and wet patches. Ms. Peabody accidentally clipped her toe and it turned into an infection. The next thing she knew a doctor was taking her leg off at the knee. Now she hobbles around on a prosthetic."

"Please tell me what we're doing here," Warsaw said.

"A good place to talk."

We shared a long moment of silence.

"In that case," Warsaw said. "I need you in court with me in a few weeks. Can you do that?"

I turned. Warsaw hadn't shaved his head in days and it resembled a seeded field. "Does this have to do with your accident?"

"Just tell me you'll be there," he said. "I need someone with me in court. And I don't want your questions."

Clouds moved over, burying us in semidarkness. I ran my fingers through the grass—my grass. The adjoining golf course was closed, but far off, there was a party at the clubhouse. Soon enough headlights appeared at the main gate, illuminating a huge obelisk nearest the entrance, a monument needed, I was certain, to hold down the dead ego beneath it. I watched the white F-150 stop in the cemetery's rotunda. Diego was as dependable as the moon's cycle. He had been in my rearview mirror all night.

"Pharmaceuticals aren't cutting it," I told Warsaw. "We were maintaining, but not now, with Nana's stroke. I know how to make enough to hold us."

Warsaw played with a patch of dry skin on his elbow as I brought him into the fold. I pointed at the F-150 truck. "That's our contact," I said. I told him how much we stood to make, and in just one night. "But I need your help."

My friend was quiet for some time. He brushed grass from his knees. "I have a question," he finally said. "Do you think someone might wave a gun at me again? I've been replaying what happened. That was, I have to admit—that was exhilarating."

"It is Arizona," I told him. "There's always that chance."

EPSTEIN AND HIS DAUGHTER were waiting on the sidewalk under the restaurant's red awning. I saw Sarah straightening the old man's tie while he did his best at fighting her off. Warsaw's foot caught my chin as he crawled over the seats to give Epstein shotgun.

When Sarah leaned down at the window, a tickle of fright wandered across her face. Her eyes went wide as she noticed my shaved friend in the back. "Don't have my father out late," she said to me. I saw her eyes bounce between Warsaw and the child's car seat. "We had a big meal and my father needs his rest." She handed me a cream-colored business card with her work and cell phone numbers. "Call if you need anything. I sleep with the phone on the other pillow."

"That should be a husband," her father said.

"Daddy, not now, not here," Sarah said.

Sarah refused to allow the door to close. She blocked it with her hip, perhaps thinking that she was feeding her father to wolves.

"You're embarrassing me," Epstein said. "Let the door go, Sarah."

"I'm just looking out for you, Daddy."

The old man finally cajoled her away, and Sarah shrank in my rearview mirror as we drove off. Warsaw patted Epstein on the shoulder. "Damn, she looks familiar," he said to the old man.

"Sarah doesn't visit often."

"Nice ass. Tits like apples," Warsaw said. "She looks familiar."

"My daughter lives in New York. You don't know her."

"Jackpot. New York. I was there with my dad. Now I remember. The hotel hot tub. That woman. I woke up with twin hernias."

"Mr. Hilarious," Epstein said.

It was game night. And game nights required a twelver of beer, chips, fresh guacamole, and cold six-packs of Epstein's vanilla nutritional supplements. The Diamondbacks were 134 games into the regular season. The team was on a slow march upward through division ranks. The Dodgers had tanked their last seven. The preliminary report about the disabled list reassured me. Game night brought us to the FoodMax, where I watched Warsaw toss shiny purple grapes at Epstein in the produce section. My permanent shadow was never far behind. Diego followed us to my street and parked in front of Alejandro's Old West outdoor gun-slinging exhibit.

"Is your neighbor some fresh kind of lunatic?" Epstein asked me as he shuffled up the walkway. A moment later he tripped and reached for my elbow. The old man leaned against me hard.

"You okay?" I asked.

"Goddamn tie is cutting off blood to my brain," Epstein said. "Lost my balance, that's all. Goddamn cheap soles on these shoes."

I tossed a bag of popcorn in the microwave. Warsaw dragged in chairs from the patio. Epstein claimed domain over the couch. The game was in the fifth inning. Zero-all. Man on second, two outs. The Dodgers were at the plate.

I saw Epstein firm-knuckle his temples. "You're having headaches again," I said.

"Forget it," Epstein said.

"He's having headaches," I told Warsaw.

Epstein showed me his palm. "I get this buzzing in my ears whenever my daughter visits. Just forget it."

"You're making an appointment with your doctor," I told the old man.

"Are you my daughter now?" Epstein said. "Is your name Sarah?"

"Three down. Diamondbacks are up," Warsaw said. He turned the volume up.

I stopped at the window on my return from the bathroom. Diego was a mere silhouette inside his darkened truck. I watched a dome light go on. Then shut off. I wondered if the man would wait outside all night, as he'd done on other nights, alone all night reading aviation magazines and God-knew-what-else. The dome light went on again. Having him around my life was a bit like having a bodyguard. I opened the front door. Diego's window went down.

"Come inside," I said. "It's game night. We have popcorn. We have beer." I walked over to the truck.

"I'll wait here, thanks," Diego said.

"I thought you wanted to be friends. Besides, what kind of asshole refuses beer?"

Diego's window rose to his eye level, and I watched his gaze slide toward Alejandro's sculptures, then back to me. At last his door opened.

He committed himself in increments. He walked in slowly, scanning the casita, probably searching for something of interest, something of importance to relay to his Mexican boss, running his eyes over an old cross and thirty-year-old drapes. It was just an old woman's former home, my home. Diego pressed his Stetson against his chest and went toward the noise in the living room.

Old man Epstein, dressed for a night out, was on the couch rubbing his temple again. Warsaw—bald, white, shaved—sat on the floor with a bottle of Tecate between his legs. My friends nodded at my guest. I shoved him into the room.

"Everyone," I said, "meet everyone."

17

I met her at the city zoo before opening hours. I hadn't been to the zoo since I'd been a teen, and my date was early, standing beside her two-door, in leather sandals, fanning her face with two tickets. Mona's toenails looked newly polished, sunlight glinting off the red.

"You have a neck rash," Mona said and reached out to touch beneath my ear.

"There was an extra razor on the counter. I thought, why not?"

"A man who seizes opportunity," she said.

"I like that color on your toes," I said. She crinkled them against her sandals. At 8:00 AM it was already ninety, and I knew by noon it would be like walking through wet cement. Mona's sundress broadcast a large yellow button placed mid-cleavage. She handed me a ticket. "I shaved," I said. "And you painted your toes. In some circles they call this a date."

"We'll see," she said.

Two other couples had also purchased tickets. I'd heard radio spots advertising the adults-only tour, called Animal Amore, and I remembered a woman's velvety voice boasting that the tour was a fun addition to any romantic relationship. Our tour guide collected tickets at a side entrance. Midway down the path I saw a man hosing the dusty cement.

Mona and I exchanged sheepish smiles with the others, who seemed relaxed in their relationships. They held hands, touched shoulders. It was obvious to me that their foundations had already settled. One woman with curled bangs seemed almost unable to contain her delight. She clutched her partner expectantly and chomped a wad of gum as gray as a rock. She was the type of hologram woman who was attractive in profile but not from the front. I watched her husband keep her close, as though they were sewn together.

Our tour guide was a thin-lipped know-it-all whose high voice brought to mind ringing bells. Her auburn hair was styled like a lion's mane, short on the sides with a sort of fluffy crown, and she was well versed in mammalian sex. She knew her organs. She knew her fluids. And she clearly knew her way around the zoo, walking backward, leading our small group from one animal enclosure to the next. She explained in intimate detail the sex lives of animals.

"The great ape's phallus has nothing to do with his body size," she told us, pushing toe to heel. "If the ape has a large harem, in fact, he'll have a smaller penis." She balled her fists. "But he'll have big balls. Human men are the most well endowed when comparing body size."

I noticed the gum-chewer smile at this morsel of information and squeeze her husband's arm. Watching the other couples interact—such close, constant, slathering contact—unnerved me. The other woman, the non-gum-chewer, began eyeing Mona and me suspiciously when we didn't hug and kiss the moment we heard how bonobo monkeys settled differences through sex. I knew an invisible line existed around Mona. I didn't know her. She didn't know me. Eventually, though, Mona started to walk slower, falling back from the group, making me fall back too, which opened enough room for brief, wondrous silences. Her tactic annoyed the guide, who waited for us with pursed lips before diving into her next spiel.

"We'd like to have cheetahs here, but cheetahs need room to roam," she said. "And as you can see, we're a small zoo. Cheetahs are downright notorious for bad sperm quality. Certainly not as bad as *human* males—" She seemed to stop herself. Her face went pink, as though she was putting the cap on something. "The point is, human male sperm is bad, but not as bad as the cheetah's."

Then the lady was off, reverse ambulating, heading to the next enclosure. All the mating talk accelerated the dating ritual. It stripped away the small-talk veneer, and I soon dropped into serious business with Mona, as though both of us were participating in an interview. Mona purposely fell behind again and I followed her lead.

"Married before?" I asked Mona.

"Once," she said.

"Kids?"

"The ex-husband didn't want them," she said. "His sperm quality was fine, I'm sure, but he himself was a child."

"Is that why you divorced?"

"Among many reasons," she said. "I'd go to the bathroom in the middle of the night and realize I was standing in little drops of the ex-husband's urine. That's when I knew."

A monkey leaped from fake branch to fake branch inside its barred prison. The two of us strolled closer to the group. The guide called the doggie chew toys inside the cage "enrichment."

"Quirks?" I asked Mona.

"Meaning?"

"Personality traits I might find endearing or repulsive."

"Indeed," she said, smiling small. "These are easy questions. You can do better."

Indeed. I knew how to get up in the morning, tie my own shoes, feed myself, but dating really made my blood rush in an entirely different way. I reached deep in search of questions to torque up the scarily candid exchange. I knew women found listening in men an admirable quality. It ranked with sperm quality, perhaps, and the willingness to do dishes. "Instability issues?" I said.

Mona blinked. "After the divorce, I popped antidepressants. The standard behavior of a divorced American woman."

"You must have secrets."

"Many," she said, smiling bigger.

We caught up with the group. Our tour guide was tapping her fingers against her bicep. She raised an eyebrow at me. "White rhinos," she said, and I heard strain in her voice, "do not breed well in captivity." The rhino sat in a patch of weeds, hulky and depressed-looking, as sourpussed as a captive outlaw. Its tusk was as large as a warhead. "White rhinos need to be stimulated by multiple females in heat," the guide continued. "Naturally, they breed best in herds. Mating happens between ten and four in the morning."

"Just like us," one of the women blurted. I saw her quickly cover her mouth with a hand. But her husband smiled, obviously happy that his sex life had been confirmed. He slung his arm around her.

"Difference is, we don't need multiple men to arouse this one," he told the group.

"We fuck at night too," the other woman said, chomping on her gum like a trucker.

"For the duration," Mona said, clearing her throat, "can we all please use the term 'thread the needle' instead? I don't like that word at all. It's improper."

The husband's neck snapped back. "You mean, instead of 'fuck'?"

"As a courtesy to me," Mona said.

"We're adults here," he said.

"I don't like that word."

"Screw, hump," the man said. "Fuck."

Mona shot him the kind of look that destroyed armies. "I prefer the phrase 'threading the needle,'" she said.

"That's *perverse*," he said.

The tour guide put her hands over her ears and pushed on. She wanted the tour to end, I was sure. Mona and I fell behind. "My turn," she said, bumping her hip against mine. "Why aren't you married?"

"Was going to. It didn't last."

"Tell."

"She gave me someone else's venereal disease."

"Sorry."

"She is too, I'd like to think."

"You miss her."

"Let's not mention her."

Mona walked ahead and I moved alongside. "Any major issues that I should know about?" she asked me. I fell silent. The group had stopped at the giraffe enclosure. The tour guide called them "hoof stock" and explained to us the flehmen response: when the male sniffed the female's urine to determine if she was breed-ready. I tried to imagine the physical act, but the routine must have looked incredibly awkward: long necks and long limbs in collision. One giraffe's ears swiveled, as though he knew the guide was talking about him. There were two sixteen-footers in the large enclosure, both regal, with bristly Mohawks along the backs of their necks. I watched their heads bob with each step. Long eyelashes, bumps rising between the eyes, they had up-pointing nostrils, like teacups. The larger of the two extended his long, purple, searching tongue and tasted the tip of his nose.

Mona waited for my answer. Issues? I thought about it. She already knew about me running pills. I rarely discussed with anyone my complicated desire for family. I was living broke, but with a fairly clean line of credit, and recently I'd been dabbling with the idea of running people over the border. "The usual, I guess," I told her.

Our group visited the mandrill baboon. Everyone became entranced by its wildly colored, humanoid, plastic-looking face. In the Asian habitat, the gibbon, with its white puppyish grin, was a tender creature. Introducing males and females was tricky, the guide said. "Gibbons either hate each other or like each other. You can tell if it's going to work right away. Scientists think it's scent-related."

My finger briefly touched hers. I didn't draw my hand away. Tingles worked up my leg and stirred the blood around my groin. The group walked on and I was disappointed when my connection to Mona ended. The other couples alarmed me—their slobberyness, how much they hugged, kissed. I watched one of the men pinch his wife's sofa-sized butt every dozen yards. All the sex talk inflamed the others' engines, and they couldn't restrain themselves from pawing, from preparing for the eventual. At the chimpanzee enclosure I stood closer to her, hoping to touch her again. As it was about to happen Mona put her hands in her hair, tightening her hairband.

"It's not off-limits," she said. "It is allowed."

"It's nice, though, building this tension," I said.

"We could be acting like these couples."

The word nipped my side. "Couple." I stepped back. "Don't you think we could lead full and productive and happy lives alone?"

"Now he retreats," she said.

"It's something I think about. From time to time."

"There are reasons, you know, to rush into it with someone."

"Don't you think people get bored? After two, three years, interest wanes?"

"There are reasons to stay together," she said. "A warm bed. A quiet walk with nothing said."

The tour guide, still maneuvering backward, stepped around a trash bin, escorting the group to an open enclosure at the end of the path. By the look in her eyes she was eager to end the tour. Three hyenas tromped around a make-believe savannah. Their wild eyes blazed in the sun, and their backs were arched, as though ready to pounce.

"And finally we come to the spotted hyena," the tour guide said. "Hyenas live in female-dominated societies. They have more testosterone in their bodies, and they're more aggressive, and larger, than males." She clasped her hands. "By outward appearance female hyenas can be mistaken for males. Her large clitoris is penis-shaped, and during birth the offspring pass through her U-shaped canal, pushed out finally through her clitoris."

I watched the two other women grip each other's elbows, their faces going off like fireworks. Both stared at their partners, as though the men suddenly looked like slabs of meat. The gum-chewer spit the gray wad into her hand. I looked at Mona, who was quietly smiling. She curled her pinkie into a question mark and hooked it around mine. Her toes, her red toes shone, and her pupils were in full, brilliant dilation.

WE THREADED THE NEEDLE on the kitchen floor. We threaded the needle in her hallway, knocking the cello case against the phone, everything tumbling to the floor. We threaded the needle standing up, unable to make it fifteen more feet, to her bedroom. Mona's enthusiasm infected me. The woman inhaled and exhaled with her entire body. She threaded the needle with the vigorousness of a sexually adventurous mid-thirties woman who hadn't threaded the needle in over a year: and she was good, she smelled right, healthy, sun-rubbed, she smelled wonderful. Every one of her touches landed on me like a small conclusion. The electric nip of her tongue fueled my performance. I watched her eyes grow distant and bright as she nudged closer, and I lost her momentarily as her hips shivered in my fingertips.

Afterward, she helped me locate the bed, and we crashed onto it like the shipwrecked do onto the beach. Mona's hair looked wind-tossed. My calves ached. Between us were questions and unspoken reservations. Things usually happened incrementally. Instead, I now knew Mona didn't shave her underarms. She crawled beneath the sheets as I tried to come to terms with the curious notion of meticulously painted toes but hairy armpits.

"That certainly earned an entry in my journal," she said.

"Always this intense?" I asked her.

"You asked for it."

"Did I?"

"At the hyenas. That glance. I read a glance. In any case, human beings are complicated creatures."

For the first time I took her foot in my lap, delighted by the lack of calluses, by the near-perfect toe spacing. Healthy feet were a good thing. Massaging her naked arch didn't even faze her, unlike many of the women I'd known. She patted down air pockets in the sheets and said, "I can understand why you go to Mexico. Anyone in your position would. In fact, my friend Elizabeth's mother once border-hopped every month for checkups. Medicine, doctor's visits, pretty much anything. Finally she up and moved. There are homes down south at one-third the price, with trained staff, and in destination cities. My grandmother lives in a home in La Paz. The same type of care, but cheaper. Of course, she's Mexican."

"I've never considered that. Mexican nursing homes."

"You should."

"You know more about nursing care than me."

"The homes are cheaper," she said.

"Use that word again and I might kiss you."

She ran a toenail down my arm, leaving a red mark. "Cheaper," she said.

I worked her feet. She closed her eyes, lashes fluttering, and I thought, yes, I did like her unshaven armpits. Mona moved her hips in a circular motion underneath the sheets. "You like?" I asked her.

She arched toward the bedside table and pulled a half-empty box of graham crackers from a drawer. Carefully she separated the rectangles. Bits of cracker sprinkled the sheets. "There's something I didn't tell you at the zoo," she said, taking a bite. "Sometimes I eat in bed. The ex-husband was not a fan. I do come with complications."

18 The taste of her salty, sun-bleached skin remained on my lips. For a day I replayed our collision, rewinding the conversations, pausing on mutually agreeable moments. In the morning she was still with me. I walked around the casita halfway dazed. I spilled coffee on my toes. I looked down and I was wearing only one sock. It was more than the sex. The sex was good, but it was her touch, her smell, her voice, smile, opinions, questions, demands. I was invigorated by the potential.

Around noon I began on the backyard. The pale sky was a day galaxy of cottony clouds pressed flat on an invisible plane. My grandmother liked the weeds because they added green to the view, but the weeds had to go if we were to ever sell the place. I walked stiff-legged to the shed, searching for gloves and a trowel, replaying the moment I'd stepped into her apartment until the moment I'd left. Mona was a dealer in pleasure.

Monsoon rain had softened the soil and the roots pulled easily. It was hard for me to tell weeds from wild desert flowers. Everything was sharp, thorny, tough, barbed. But consumed as I was by her taste, consumed by the idea of seeing her again, the chore became mechanical. I mined weeds with the trowel and tossed the carcasses into a bag, lost in sensuous daydreams, remembering my fingers grazing along the peach fuzz in the hollow of her back, remembering the circus act with her leg, so acrobatic, in the air just so. The handle of the trowel brushed my penis and my inner thigh tingled. I did not use protection. Another weed got a deathly yank. Soil clung to roots. Four times I did not use protection. I didn't know whether to feel terror or joy. You could earn a blue-ribbon disease or an unexpected child with that type of behavior. A routine developed. I bent over, dug a weed, and brushed my penis with the trowel. I was hard after a dozen more weeds. Sweat rolled down my back. My bald spot warmed. Mona's leg in the air—just, perfectly, so. Knees on the ground, I removed my glove, unzipped my jeans, and fit my hand through the opening. I moved slowly, closing my eyes and working until the veins were as hard as plastic tubing. Bloodred light pulsed behind my eyelids. I thought of hair falling across her pretty nose and the openmouthed, pained look of satisfaction.

I heard the creak of a loose board. I opened my eyes and Alejandro was standing on his porch and looking into my yard. Alejandro was sipping from a mug, watching me become pornographically compromised. He just stood there, refusing to break eye contact, scaring the shit out of me.

"Alejandro, hello," I finally said. "I didn't see you." I removed my hand from my jeans as casually as possible. Without a word Alejandro took another long, slow sip.

DIEGO PICKED ME UP outside Paseo del Sol's entrance gate. Jutting from the bed of his truck was a large wooden surfboard, a little yellow flag tied to the fin. Diego had failed to mention that there would be a third person along for the ride. In the compact area behind my seat was a mestizo boy, no older than twelve, with a diamond in his left lobe, who crouched on the hump seat, knees to his chest, hidden beneath the window. I noticed a steely look in the boy's eyes.

"Never knew there was an ocean around here to surf," I said to Diego.

"El Bebé gives me errands," Diego said. "Do *this*. Do *that*. It drives me crazy."

"And the kid?"

"Oh, he won't bother us."

The drive south was desolate and striking and I allowed my heart to open to it. Home supply megastores turned into fields thick with purple prickly pear and teddy bear cholla. Pink, turquoise, and mauve tract homes gave way to blighted highway architecture, shacks without roofs, and abandoned gas stations with their guts plundered. The desert emptied of people, of buildings, of everything. To the east I saw swollen clouds drifting over the parched sweep.

Diego cycled through radio stations, hunting around the dial like an explorer, finally settling on an accordion-heavy corrido, but my Spanish needed work, and I was left to guess at the dramatic tales being sung about: border crossings, love triangles, drug moving. It didn't surprise me when I noticed a build-it-yourself toy model airplane at my feet.

Ten miles before the southern Port of Entry, Diego pulled over on the highway's pebbly shoulder. He turned to the boy and spoke to him in Spanish. I understood tone more than words. The kid nodded. Then the mestizo kid climbed over my seat on his scramble out the door, and I watched him frog-jump a low fence, heading for a small oasis of tract homes in the near distance.

Something like pride played in Diego's eyes. "He's one of our best polleros," Diego told me.

"That boy works as a smuggler?"

"He earns salary. He escorts families across the desert to prearranged houses. And we have many houses," he said, putting the truck in drive. "By that I mean seventy-two. Bebé gets most of the payment, of course. His father gave him control over that part of the family enterprise."

"That part of the family enterprise."

"People," Diego said and turned his blinker on.

I understood that El Bebé was the puppet master around here, but I was not amused that he employed kids. Every organization had a figurehead, sure—someone watching over the worker bees—but using young kids?

We passed numerous Border Patrol vehicles along the highway before driving into Mexico.

The town of Catedral didn't look like much from a distance, but by the time we got to the center of town we were held up by traffic jams. Catedral was frequently mentioned in the newspaper. Sixty clicks southwest of Nogales, intersected by Mexico's Highway 2, it was a chalky rancho on the downslope of scorched alluvial plains with views of nearby mountains. I knew mass migration had transformed the town, and I knew travelers from across Latin America and elsewhere gathered here, but I'd had no idea it was an inland mecca.

People were everywhere—inside cars, outside cars, crawling into cars, riding on top of cars. The place amazed me. Double-decker transit buses with digital LED displays publicized the only destination: Gringolandia. It seemed to me the town was celebrating an instant holiday, only one not marked on any calendar. The streets were full of spirited vendors and men whistling up business. Storefronts advertised heavy discounts on merchandise necessary for desert trekking. Water jugs, duct tape, Band-Aids, flashlights, saltines, black clothes for night travel, backpacks, sleeping bags, chewing gum, baseball hats, salt pills, diet pills, cotton swabs, tennis shoes, and packaged lotería cards. We were no longer in the fantasy land of Chiclets and five-dollar cervezas. This seemed to be the nucleus. A dry water fountain in the centro comercial looked like a good place to lounge, and I saw a man with an accordion strapped to his chest entertaining groups of old-school campesinos and teenagers wearing gold Lakers jerseys. The accordion player sported a frayed white suit with purple piping. Cash-wiring outfits lined the sidewalks. One old woman sold packaged tube socks. Government Grupo Beta officers offered assistance to travelers in a parking lot. Here, the state police presence consisted of low-riders trawling the streets and bragging with shiny, spinning rims.

Diego drove to the south side of town and pulled into a block-long compound, an enormous castillo surrounded by twenty-foot walls capped with spiraled concertina wire. An impressive arched entranceway opened onto a cobblestone drive. Men with submachine guns propped on their shoulders stood around looking partially stoned. Despite the air-conditioning, I felt streams of sweat leak down the front of my chest. I half expected to see Villistas assembled by the ornate tile fountain, suited up in brimmed hats and bandoliers. I had never been face-to-face with a narcotraficante, never any reason, never had had much desire to touch, even remotely, the fringes of Mexico's narcocultura. I removed a square of aluminum foil from my wallet and pooled enough spit to swallow two pink pills.

"What was that?" Diego asked me. "You getting high?"

"Beta blockers," I told him. "Keeps my heart from leaping through my chest."

"Relax. El Bebé will take care of you," Diego said. "When you work for him, you're family. He loves Sonora. He loves Catedral. People here are family. And that you care for your grandmother impresses him. He is close with his abuelita in Culiacán. They talk on the phone. He has her number on speed dial." The image of an elderly woman brushed across my mind, her age-lined lips instructing her grandchild on how to properly package parcels of marijuana. "He takes care of us," Diego said and squeezed my forearm. "See? He even bought me this truck."

Diego eased behind an older model BMW in the circular driveway.

I was guided down a path leading away from the main residence, a red-tiled hacienda, toward a smaller, two-story casita with thin, spindly vines hanging off the portico. Bolted to the walls were surfboards. Alongside these were framed photos of surfing celebrities. The photos showed glistening pecs and foam boards slicing through frothy waves. Someone here was a big believer in fans. I counted ten blowing at different angles. The ceiling fan pushed warm air over my wet neck.

Diego dragged the wooden surfboard into the room. He hoisted it onto a mahogany pool table. Sweat stains had darkened his collar. "It's one of Duke Kahanamoku's long boards," he explained between breaths. "He was this famous surfer."

"Who surfs around here?"

"El Bebé," Diego said.

"We're in the middle of a desert."

"Act nice," Diego said.

Muted on a flat-screen TV was a telenovela, all counterfeit tits and melodrama, and beyond the double doors I saw a swimming pool with a well-tended desert garden behind it. I asked Diego, "What now?"

"You wait," he said, before leaving. "And you act nice."

The telenovela ended and another began. I sat on the leather couch, reconsidering my decision to come, knowing that El Bebé's father was the captain in Culiacán, Sinaloa. El Jefe de jefes. El Patrón. The scariest motherfucker in the universe.

He arrived midway through the telenovela with a Popsicle in his mouth and said to me, "I'm Bebé." I didn't respond. I sat quietly, acting nice. He was young, and I was surprised by his defined jawline, his worked-out biceps, his knee-length surf shorts and black flip-flops. The kid sank into the couch beside me and set his fist on his knee. Under each eye was a bold stripe of white zinc. Black hair dangled to his nose, which he swiped to the side in order to catch sight of the television. Following El Bebé into the room was a stern fellow, thin as a wraith, in a black suit. He bludgeoned me with his scowl. I tried not to make eye contact as the man positioned himself behind his younger counterpart, touching his necktie with his pinkie. He leaned down to whisper into El Bebé's ear, considering me with one yellow eyeball. Their whispering turned into a disagreement, from Spanish to English.

"Remember, business," the older man said. He pointed his skeletal chin at me. "Ask him. Our money." The man looked to me like some sicario or lieutenant or advisor or something.

El Bebé flapped his elbow. "All right. Let me ask him a question first." El Bebé pursed his lips and blew the bangs from his eyes. "Do you like music?" he asked me.

I watched the advisor put his hand to his forehead.

"I like a lot of music," I said. "Depends."

"Do you like norteño?"

The accordion; that polka rhythm; I absolutely did not. "Do you like Waylon?" I asked in return.

We exchanged vinegary glances.

"No, I like norteño," El Bebé said.

"And surfing, apparently," I said.

"My family sent me to school in Malibu." He shrugged. "I picked it up."

"Right."

"But anyway, I need a song, at least *one* song, about *me*," he said.

"You need a song?"

"In this business you get known by corridos," he said. "My dad, everyone knows about him. He's *known*. People know what he's *about*. I need a song so people will start taking me more seriously around here. Like El

Mosquito. Corridistas wrote *ten* songs about him. The albums fly off the shelves at the tiendas." I watched his eyes grow wide. "But shit, dude, what about me?"

Over El Bebé's shoulder, his advisor swept back his jacket to show me a gun. The guy smiled. The gun, tucked in his belt, was large. Heat gathered in my stomach, swam to my arms, and pulsed liquidly to my fingertips. My beta blockers had yet to kick in. El Bebé licked Popsicle juice off a knuckle. "Tell me," the kid said, hoisting his knee and gently touching my arm. "Do you think I should change my name? There must be better names the corridistas might like. Can you think of one?"

"A better name?"

"Yeah."

From the slither of his syllables, and his soft touch, El Bebé struck me as a switch-hitter. "Sorry. Out of ideas," I said.

"Sure, I understand. I'm the youngest in the family," he said. "So I got stuck with this name. But who the hell wants to sing about *the baby*?" The kid grabbed my arm. "Here, come, I want to show you."

In an adjoining room was a professional recording studio. The instruments in the domed room sat unused: accordion, drum set, and twelve-string bajo sextos. "Everything's here," the kid said to me in all seriousness. "Everything but the musicians." El Bebé showed me dials and knobs inside a mixing cubby. The gear appeared to be new. "I have everything any band needs. I spared no expense. Good enough for Chalino Sánchez. I even sent out word. Come to Catedral and record your album for free. But you must record *one* corrido about me. Please, I said. Look, I said. I move moto north in gas fuel tankers. I employ armies of Zapotec girls who sew dolls full of chiva. Pay attention, I said. Listen carefully, I said. I melt diet pills and send the methamphetamine—" The kid stopped and looked over at his advisor, who was hovering. "Fausto, how the hell is that done again?"

"You send meth over on the backs of mules," Fausto said in a monotone. "Remember your lines. You didn't do your homework. You should memorize better next time."

"Oh, right. I send meth over on the backs of mules," El Bebé said. "Still, no one gives a shit. Stupid pinches corridistas only care about what happens in Juárez and the Gulf and Michoacán. No one cares about El Bebé en Catedral." I watched El Bebé's eyes fall as he shoved the Popsicle into his mouth, his cheeks expanding and protruding. "I could gain weight, I guess," he said. "I could get fat. Or I could start acting unpredictable. I could make people think that I'm not all *here*." El Bebé pointed at his temple. "What do you think of the name El Mono Loco?" The kid gripped my arm and waited for my answer.

"I don't like it," I said.

"Okay, what about El Machin? It's never too late to change my name."

The kid was talking a sharp line of lunacy, but I listened. I listened because I'd come to Mexico to listen. El Bebé escorted me through another door, which turned out to be the nicest lavatory—showers, sauna, steam room—and out to a flagstone sundeck that descended via steps into an infinity pool. I was struck by the view. Open blue sky dueled with russets.

I watched Fausto whisper into El Bebé's ear again, and El Bebé made it clear he didn't like speaking Spanish. Their argument turned into English.

"Ask him," Fausto said.

"Give him some time to get comfortable," El Bebé said.

"Ask him now. You have to learn."

"Leave me alone."

"Like we rehearsed," Fausto said.

El Bebé placed a finger against the man's lips. "So," the kid said, turning to me. "Why don't you pay me? No one does business in my plaza without my approval. Sonora belongs to me. All this"—he threw out his arms, as though hugging the state of Sonora—"all of this belongs to me." He looked at Fausto. "Was that good enough?"

I read exasperation or resentment or anger or some combination-of on the older man's face.

"Oh, just go," El Bebé said, shooing Fausto away with the backs of his hands. "Leave us. You make me so tired." El Bebé collapsed onto a chaise lounge, as though struck with fatigue, his foot dangling over the side, his toe knocking against my shin.

"Your father instructed me," Fausto said.

"Go. Leave," El Bebé said.

"Your father said you must learn," Fausto said.

"You're not my tutor anymore. Just leave me alone."

The older man bumped my shoulder and walked to the far end of the sundeck, where he stood with his hands clasped, shaking his head. El Bebé peeled off his T-shirt. The young man's chest reminded me of Juliet's: lean, ribby, a cosmos of freckles. He squeezed globs of lotion onto his knobby knee while I stood over the pool, looking at red, white, and green tiles on the bottom, and I finally began feeling at peace. The beta blockers were working. I breathed in this land of contradiction, full of such excess and such poverty, and I thought of Nogales, where I felt more comfortable, picturing the shacks stitched side by side on the hills, dirt streets sprinkled with batteries, spent water bottles, and my lovely pharmacist, Amelia.

"This is all about family," the kid said.

"Isn't everything?"

"My dad gives me responsibilities because it's the family business, but to be honest"—El Bebé looked over at Fausto, presumably making sure the man was out of earshot—"I *never* wanted to do this." El Bebé leaned forward, smiled. "I really want to be a musician. But more than that, I want someone to write that one great corrido about me. Be honest," he said. "You must have a dream."

"I want my grandmother to have the best life."

"That's not a very good long-term plan."

I shrugged.

"You also want to move people," he said.

"I figure, if they want in, for the right price, I'll be a chauffeur."

"Okay, I'll pay you a fair amount," he said.

"And what's fair?"

"Whatever I say is fair," the kid said. "Besides, I don't want to deal with the headache anymore. Your border police frighten me. They bury sensors in the ground. They have drones flying through the sky, taking pictures. It's crazy."

"Just doing their job."

"But if I help you, you must help me. Give me a cut of your pharmacy business. That must be great money. Very inventive."

"But I use everything," I said.

"You must have something left," he said.

"Every nickel pays for my grandmother."

"Listen. From now on, give me a quarter of your monthly earnings," he said.

For a quarter, I would need to sell the casita immediately. Giving away a quarter of my business would ruin everything. "That's too much," I said.

"You better think of a trade, then. Me? I don't really give a shit." He smiled and added, "But that guy standing over there? Fausto likes to shoot people in the feet when they don't pay."

19 Thursdays and Fridays felt more or less like Tuesdays, not much unlike Wednesdays, each day the same, rewind and play, rewind and play. Repetition stapled the days together into an undistinguishable heap. I spent time on the casita, caulking the leak under the bathroom sink, installing blinds in the spare room, and checking the fuse box. The days were long and cauterizing, the air dusty and stirless. Each was difficult to move through and easy to forget.

I visited the nursing home almost every day while I waited for things to move on the Mexican front. I sat with Nana, patting her arm, waiting for improvements in her speech, listening to her labored words. I missed our long talks and arguments. A criticism would have felt welcome, a cause for celebration. Too often I caught myself staring at the corners of her slowed-down mouth, searching for signals.

The Activity Director—that hyper-caring woman—had given me a sheet with helpful instructions. I'd asked her if I could volunteer.

I followed the instructions like a dutiful son. I smiled, and I tried to help, but there were days when all I saw was loose skin draped over skeletons. Transferring Ms. Silverstein from chair to bed felt like lifting a plastic bag full of wooden hangers. Ms. Montague had lost weight; her elbows in my side were scalpels. I enjoyed wheeling Ms. Collins to her clinic room appointments because she was a storyteller. I walked through the building and patted gaunt shoulders and touched cheeks blooming with eczema. I rescued shoes that had gone missing. I taped streamers across the hall that announced the monthly birthday party.

It was okay to tell therapeutic fibs. But never contradict yourself.

Hand-sanitizing dispensers were every twenty feet.

Visitors on average were in their mid-fifties. Sons and daughters had eyes full of worry and loss.

I found the building at the end to be not unlike preschool. There were the occasional pissy smells and unidentifiable wet globs in the activity rooms. There was singsong hour and reading hour. Some days I found the place wondrous. At any moment utter nonsense could come from any resident, which I enjoyed, which I'd come to appreciate, above all because the nonsense was often more edifying than the standard rote hits popping from doctors' mouths.

One hundred and ten women and ten men called the building at the end home. Thinking about the numbers made me shudder. There were only ten men—just ten. Each visit was a reminder that my male reptilian circuitry was already starting to fray. Each tug at my sleeve and each gapped smile reminded me where everyone was headed, with my gender leading the charge.

PANDEMONIUM erupted one bright morning. I arrived to find the residents scattered in the sun, as though the building at the end had disgorged them. Orange highway cones were propping doors open, and from inside I heard alarms. The emergency had happened during breakfast, and each resident had a cloth bib around his or her neck. I witnessed one nursing assistant panic and lasso together four women with rope, which prevented them from rolling down the path toward the lake.

I searched for my grandmother amid the chaos, surprised to find Mona at her side. My grandmother was wearing a straw hat.

"Alarms blew twenty minutes ago," Mona said to me. "So I grabbed your grandmother." I watched her play with the hem of her skirt. Sunlight distilled through a cottonwood's waxy leaves and speckled the pavement. "The zoo was fun," she said, and into my mind came the zoo, her leg, the contortions, up in the air, just so.

"We need to do that again," I said.

Mona smiled.

Eventually the Nursing Director cupped her hands around her mouth, mimicking a bullhorn, and yelled, "There was a scorpion in the alarm system! Nothing to worry about. False alarm. No fire." I watched her move from group to group.

Barbara Gordon, fat as a hornet, waved at me from across the wheelchair traffic jam. She grabbed the handles on her father's chair and pushed him over. Mr. Gordon's plastic gun sat snug inside its holster, and the old gunslinger was decked out in cowboy hat and ostrich-quill boots. "I assume you have something for me," Barbara said. She ran her ringed fingers through the feathered hairstyle of a distant decade.

I dug the woman's blood pressure meds out of my postal bag and Barb handed me a personal check. Our exchange happened in front of my grandmother, who didn't, because she couldn't, complain.

"I'm taking Pop-Pop to the firing range," Barb informed me. "Even though he's late-stage dementia he hasn't forgotten the feel of his guns. It's so life-affirming. To see Pop-Pop goggled and earmuffed and plugging away at paper targets."

My grandmother squirmed. I watched her brace the chair's armrests and attempt to lift herself out. When she gave up, she set her hands on her knees, and an ugly, sad look entered her eyes.

"Talk later?" I said to Mona.

"Later and again," she said, "and soon."

I wheeled Nana to La Santa Rita. The doors glided sideways and the air-con swept over us. In the periwinkle hobby room, I saw Ms. Haybroke's eyes brighten when I came through the door with my grandmother. Nana's other friends were around a hobby table with bundles of yarn in their laps.

"Thanks for bringing her," Ms. Haybroke said. "Mary Beth may not be able to handle the needles, but we can update her on the gossip. Always plenty of that."

I made my rounds, knocking on doors, delivering white paper bags, collecting my service fees. I smelled incense when Ms. Vallance opened her door. She tried to pull me inside. I stopped her. I told her I was in a hurry.

"I need a favor," I said.

Ms. Vallance smiled and touched my knuckle. "For you? Anything."

"I need you to spread a rumor about Nana."

"What? I will not."

"Please, one rumor. And I need it to be good. And I want to make sure it gets back to her."

Ms. Vallance crossed her arms. "You're talking about your grandmother and my friend."

"For example, maybe she fooled around with Errol Flynn. Maybe she was a bank robber. I don't know. You're the expert on these things. Make something up." A small smile appeared on her face. "Please," I said, "do it for her. You should see Nana in that chair. She needs a rumor."

"Okay, okay. I get why you're jumping. Carlie Arthur at the newspaper owes me. Let me see what I can do."

Mr. Carter received his standard seven bottles, two packets of push tabs, and foot ointment from the FoodMax pharmacy—Amelia did not carry the brand. After Mr. Carter, I stopped at Mr. Garland Bills's door and pulled the howling coyote knocker. His hand emerged. I placed the bag in his fingers. The door closed.

Chloral hydrates, Tylenol with codeine, bisphosphonates, stool softeners, dopamine agonists, lipid-regulating agents. Watch for interactions whenever ingesting alcohol, whenever driving or operating heavy machinery. Adverse reactions: moodiness, drowsiness, diarrhea, and loss of balance.

I stopped by Ms. Wetherbee's apartment.

"Let me in," I said through the door.

"I will not."

"Then I'll tear the door down."

"You're not man enough."

"I can try."

I kept knocking until the crazy old woman surrendered. It was obvious to me that Ms. Wetherbee was in the middle of a meltdown. Since I'd discontinued her supply, it looked as though she had been throwing her money away on more junk. Packages from the Shopping Network were stacked nearly floor to ceiling. One window was completely blocked. Her apartment broke every regulation in the fire manual.

"You don't have sympathy for anyone," she said to me. "Look what you've done to me. I'm a wreck."

"You needed to quit."

She crossed her shivery arms. By some miracle her hair was growing back and the bald spots were filling in. She turned away from me, but I grabbed her. She stiffened in my arms. She smelled of old skin and aerosolized lilac perfume, but after a while her arms came around me. She held me as though it was the last time she would ever touch another human being, and finally, finally, finally she cried.

Later, the old man was wearing a clean, tight, white wife beater, and he looked tired and small and unwell. His drapes were pulled and only one dull lamp was on. "She's gone," Epstein said to me, standing in his doorway.

"Your daughter would exhaust anyone," I said. "She has efficiency down to a science."

"I'm not talking about my daughter, you idiot. I mean Effie," he said. He turned and disappeared into his murky cave. I followed and saw a lamp trained on a photo atop his coffee table. It threw an oval spotlight onto his dead wife's smile. Epstein collapsed on the couch. "I was at the medical arts complex all day," the old man told me, and he said, because of me, because I'd insisted, his doctor had ordered more tests. The old man spat the word out as though saying *pests*.

"Tests for what?" I asked.

"He wants to clear his suspicions."

"Clear what suspicions?"

The poor old man looked spent. Bags drooped under his eyes. His sport jacket lay in a crumple on the floor. The laundry basket with the exercising paraphernalia was beside it. I sat, and both of us stared at his wife's picture.

Effie had been a round-bodied woman with tightly cropped hair. In the picture she stood beside a large gray statue, some European monument. A blur of cars passed behind her. I wondered how long Epstein had been sitting in the dark, staring at this photo, warmed only by his wife's smile. It saddened me to see love demolished by death, and I thought about Mona and the future, growing old, growing infirm, both of us clutching to each other.

I opened the drapes. Below, two men were playing horseshoes in the pits, their game guided by shouts and luck.

"That Mexican at game night was nice," Epstein said. "Very polite, that guy."

"He's not Mexican. He's American."

He looked up. Half his face was shadowed. "Kid, listen," he said to me. "I know you've got something cooking with that Mexican American. Whatever it is, I want in. I'm old. And old men don't have that much time left."

ANOTHER VOICE MAIL. I listened outside in the parking lot.

"We could have had a son, Sid, or a daughter, two daughters, an entire swarm. That night you set your hand on my belly and told me stories. I listened. I heard everything you said. That night we sat by the radiator and you told me you wanted as many children as you had toes. We could have had children together, a family, we could have—"

I hit ERASE. I had enough children, Juliet.

20   Coronado High School wasn't far from the casita, an easy ten-minute bike ride, and it was exactly where I wanted to begin some kind of career. During lunch hour I sat outside the administration offices, hoping to befriend the principal, a woman with Technicolor blouses and cosmetically tattooed eyebrows. Not the prettiest fruit in the basket, but she cut a commanding figure as she led a colleague into her office and slammed the door. A plastic vase vibrated on an end table. After some time her door opened and a teacher limped out.

"In my office," she said and pointed at me. The woman scared me. Joanne Rahlson parked her hip on her desk, beside her nameplate, crossed her panty-hosed legs, and swung her foot back and forth as she scanned my résumé. "So, you want a job, Charlie?"

"It's Sidney."

"Happens to be your lucky day. This spring I need a new phys ed teacher. Interested?"

"I teach English."

"Beggars can't be choosers, Charlie." The more I examined her false eyebrows, the more they looked drawn on by black marker. "Listen, okay, look. How's this?" she said. "Three periods phys ed, two periods English, and I'll throw in donuts every week. You serve me well and I'll see about bringing you aboard next year as English faculty." She licked her finger and ran it along her temple, waiting for my answer. I already knew it.

"Shouldn't this be a more formal interview?"

"This is it, Charlie. You have five seconds to decide."

Everything about the school, when I left her office with a job, felt cinematic. Someone may as well have been filming the quarterback preening in slo-mo down the hall as girls' heads turned in admiration. All around me athletes sported red letterman jackets with blue C's over their hearts. Cheerleaders wore uniforms too, showing off bright red kneecaps. Here everyone had a place, including me. Kids were excited to be living the legend. I knew their lives were thick with gossip and budding romances. Everything seemed tinted with promise.

When I returned to my fifth-period class, the students were waiting for me. Five boys in hoodies had wandered away from their biology textbooks. They were now huddled in the back of the room. I parted the crowd and saw one of the boys brushing a wad of cash against his chin. I pointed at the boy with braces. "You gambling?" I asked him.

"Just tossing dice against the wall," he said.

"Come on, guys. Toss dice during lunch, fine, but no gambling during class."

"You're no teacher," the kid said. "Just a substitute."

"Not anymore. I'm new," I said. "Plus, you ruined my mood. Plus, I could easily kick your ass across this hot room. Put the dice away."

WHEN THE SCHOOL DAY ENDED, I drove to the park. Parents and children claimed one large section, next to the brown soccer fields, where there was a playground with swings, monkey bars, slides, sandboxes, the works. Encircling the playground ran a track where women worked their glutes while pushing newborns in cross-training strollers.

I lugged the child's car seat around, hanging it from my elbow. I wanted to briefly sample the idea. I was ignored for the most part. I smiled back when smiles came my way but said nothing. I pretended the wife had gone ahead with the littler one, and this was my lot, the willing paternal mule. I was the man who carried the car seat.

One lady without kids, lost in this section of park, stopped to ask me directions. She didn't appear to suspect subterfuge. I gave her my best guess and quickly hurried, overjoyed, to the car.

21 Mona nudged me awake by gently rolling her knuckles along my ribs. I was half-asleep, my ears clogged with nonsensical dreamscapes, when she crawled on top. Her musky hair tickled my eyelashes. I opened my eyes and saw her heart going in her neck. I reached for her hair and grabbed with my teeth. She eased down with a tug. It was nice.

"You grind your molars when you sleep," she said. "It's like sharing my pillow with a cement mixer."

"Stress."

"I know something that helps," she said. I felt her tongue on my earlobe when the report of a gunshot echoed outside her bedroom window.

I bolted upright. She rolled off. "What was that?"

Mona sighed. "The neighbor's kids again."

"Kids? Again? What kind of neighborhood is this?"

"I'm a social worker," Mona said. "I can't afford the hills." Mona dragged the sheet from the bed, wrapped it around her middle, and stood beside me at the window. Another gunshot went off. I pulled her down.

"Two boys," I said, "one gun. Should we call the police?" I popped my head up. Mona's apartment overlooked an alley. Below I saw two boys taking turns with a medium-sized pistol. They appeared to be elementary school kids. They were firing at an old bottle of bleach propped atop a green Dumpster. From this distance I couldn't make out the gun model. But I saw sand trickling from the bottle— fresh wounds. I watched an older boy brace himself in anticipation of the recoil. After he fired, the younger boy grabbed the gun's barrel. I was insulted by how they handled the thing like it was a toy. "We should do something," I said.

"I usually wait until they finish," Mona said.

"This happens a lot?"

Mona palmed my shoulder and pushed herself up. I heard her scooting around in the kitchen. But I was riveted. I felt the next gunshot ripple through my spine. The younger boy had fallen, seemingly unable to withstand the force of the gun. The kid clutched an elbow and his face was on the verge of tears.

I couldn't find my jeans. My jeans had been the first item off. So I threw on my T-shirt and tennies. I felt a great urge to set down rules, and unarmed, I tramped outside, naked from the waist down, and grabbed the gun from the elder boy's hands. "No," I said emphatically. The kid looked startled, and he focused on the asphalt and kicked at a pebble. "No," I said again. "Understand?" The kids were silent. "I said, understand?" They nodded. "Good, good."

Hands trembling, I marched inside, terrified and proud, and I set the gun on the kitchen counter. Mona was layering mayonnaise on a slice of bread. I couldn't believe it. Two boys handling a firearm outdoors, yet here she was, preparing a sandwich.

"It's for you," she said. "You probably have a busy day. I thought you might want lunch."

Day-old bread, Swiss cheese, mayo, yellow mustard, rolled slices of honey turkey and half-wilted lettuce. Three slivers of avocado. No tomatoes. Mona was making me a sandwich. I watched her slice diagonally and put the sandwich into a clear baggie. I dug a fingernail into my palm. Mona was making me a sandwich. It was the nicest thing anyone had done for me in the longest time.

I FOUND MY JEANS, but Mona was determined to keep unbuttoning them, so I was late, unsure which building to enter, which door was right. The historic, green-domed downtown courthouse was crawling with a busload of Japanese tourists. They were snapping pictures and touching the exterior walls and loitering in the arabesque breezeways and getting in my way.

I wandered aimlessly around Justice but couldn't find the room. I called my friend. "No, you've got it wrong," Warsaw said. He told me to get to Superior. Superior, it turned out, was in a black glass building with a second-tier security guard in the lobby who leaned back in his chair, his fat fingers crawling across his stomach like a tarantula. He refused to give me directions.

"Oh, that way," the man said. Moments later he said, "I mean that way." The man wanted to joke around, but I was late and in no mood for jokes. I passed lawyers in linen suits standing beside terrified clients who looked like they would rather be chewing on glass.

Finally I located the informal courtroom. Running commentary came from a presiding judge, a man with sagging cheeks and a triple chin. Spectators wandered in and out. A clerk behind a lesser bench passed paperwork to an even lesser clerk.

Warsaw snapped his fingers and snagged my attention. He was at the front. "You didn't have to wear a tie," Warsaw said to me. My friend was in tattered cutoffs, flip-flops, and tank top.

"It's a courtroom," I said. "This is how you dress. You never told me what this was about."

"At least you showed up," he said.

The next thing I knew the clerk called Warsaw's last name, and suddenly I was at the podium with my friend, both of us watching the judge scribble on a piece of paper. The judge looked up. "You are Peter Wozniak, is that true?"

"I am, true," Warsaw said. His stance struck me as submissive, hands crossed at his waist, head bowed. I watched the clerk show the judge Warsaw's passport, and the judge whistled as he flipped through it. Hot on my brain was how much this little circus was costing my friend, and for what?

"I understand you want to change your name," the judge said.

I felt the heat of grand embarrassment rising in my chest.

"Before we continue," Warsaw said, "I want confirmation. Legally, I need one name, right?"

"Meaning?" the judge asked.

"I can't opt for a blank line, right?" Warsaw said. "In lieu of a name?"

I watched the judge breathe hard through his nostrils. He stared down at us as though considering twin criminals. "You need one name," the judge said.

"Fine," Warsaw said.

The judge then pointed his pen at me. "And this is your witness, true?"

I was too shocked to respond.

"Yes, true, this is my witness," Warsaw said.

The clerk asked for my driver's license, and the judge prolonged the insanity by taking a long gaze at it, half-asleep, as though this was his career-ending purgatory. The judge read briefly from a laminated card. "And you have no felonies within this county, within this state, and within this country. You have no outstanding debts. You are not in hiding, in any way, from previous financial responsibilities that this name change would enable you to avoid. Is all of this true?"

"All one hundred percent true," Warsaw said.

"You understand, from this day forward, you'll be legally known as"—the judge read from the form—"known as Warsaw."

"Yes," Warsaw said.

"That's a Polish city," the judge said.

"The capital," Warsaw said.

The judge pushed his glasses against his eyes. "You don't seem to have any eyebrows."

"That's right," Warsaw said.

"Why?"

"I shaved them."

"Regardless," the judge said. "You must understand that for banking purposes, and for passport and licensing and such-like, such as airline tickets, you'll need to use your chosen name twice. Do you understand?"

My knees nearly gave way as I entertained the idea of an overhead paging system, somewhere in the future, calling out *Warsaw Warsaw! Warsaw Warsaw!* The judge was leering at me. So was Warsaw. The same went for the clerk. "And you do attest that this man beside you is the person he claims to be?" the judge asked me.

"Say you attest," Warsaw said and bumped my elbow.

"Yes, I attest," I said. "I attest."

The proceeding ended as quickly as it had begun. The clerk gave Warsaw his passport, the judge signed the form, and I was dragged outside by Warsaw, into the open-air plaza, feeling flogged by the sun, when I was finally able to say, "I attest that you're a major asshole. Jesus. What was that in there?"

"But you did attest," Warsaw said, full of smiles. My friend spread his arms wide, palms at the sky. He looked like a new man, absolutely buzzing with newness. It was as though, with only one name, he felt lighter.

"I suppose you think this is hugely clever," I said.

"I wouldn't use the word 'clever.'"

"I can't deal with you anymore. What's happened? Are you losing your mind?" Warsaw's smile dropped. "Shaving your body. Giving away everything you own. Reading and rereading your stupid book. Hell, moving back to Arizona! You were supposed to have the career, and the family, and all of it. Wealth gave you every opportunity. And you're wasting it. Is everything a joke to you?"

My old high school friend spat in the courtyard's fountain. "He gave me everything, except one thing," Warsaw said. "How far do I have to take it before he notices?"

"What are you talking about?"

"My dad," he said. "That I count, that I'm here, that everything's not about him. That he has a son."

My lungs felt hollow. We never got over them, I supposed. A headache approached the corner of my eye. I watched my friend dip a hand in the fountain and cup some water. Mist settled on our cheeks. My friend was slowly pulling the vanishing act, and I didn't know what, if anything, to do. Was there anything anyone could do? I touched Warsaw's arm. He tried shrugging it off. I didn't let him. I stood with him, touching his arm. Sometimes this was enough.

22 Five people inside the casita's small living room brought the place to capacity. I watched Warsaw assist Danni with the large topo map. He pegged the corners to the floor with our empties. Warsaw had wanted to use my grandfather's urn, which I now kept in the living room, but I refused.

For a while Epstein stayed quiet, and I saw him admiring Danni's forearms. Warsaw was apparently taken with her too. He shushed me whenever Danni wanted to speak. Both of them watched her move through the room carrying that solid confidence and gliding seemingly by radar, like a bat. It was clear to everyone that Danni understood the thrum of her body in movement. But Warsaw was just a pallid blur anymore—two watery eyes overhung with shaved Cro-Magnon eyebrows—and I thought that if my friend had looked even partially human, Danni might have given him an appraising glance. But tonight, for her, for us, it was about what we would move through the desert.

Danni reached for her rucksack and grabbed a laser pointer and flipped it on. A red dot appeared on my grandmother's crucifix on the wall.

"Sidney and Warsaw, you'll be going north, skirting this mountain range on foot, right here," Danni explained to us. I watched the red dot move along the map's squiggly lines. "Mr. Epstein, and me, we'll be in the van, waiting here." Danni touched eyes with each of us. The plan as I understood it: We pick up the shipment in Mexico, drive north to the border, where Danni drops us, she drives safely away in an empty van and into her nation, Warsaw and I walk the shipment into Arizona, meet the van at a safe point, and drive away. Easy, she said, simple. She told us she had done this before without complications. "And we choose a moonless night," she added.

Warsaw scratched his ribs as he scooted back on the couch. I saw his jaw muscles tighten. "That's twenty miles, you said?" He parked his chin on a fist. "No one said anything to me about hiking twenty miles. That's not in my personality. I've never hiked five miles. I don't even own the right kind of shoes."

"Buy the right shoes," I told him.

"This is night, along the border, in the middle of nowhere, with snakes and invertebrates and a shipment of strangers."

"*This* shipment, *that* shipment," Epstein said. "These are human beings. We're making this enterprise sound as though we're moving toilet paper."

"I don't know about this," Warsaw said. "I just survived a car wreck."

"A fender bender," I corrected him.

"The door is *totaled*. I could have *died*," he said and eyed Diego, who was sitting with his back against the wall and saying very little. "And what about you? What's your job?"

"I'm here to listen," Diego said.

"My question remains unanswered," Epstein said. "Mind telling us who we'll be moving?"

"We don't know," Danni said.

"When will we know?" Warsaw asked her.

Diego cleared his throat and spoke up. "As soon as Sid receives the call from us, he'll drive south and meet the group," he said. "At the stash house."

"They won't be itinerant workers," I said. "Whoever they are, we'll be paid extremely well for safe passage."

"Bolivians, Vietnamese, Filipino, who are we talking about?" Epstein asked, apparently cemented on the detail.

"Does it matter?" Warsaw said.

Epstein swiped his hands as though ridding them of crumbs. "Of course it *matters*. These people aren't stepping onto Ellis Island. We're bringing them illegally. I want to be the voice of conscience."

"Epstein's right," I said.

"Having a conscience interferes with business," Diego said. And I knew he was right too. But I also knew the man had gone terribly wrong with the application of his cologne. It was so strong that I felt the scent behind my eyeballs. Diego had arrived late, and now he sat across the room, away from everyone, and he refused to make eye contact with me. Like he was angry, or something. I noticed him focusing on the grooves of his palms.

"Chinese or Brazilians," Danni said. "There's a high probability we'll be bringing in either Chinese or Brazilians. Okay?" She nodded at Epstein. "Happy?"

Epstein slowly stood, as though he was preparing to deliver a speech. "I can live with Chinese or Brazilians," he said. "Chinese or Brazilians suits me. I have no problem with either Chinese or Brazilians. And another thing," he said and clutched his side. "Because my presence is unnecessary, I'd like to donate my cut to Sid."

"Isn't that just peaches?" Warsaw said.

I watched the old man hurry down the hall. I heard the bathroom door shut. One of his pills was a diuretic, so it was understandable.

Danni's army rucksack was a nest of treasures. Inside were square gadgets, beeping gadgets, and electronic gadgets. One hissed as she flipped it on. She passed equipment around, showing us how to handle the radio. Then she lifted a small bottle. "Salt pills will replenish whatever you sweat away," she said. "This is a long walk. A brutal walk. You need to be prepared."

Warsaw made a fist, and up popped his special finger. He squeezed out a strained smile at me.

MONA ARRIVED EARLIER THAN I EXPECTED with a large overnight bag slung over her shoulder. She kissed me on the cheek and looked eager for bed, fresh breath, pores scrubbed, her hair secured with a sapphire band. She stood bright-eyed in the doorway, her feet in pink flip-flops, vaguely smelling of night lotions.

I saw Danni glare at Mona on her way out, clearly displeased by the arrival of another woman, at this time of night, at my door. Without saying good night, Danni caught up with the others on the sidewalk and latched her arm into Diego's.

"You're early," I said to Mona.

"Couldn't wait." Mona considered the scattered beer bottles, the half-empty bowl of popcorn. "I didn't know it was potluck night." Her sharp, bony shoulders poked from a blue tank top.

"You brought a bag," I said.

"Girls need things."

"A big bag."

"Toothbrush, socks, wall calendar. The picture frame won't take up much room. I framed our zoo tickets." Mona set her bag beside the topo map on the floor. "This doesn't look like any old potluck."

"Business," I said.

"Mind clueing me in?"

I said nothing. Drop that first lie and the second came too easily. "I need money," I told her.

"Don't we all?"

"Caring for Nana is expensive."

"I know that part."

I fiddled with my watch. As I explained to her the break in the fence, the open lane across the border, the lines beside her eyes hardened. I gave her Danni's reasoning. People crossed every day. As human beings, people were meant to move from one place to another. I would just be helping people out. It was really nothing, I assured her. I watched Mona assume her best game face, but her feelings filtered through. She crossed her arms, uncrossed them, pulled down her lip, squeezed her nose, and scratched her forearms. "Moving people over the border," she said.

"That's the gist."

She breathed in a slow, deliberate lungful of air. Then she re-looped the bag's strap over her shoulder. "How big was the bolt that came unscrewed in your brain?" she asked me. "Pills I can handle. Pills, sure, but this?" She pushed me aside and went for the door.

"You're leaving?" I asked.

"The residents have puppy therapy in the morning anyway. I like to be there."

"You can't leave."

"I can't?" She tilted her head. "I own these two feet," she said.

23 We were not square. We were several Benjamin Franklins away from ever being square. The balding old bird owed me hundreds of dollars, but now there was a professional compound bow in her kitchen, not to mention a Nubuck quiver full of razor-tipped arrows, and it was clear to me the old woman was not well.

"The meeting only lasts an hour," I explained and watched her eyes slide away. "These meetings will help."

"I don't know," Ms. Wetherbee said. "That kind of thing's not for me."

She rocked back and forth in her puffy armchair, the queen bee of her messy hive. Pink lipstick gleamed wetly on her teeth.

I stepped around a ceramic reproduction of the Little Mermaid. "You can come on your own or I'll pick you up and carry you. You must weigh—what?—a buck and a dime?"

"Some choices."

"Either way, you're coming with me."

Eyelashes fluttering, Ms. Wetherbee squeezed her hands. She looked at her mantel and the portrait above it. There she was, posed in a velvet chair and backed by her two sons. Oh, I would have loved to get them alone in a room. It would only take an hour—one hour behind a locked, soundproof door. They never helped her. I knew her elder son was a lawyer, and her other, an architect, was always busy, always too, too busy.

"Time's ticking and I'm not in the mood for arguments," I said. "My new girlfriend left me. So I'm fresh out of patience."

Ms. Wetherbee put her foot down and stopped rocking. "Let me get my coat."

"Fine." I'd just about had it. These old-timers! With their coats and hats and special socks and woolen gloves! Ms. Wetherbee went to her bedroom while I rooted around the horrible magnificence of her apartment. A fly lit on a large purple glass egg and rubbed its tiny hands. All around were boxes and boxes of useless stuff. Where did she get the money? I knew serious debt could be in her future. With my other clients, money moved through channels with safety measures. Lawyers, family members, and DPAs gave out monthly allowances. But Ms. Wetherbee spent hers like it was her job.

I waited. She remained in her bedroom for a suspiciously long time. When she didn't answer her door, I tried the handle. She was in the middle of a California king, perched amid piles of orchid-patterned pillows. And she was holding a smoky-orange pill bottle. The lid was off. She was reenacting the crying routine again. "I swallowed three," she said.

"You told me you stopped."

"I fell off the wagon."

"You promised."

"Can't you see that they make me feel delightful?" she said. "They make me not feel anything."

I examined the label on the bottle. Thirty-milligram scored tabs of morphine sulfate. They looked new. I could use them, re-bottle them, but I wanted to set a precedent. I marched the pills to the toilet. While dumping them out I noticed a sticker attached to the bottle. It was the image of a black bull. A bull. A black bull.

Ms. Wetherbee was on her side, sucking her finger, when I returned. "I'm *soorrrrry,*" she said.

"It's my fault. We know it's my fault. Just tell me about the rest."

"That was everything."

"You're lying."

"I'm not," she said.

I told my old friend that we might miss the meeting, we might miss next week, but I was not leaving her apartment until she showed me the rest.

"Leave an old woman alone."

"I'm not leaving."

By the look I landed she had to understand that I was serious. She stopped her antics, as though I'd flipped the magic switch, and reluctantly pointed at the closet.

It would have been implausible if I hadn't witnessed it myself. Lining five shoeboxes inside Ms. Wetherbee's closet was enough dope to kill an elephant. Oxycodone tabs, hydrocodone caps, hydromorphone rectal suppositories, Demerol syrup, Lortab liquid elixir, 20-milligram doses of MSIR oral solution, even a goddamn tube of opioid nasal spray. I knocked every shoebox to the floor.

"Unbelievable." I calculated how much there was, translating the stockpile into dollar amounts. Even the druggist at the FoodMax pharmacy would have been shocked. I lifted a blue box from the carpet. "So you got your hands on some," I said. The box contained flash-sealed strips, opiate arm patches, seventy-two hours of bona fide pleasure. "I don't recognize *any* of this. Where did you get it?"

"That nice Mexican gentleman," Ms. Wetherbee said.

I saw another sticker on this box. Another black bull. "Does this man drive a big white truck?"

She nodded, as I knew she would, and I began devising a lengthy mental list of Latin American tortura techniques: acid in the eyes, mock suffocation, drilling holes into that gold-toothed, pinche's toes. "This man has a smile with gold in it, right?"

"Isn't he your cousin? He told me you worked together."

"My cousin?" Diego had crossed the line. Now I understood why he wouldn't look me in the eye at the meeting.

A red bird jumped from a clock above her headboard, scaring the shit out of me. It chirped twice and disappeared behind its bright yellow door.

"We're late," I said. "Grab your coat."

"How can I attend the meeting now? I took pills. Three pills. Big pills."

"I'm sure people show up wasted all the time." I dumped a pillow, gathered the bottles and packets in the pillowcase, and cinched the end. Ms. Wetherbee watched hopelessly as I removed the candy from her grasp.

"Don't make me do this, Sidney. Please let's don't."

"Let's go."

"I'll kill myself." Her hands jumped to her thinning hair. "I'll do it. Like Sophie Hamilton. With pills."

"Don't say that."

"I will. I'll do it."

"No, you won't."

"And why won't I?"

"Because you love how much I bother you."

She blinked, her face blank as the porcelain doll beside her.

I drove her eight blocks to the Catholic elementary school. Classes had let out for the day. A photocopied sign on the entrance door directed us to a classroom, where a motley group had arranged themselves in desks meant for seven-year-olds. I smelled the familiar whiff of chalk. Styrofoam cups sat next to a portable coffee machine. We were late, and a young woman was already standing at the blackboard. She went quiet when I pushed Ms. Wetherbee inside.

"Terribly, very sorry to interrupt," Ms. Wetherbee said. She patted down the air with her hands. "He made me. He forced me." Ms. Wetherbee struggled to fit into a desk. I took the next one, my knees sticking out. There were eight others. Two wore the white collars of the priesthood.

The person in charge was a middle-aged man with a frayed yellow bandanna around his neck, and he scolded me by tapping on his watch. Then he turned to the woman at the blackboard. In a calming voice he said, "Sorry about that, Suzie. Let's please continue. We're listening."

Suzie was young and twitchy and, considering her bandaged hand and leg cast, quite a gruesome sight. It looked to me like years of abuse had punched her face into a haggard mask of skin and bone. She was an experiment gone wrong. I knew she could make even the meanest man's heart feel tender.

"Anyhow, like I was saying. I wasn't wearing a seat belt." I watched her fondle her bandaged wrist, clear her throat, and gather courage. "I was high, but you already know that. Anyhow, like I was saying, I passed out with the door open while the car was rolling. Fell to the street, cracked my head. That's when I saw the rear tires moving over me. That's the story, since you need to know. That's the story of how I ran myself over with my car."

Ms. Wetherbee shot me a desperate look, but I stayed with her for the entire meeting, for the entire hour, listening to everyone's tragedies. I stayed with her and listened, because people were friends here, because this was a place without judgment, and because this was the only way I knew how to make an old woman well.

24 Early morning I received a phone call from the Mexicans. El Bebé's advisor spat directions into the phone. I wrote them on the back of the sports section. I shut my phone. The casita was quiet. A clock ticked. A floorboard creaked. Something was blooming this time of year, and I sneezed.

I drove south out of Tucson and passed through the twin border-kissing Nogaleses, and into Mexican sun. Shape-shifting figures skipped across my car's hood as the red morning sky cooled into icy blue. I followed the dusty two-lane road between Catedral and the international line.

I slowed when I saw the motel in the distance. Bulbs were shot out of the motel's old neon sign, and the ramshackle building bent U-shaped around a dirt lot. I didn't trust the place. Except for a horse trailer in front, the building looked deserted.

My car door creaked open and the smells hit me: sagebrush, tropospheric dust, oil, gas. Dry air sucked moisture from my lips and the sun drilled my bald spot. I looked around. I was alone out here. Sunlight dabbed out the farthest range, some twenty miles away, smearing the ridges into the blue-white sky.

The room number was affixed to the door with cheap gold numerals. Sweat had collected in the hollow of my upper lip. As instructed, I knocked on the door three times, took a breath, and knocked once more. A drape in the window swayed and went still. Very quickly the door opened, fingers clamped around my throat, and I was yanked inside. A strong, short man kicked the door shut and forced me against it. I felt the cold, sharp tines of a fork against my Adam's apple.

"Los Tigres del Norte," I said, feeling my adrenal glands empty. The password came out in a spray of spittle. "Los Tigres del Norte." An onion stench eased off the man. His forehead hovered at my chin. Without warning he nicked me on the pull and I felt heat on my jaw. "Hijo de puta," I said.

"Lolli," the man said in response.

Black sunspots dissolved in my eyes. The man was wearing a policía uniform with sweat stains at the pits. A revolver stuck out from his fanny pack. The frigid, dank room smelled heady.

"I've come to check the people," I said. Blood leaked onto my neck.

"Diego?" he asked.

"Diego's not here."

"No here?" the man said.

"Just me."

The man pressed me against the door with his forearm again. "Lolli," he said vehemently. The man's breath was a blast of chemicals, ripe with gasoline and pipe cleaner, and I knew he'd been chewing the wrong kind of Chiclets, which could turn any man shitbird insane. His yellow eyes signaled a failing liver, and his two front teeth were chipped down into stalactites. "Lolli," he said again and kneed my thigh, forcing me to the floor.

Behind the man was an adjoining room, and for a moment I thought I'd drifted into a hallucination. In the other room I noticed long, regal, dotted legs standing motionless. I was expecting Brazilians. I was expecting Chinese. Droppings littered the carpet and looked like brown mashed-potato bombs. The animal had kicked over a twelver of Carta Blanca. Bottles lay strewn. The giraffe was younger and shorter than the giraffes at the zoo. An adolescent. Undersized, able to fit inside a motel room.

"Where are the people?" I asked the man with the fork. "I'm supposed to move people. This isn't funny."

I watched the animal's long neck scuff the ceiling.

"Lolli," the maniac said and pointed the fork at my hands. He meant that I should warm them with my ass. I did. Dirt embedded in the carpet scratched my palms. By the look of the pesthole scum motel, the place was used often. Tattered wallpaper showed a tropical coastline—green fronds, beige sand, the sea. The maniac padded around. I watched the sides of his mouth jerk wildly.

Over my shoulder the motel's door opened and hit me.

"Que te pasa?" another man said, trying to push in.

The maniac leaped toward the door. "Agarramos un gabacho," he said.

"El es el coyote," the other man said.

"Lolli," the maniac said.

I rolled to my side and slithered out of the way and saw another uniformed municipal. A black, untrimmed mustache overhung his bottom lip. When he bolted the door, the lock broke off, and he stared at the thing. He threw a plastic grocery bag at the maniac and lollipops fell to the floor. The maniac webbed the carpet with his hands and tore the wrappers off and shoved three inside his mouth. His eyes wandered to the back of his skull.

"Este es el hombre de Diego," Mr. Mustache said to the maniac. Mr. Mustache smiled down at me, saying, "All is good, yes?"

"No, all is not good." I touched my jaw, wanting the man to understand. Blood was dribbling down my neck. My heart was going. "That man assaulted me."

"You take it?" He spread his arms toward the adjoining room, meaning, of course, the giraffe.

"I came here to count the number of *people*. There are supposed to be *people*. El Bebé's man called. He told me to check the cargo. *Cargo*. By *cargo* I thought he meant *people*. What am I going to do with a giraffe?"

Mr. Mustache nodded, and then unexpectedly, in flawless English, he said, "Your wallet, please." He kicked my thigh lightly until I rolled over. Then the man skillfully removed my Velcro wallet from my pocket. A small aluminum foil packet dropped on the carpet. He unfolded the foil and looked at the pills inside. "What's this?"

"For emergency situations," I said.

"What emergency?"

"Right now. *This*. This situation is an emergency."

The man was more interested in cash than my pills. He shoved the thin wad into his pocket. Juliet's phone number was scribbled on several.

"You were speeding," Mr. Mustache said, perfectly.

"How was I speeding? I'm sitting on my fucking hands."

The maniac adored his partner's idea. He tossed the fork into the sink. The lollipops bulged inside his cheeks and he looked like a deranged chipmunk. He kicked at my tennies. He kicked again and said, "Please. Speeding. Please."

THE PISTOLERO at El Bebé's gate stared at my bare feet. The maniac at the motel had even removed my socks.

"I need to see him," I said. The pistolero blinked. He looked like he distrusted sockless men. I could read that much. "Tell him Sid Dulaney. Tell him that name. I need to see him. Okay? Right now."

El Bebé's stately hacienda was off-limits again. So I was escorted to the two-story casita, where a boy was scrubbing at a deep red stain on the pool table. All the fans were off and it was sweltering. I watched the boy twist a yellow sponge over a water bucket. Pink foam drained off it. The boy's scrubbing was in vain, though, as he was just spreading the stain across the felt.

Finally the doors to the studio opened. El Bebé was flanked by two guards with rifles held to their chests. The men appeared well trained, athletic, gorilla-like, a detached robot glaze in their eyes. Today, for some reason, El Bebé was dressed like a desert cowboy, with jokey boots, and a crisp button-down shirt tucked into tight blue jeans. His sleeves were folded back. "Musicians need peace," he said to me. "Musicians, like me, hate interruptions. We're recording my debut. If no one will sing about me, then fuck it. I'll sing about myself. The band, by the way, is from San Diego."

Behind him, in the studio, I saw four men—a band—on a break. "Tell me. Why are you here?"

"You don't know?" I said. "The *giraffe*? You want me to move a zoo animal over the border. Wrap that around your neck. Why am I here?" I said. "Christ."

El Bebé narrowed his eyes on my bare feet. "You don't understand. It was getting horrible treatment." He reached out and torqued my chin, inspecting my wound.

"You said nothing about zoo animals," I said.

"Black market," he said. "You have no idea how long it took us to steal. We fly them from overseas. Collectors."

"We never agreed on zoo animals."

"Where it's going, it will have an improved life," he said. "Plus, it's really good money. I'm trying to branch out." El Bebé's advisor stepped into the room with a black cowboy hat in his hand. "Anyway, you asked to be involved, remember?" El Bebé snatched the hat. He set it, like some trophy, on his head, but his smile fell when he noticed the ruinous stain on the pool table. "Idiota!" El Bebé screamed at the boy. The boy dropped the sponge and sprinted out the door toward the pool. El Bebé directed one of his guards with a finger flick. The guard mechanically handed his weapon to his counterpart and went in pursuit.

"I don't know anything about giraffes," I said.

"Pick it up at point A and deliver it to point B. Simple y facil," El Bebé said.

"This is insanity."

"This is Mexico, pendejo," he said. "I don't have time for this anyway. The other families now want more," he said. "My family is under pressure. Not *half* of Sonora, as originally agreed. The other families want *all* of Sonora, the entire highway, including my thin slice. And if they take it, they'll force me back to Culiacán, to my family, under my dad's thumb, but more importantly, nearer my sisters." And, he said, ending his brief lesson, he didn't want to return to his sisters. "They're fucking prudes. I'll have no privacy." He rubbed his temple with two fingers. "I just need to finish these songs. Everyone will see."

Through the glass doors I saw the guard carrying the young mestizo boy sideways with one arm. The boy was stiff as a board.

El Bebé's advisor clasped my hand. I could smell Fausto's neat, tidy cologne. "Do not come to us again with complaints," he said softly.

"But that animal can't cross the desert. It needs to be shipped back to Africa or wherever it was born. That's not part of our deal."

A cathedral bell chimed in town.

"Finish it," Fausto said. "And then you and El Bebé, your business together is done."

Riotous shouts were piped in from the recording studio. It was the boy, his voice amplified.

El Bebé clutched Fausto by the shoulder. "Dude, I like his voice," he said. "We can use him on the album."

A door opened, slammed. Another door opened. The kid tramped out, pants around his ankles, his ass red and waffled and recently spanked. El Bebé watched with reverence as the boy hustled toward the swimming pool again. The guard followed with a Ping-Pong paddle. El Bebé breathed deeply and readjusted his cowboy hat. "Musicians, like me, can't handle all these distractions. Musicians, like me, need boys like that. Get that boy. Get him for me."

"What about the giraffe?" I asked.

"Do your job," Fausto said. "Take it north. And if you refuse, we will use the paddle. Or, we have other methods." To illustrate, he shaped his hand into a gun and pointed at my feet. He squeezed his index finger like he was pulling a trigger.

I felt just-punched. Nodding dumbly, arms wrapped around my chest, my legs liquidy, I floated unfocused down the casita's pathway. Dangling vines gray as veins scratched my neck. An armored military vehicle now idled in the cobblestone driveway—and why, of course, why wouldn't there be an armored military vehicle? Plumes of exhaust roiled from its pipe. The vehicle looked vaguely Russian by design. A soldier wearing a square helmet peered down at me from the gunner's turret. He manned a massive gun. He smiled. But I felt too out-of-body to return anything other than a glance.

More heavy vehicles were waiting outside the arched gate. Men pointed the muzzles of their guns at the ground, their bulky uniforms overlaying body armor. Men humped artillery racks and ammo belts and boxes full of ordnance and camouflage mesh netting. One truck blocked my Honda. My car looked tiny and pitiful by comparison. The soldiers' movements were synchronized and expressionless, as though they abided by the same note. They looked to me nothing like the Mexican army. I'd seen Mexicano soldiers at the Port of Entry. This wasn't the military. This was a private army. This was Los Toros.

I sat in my car, the doors locked, windows rolled up. My new thrift-store cassette tape had melted inside the stereo. A lone cloud floated in the sky, so close I could have taken it out with a rock. I heard distant popping noises—firecrackers, gunshots? I wanted to be with Mona in some far-off place, her feet touching mine, her breath at my neck. Instead Danni listened on the phone as I reviewed the fleabag motel outside of town, the giraffe, the mess we were in, the tanks, El Bebé recording an album, the fork wound, how it hurt. How it hurt!

"I'm studying the moon's chart," she said over the phone. "According to this, there's a new moon in three nights. The desert will be dark. We do it then."

She wasn't listening. I told her about the giraffe again. This was a giraffe. I couldn't stop thinking about the animal trapped inside the motel. I had a thing for animals, especially animals with adorable young animal faces.

"There's nothing we can do, soldier," Danni said. "We need to move it, as instructed. Then we get paid. These people scare me."

I knocked my head against the headrest. "Give me some good news," I said. "Give me anything."

Suddenly the mestizo kid ran out of the compound and bumped into a soldier's leg. I saw the man smile and pat the kid's head. Then the kid was off again, running, running down the street.

"Your team won," Danni said. "I heard on the radio. That's your good news. The Diamondbacks really handed it to Milwaukee."

25 Four new voice messages: all Juliet. I couldn't bear to listen. We were once a family with a shared grocery list. We gardened. Stained two bookshelves. Then she did what she did, and now the idea of her long, delicate toes grew more vague by the day. I erased the first three and listened to the last.

"I'm waiting to hear from you. Why haven't you called? If you've found someone, okay. I can live with that. I apologize for hurting you. You hurt me plenty of times, too. In any case, I thought you might want to know that the weather is turning, the tree out front is about to go red, and I don't know how many more times I can tell you I'm sorry."

FORTY WHEELCHAIRS were parked in the main room during the weekly community meeting. The Activity Assistant, a pretty blond with an orthodontic grin, led the discussion from behind a podium. I watched her travel down a list with a pen as she asked lifestyle-related questions into the microphone. "Who enjoyed yesterday's yummy cheesecake?" she asked the gathered residents. Several hands went up. She unlatched the mic and thrust it into Ginny Olgermeyer's unsuspecting face.

"More butter in the crust," Ginny said.

Thankfully my grandmother was near the back. I maneuvered through the wheelchairs and touched her warm shoulder. She smiled at me with the working side of her mouth.

"Okay, last question. If you could do one thing tomorrow," the Activity Assistant asked, "if tomorrow were the perfect day, what would you do?" She dipped the microphone in front of Gertrude.

"I'd work in my garden at home," Gertrude responded

"How lovely," the Activity Assistant said. "David, what about you?"

The old man clamped his hand around the microphone and pressed it to his lips. "I'd fuck you!"

Management rotated the art on the walls every month. August had been southwestern portraits. September was reserved for watercolors painted by residents. I wheeled Nana down the hall, detouring at the nursing station before turning at Agave Trail. Midway down the hall I saw Mona, sitting on her heels in her unattractive tennies. She was helping to adjust an old woman's robe.

"You're still upset at me," I said to her.

Mona rolled her eyes. She gestured to a quieter spot down the hall. When we were out of Nana's hearing range, she whispered, "I didn't sign up for this. What happens when you get caught? What happens to your grandmother? You're not thinking."

"We won't. Danni knows the way."

"What makes you think you're so special? You think—what?—you're some white knight sent to help poor, pathetic Mexicans walk across the desert?"

I didn't respond. I didn't tell her about the giraffe. I watched her cheeks redden. Her long silence was a disappointment. "I thought you might be different." She shook her head and began walking away.

"Wait," I said.

Mona stopped.

"Please, try to understand."

She disappeared around the corner. My grandmother was now leaning forward, trying to scratch her leg. Her ankle had been retrofitted with a WanderGuard, a square transmitter grafted onto an indestructible hospital band. The wardens in charge didn't want elderly inmates wandering off the grid. I took her handles and pushed fast.

In her room I wheeled her beside the open window. Cool night air pulsed in. I firmed the parking brake. I heard voices outside on the putting green.

Nana looked smaller to me. She pointed at the duct tape on my jaw—no bandages at home. "Shaving accident," I said.

I sat with her, and we listened to the men. They were only shadows. Fluorescent glow-in-the-dark balls seemed to move across a flat plain. I took Nana's hand, and I could tell she tried her best to squeeze. If she only knew what I was planning, would she hold me, would she refuse to let me go? I was doing it for her, but the thought of getting nailed still nagged at me. With me in jail she would have no one to look after her, except Management.

My grandmother set her elbows on the chair's armrests and straightened herself. She looked from the window to me, and said, struggling with her words, "I like Mona."

I clutched her arm. "What?"

"Marry her, you dimwit," Nana said.

"It's complicated, Nana. We had a disagreement. I sent flowers."

Nana sighed "Flowers are for bees."

Her loose skin slid over her arm like silk over bone.

A CLOUD OF SMOKE followed Epstein into the hallway when he answered his door. I pushed him back inside and turned the lock. I looked around. It was as though the old man was hosting a party without attendees. Wet socks hung limply from lampshades. The television flashed. Scattered everywhere were fitness videos and magazines and other fitness paraphernalia, including, on the floor, a yoga mat.

"I'm surprised the fire alarm hasn't blown," I said.

"Just a little smoke," Epstein said.

"Look at this place. Are you living in a dorm room?"

"Just burned through a few," he said. "No big deal."

"Burned through a few?"

"Don't play dumb," Epstein said.

"So now you smoke marijuana?"

"A toke, now and then."

"Where'd you get it?"

"Bunny Vallance," he said matter-of-factly. "That's where everyone gets it. Why are you playing dumb?"

Apparently the old man was cataloguing his fitness collection like some mad librarian. Magazines were organized in one pile. DVDs, leaflets, and massage lotions belonged in another. I inspected a banker's box with every *Sports Illustrated* swimsuit edition and pulled one out. A lady named Babette March graced the cover in 1964. I had no idea the old man owned this much stuff. On TV a fitness instructor's shouts bled through the speakers, high and tinny, sounding like some mouse-person.

I opened a window and smoke flowed out in currents. Epstein sat back down on the yoga mat and returned to squaring his mags. I saw him gaze lovingly at the cover of *Fitness Monthly,* but there was something odd in the old man's manic shifts. Something odd about all of it. I sensed a soft hostility in his bloodshot eyes, which slammed shut and opened with renewed focus. His aim lay over my shoulder. His aim landed on his dead wife's picture on the mantel.

"Is everything okay?" I asked.

Epstein flung the top off another banker's box, spilling the contents on the carpet. He stacked *Shape* with *Shape, Allure* with *Allure.* The piles resembled chimneys.

"Are you ready for tomorrow night?" I asked. "Because there's something you should know. We won't be helping people."

Epstein reached for a pillow on the couch, an embroidered number with birds on it, and let out an unexpected, damp whimper. It was the sound a wounded animal made. My skin felt damp as the old man smashed the pillow against his face and wept into the birds. I'd never seen him like this before. I watched him seize the DO NOT REMOVE tag and, failing to rip it off, he threw the pillow across the room. His wife, Effie, was four years in the ground, and I thought this was a delayed aftershock. Epstein set a hand on his head. He seemed amazed and frightened by his own behavior. "I'm old," he said.

"Only eighty-two."

The old man laughed. He picked at his cuticles like an expectant kid. He sank into the couch and began speaking dispassionately, in monotone mumbles, but his words soon took flight, as though the birds rose from the pillow, clutched onto them, and spirited them into my brain. I listened to Epstein limp through ancient memories, recalling his long life, the people in it, the stories, and when I caught up with where he was headed, the room seemed to go dim. At night, Epstein was anxious to fall asleep. In the mornings, he couldn't stand waking up. He was ambulatory—for now—but any morning he could wake up and not even remember his own name. Illness could appear overnight, he said. Take a look at my grandmother, Epstein pointed out. Look what happened to her. He was old, Epstein told me. There wasn't much time left. He was old, old, old.

"You're sick," I said. "You saw your doctor. Those bells in your ears. Is that it? Is that it? Are you sick?"

"I'm not sick. The bells are tinnitus. I'm old," Epstein said. "That's the issue."

"Is that all?"

"That's everything!" he yelled. "I can't end up in that building down below. I can't live like that. I won't. I refuse." His voice downshifted, and he spoke mechanically again, as though he summoned his younger self—the professor—the man fluent in problems and how to solve them. "I'm leaving," Epstein told me. "I've decided to accompany Bunny on that cruise ship."

"That's great," I said. "I didn't know you two were serious."

"And I won't be coming back," Epstein said.

We stared at each other. "You mean to say you won't come back this winter."

"Ever," he said. "I've decided to keep going. Go until the engine gives out." The old man tapped his chest.

"You can't," I said.

"Besides, what are we doing here? We're just waiting. Waiting for the long arm to touch us. Not me. I refuse. I'm going to use what life I have left and live it."

"Every cruise ends. You can't stay aboard forever."

Epstein smiled. "There may come one night down the line when I'm on the deck, alone, the wind tossing around the little hair on my head. Bunny and I will have just made love. She'll be asleep. The deck will be long and empty. Moonlight shimmering in the water. That's how I want to go, kid. Deep water. It could be there, or somewhere else, but I want the choice. I need the choice. I want your blessing."

So this was how our conversation had to end, with a cruel punch. I resented the old man's use of the trump card, our friendship. There was no counter. I tongued the soft lining inside my cheek and bit and tasted blood. I watched the old man's head fall back. Epstein examined my reaction through his tortoiseshells. He was trying to read me, but I disliked being read. I filled a glass with water in the kitchenette. The glass was at my lips when I realized how violently my hand trembled. Bubba died. Dad died. They were gone. Mom was in Alaska. Nana was on the ladder out. An ache expanded in my chest, and it felt like my ribs might crack. I flexed my fingers against the countertop, trying to formulate an alternate plan, a better plan, but all exits were blocked. I began with a more reasonable avenue, followed that where it led, but again, the end cinched. I floated other possibilities: Epstein could come live with me.

Halfway across the room Epstein sat on the couch glassy-eyed, his hands folded neatly in his lap.

"I'm trying to build something here," I said to him. "I need you to understand. You're part of it."

"I need to leave. And I will."

"You hate me," I said.

"Kid, I don't hate you. Why would you say that? You're a friend. I thought, of anyone, you would understand," he said.

"I should call the campus psychiatrist."

"Maybe, instead, I'll fly to Tangiers. Or Asia. I've never been to Tangiers. But I want the choice. What I can't do is sit around like everyone here, waiting."

I drank the water, refilled the glass. The refrigerator hummed. The ticking clock sounded like repetitive thunderclaps. Life was about deletion. Life invented ways to wipe you out. The trick was surviving. You had to hold fast. Hold fast with the people you loved. I couldn't look at Epstein for another minute. He was old, but so what? I slammed the door and hoped every resident on the floor could hear my anger. I hit the elevator button. At night mushroom-shaped lamps illuminated the outdoor pathways and I dislodged one with a solid kick, its tip sailing into the dark night.

I punched the code and pulled the door. The building at the end had gone into hibernation. Dimmed track lighting made the halls look even more like airport runways. Harp music played softly from a radio somewhere. Down Yucca Drive I heard a resident sundowning, calling for her father, her cries padded by the thrumming in my head, and for a moment I considered going to her room, curling up next to her, and helping soothe her despair.

I walked up and down the halls, searching.

I found Mona in the laundry room. She was folding towels. Her beauty, even from behind, reached out and stung me. Simply looking at her broke me. She turned around when the door shut.

"I know you disagree with my decision," I said with famine in my voice. "I know you think I'm some sort of criminal. But I need to make this one run. I need you to understand. And I don't want it to affect us. I want to follow what's between us."

Mona stood on the side of her foot, towel draped in her arms. She drove her forearm into a towel, halving it. "You sound like you want to be rescued," she said.

"Don't we all?"

"I don't do rescues."

My temples burned as I imagined different scenarios. I imagined her leaning into me and caressing the wound on my jaw. I imagined her wrapping her arms viselike around me, my hands tangling her hair, my hands shivering down her back. Her soft lips and forgiving eyes. I was hungry with elemental need. I hadn't felt so gut shot since that cold morning in Northampton, sitting outside the duplex in my car, organizing pain into motion.

The industrial laundry machine released a blast of air. Mona folded another towel, waiting for me to say something.

"Look at your chin," she said. "You're hurt. What happens when they really take your head off? These are dangerous people. And what happens to me?"

"I want to be with someone who could write an honest account of my life."

She turned, her heel squeaking on the linoleum. "Are you living an honest life?" she asked.

26   I saw a cheap gold numeral pop off the motel door the moment Danni slammed it. Her boots scattered gravel as she marched across the dirt lot toward us. She rolled up her sleeve and examined her hand in the van's headlights, pressing the flesh around her very red knuckle. "That dirty cop tried reaching for my ass," she told us. "You never reach with me. He's on the floor thinking over his mistake."

Epstein smiled brightly.

"A girl needs to know things," she said.

Danni had parked the van with the trailer jacked, like a half-open Buck knife, and Warsaw was slowly coaxing the giraffe up the ramp and into the horse trailer. There was a rope looped around the animal's neck.

"Not only twenty miles, but twenty miles with a giraffe," Warsaw called out to me. "This indeed should be scary."

At midnight Danni drove us north toward the border. Epstein sat in the back of the van, next to me, with a pickle jar in his lap. "You sure you don't want one?" he asked.

"I want to get this over with," I said. I shoved my shoes against the seat and pulled the laces tight. I checked my equipment. In my postal bag I had water, the Smith Wessy, compass, two-way radio, and Danni's GPS contraption, in case we got disoriented. Epstein continued holding out the jar, as some kind of offering, the liquid inside rippling. "For the hundredth time, will you please put that away?"

"I don't want my decision to affect our friendship." Epstein pointed the nibbled end of a pickle at his chest and then at me.

"That's the dumbest thing I've ever heard. Of course it's going to affect our friendship. You're abandoning me."

"I'm old," he said. "I need a last hurrah."

"You're not that old."

"I'm not going to be around forever."

Headlights filled the van and then it was dark again. Danni eased onto a dirt road and I heard the trailer whine on its hitch. After a while Epstein rested his tortoiseshells against his forehead, pinching the bridge of his nose, and I caught him staring at his transparent reflection in the window. I wondered if that was how you began seeing things, at eighty-two, studying yourself, realizing what was erased when the clock stopped ticking. Your eyes, your feet, even your belly button lint, all of it unique, yours, and wiped from the map. Epstein's decision had filled me with a kind of hangover, a strange sort of exhaustion. Thinking about him aboard a luxury cruise liner, champagne tingling on his lips, drunk as a duck, straddling the railing and dropping into deep, cold, black water . . . Anyway, if the man was so sizzling on his suicidal-hero idea, he could always hop out of the van and start walking into the desert by himself, walk until his face melted off, walk until the sun burned through his amber lenses and his vision filled with coronas and his tongue shriveled to the back of his throat.

Warsaw was the first out at the drop-off point. I stood with one foot in each country as my friend led the giraffe down the ramp. Warsaw was dressed in cammo with black face paint across his head and neck. He even had a Vietnam-era rucksack with him. But what worried me more was the sword strapped to it.

"I don't know why you're bringing that sword," I said.

Warsaw's eyes were white spheres inside a black mask. "Protection."

"A sword won't help," Danni hollered from behind the wheel.

The sword wasn't our biggest issue. Giraffes weren't meant to blend with green Sonoran mesquite. The desert was dark, but when daylight came the animal's orange square spots would be easy to see, which was why we had to stay on course and on time. I circled the animal. The giraffe was a foot taller than Warsaw, with an adorable mane standing up along its neck, like a scrub brush, and it smelled of old, sunbaked leather. I thought about the zoo tour. I was unnerved that I knew the mechanical details of the animal's reproductive routine.

"And don't use the radio," Danni yelled out the window. "If you see head lights or hear helicopters or vehicles, run. BP will collect the animal. Find a cozy place to hide and sit tight. I'll find you. I'll have you on GPS."

"Did you hear that?" Warsaw said to me. "Now she wants us to hide under a fucking bush."

We watched the van's red taillights grow faint, and soon we were surrounded by a dense night that seemed to close in around us. The giraffe's pornographic tongue tasted the night air and it stomped a hoof. In front of us lay darkness. It was a chilling proposition.

"Twenty miles," Warsaw said and tugged the rope.

At 3:00 AM we ascended a low-lying escarpment overlooking a shadowy desert sea. Stars fell and died, hot white tears skating across black glass. My breathing synced with Warsaw's and my heels ached. I grew to appreciate the giraffe's company, for its size, for its body mass, as though it was our protector.

This was the scariest kind of dark, especially with the facts Danni had shoved into my head. Every weird sound put me on alert. Out here ranchers had been known to unload shotgun scatter at migrants crossing private property, and now Warsaw and I were passing midway through the gauntlet with a giraffe. Simply thinking about the reports in the daily newspaper pushed shivers up my spine. A month ago, an SUV had barreled across la frontera and crashed. At night this loonshit land may as well have been a bad dream. Renegade bajadores loved seizing entire groups, holding them hostage and demanding payment for release. Then there were the reported rapes and beatings by coyotes—and of course some nameless, faceless, piece-of-shit serial killer, still at large, who set a rifle on the hood of a truck, scoped with infrared, and picked crossers off as though unloading on tin cans.

Without moonlight we mistakenly entered a box canyon, encountered steep cliffs at the end, and had to turn around, wasting an hour. As we walked we dialed up memories, old damnable past-life bullshit.

"Yeah, well, anyway, I'm glad you left her," Warsaw said, talking about Juliet, after listening to me talk about her again. "She liked bossing you around. Like your girlfriend in high school. Old what's-her-name."

"Erica."

"Yeah. Erica. Yeah, well, Erica sleeps with someone else and then wants you to stay together with her. Can you believe? And you *did*. You did. What a *pussy*. I'm glad you knew what to do this time."

I walked in silence, the sound of my friend's footfalls keeping me company.

Up above and far off I saw a beam from a flashlight. Warsaw quickly took a knee. "Did you see that?" he said. "This is the worst idea you've ever talked me into."

"More light on the hillside," I said.

"It's someone guiding another group."

"Danni said there would be others."

I reached inside my postal bag and felt for the radio. It calmed me to know Danni was traversing dirt lanes in the night. She wasn't far. She was familiar with her homeland. If BP stopped her, she would show them her tribal ID. It wasn't a crime to drive around in an empty van. She also understood the traps. She'd carefully explained them to us. BP had turned the desert into a crazed gridiron—seismic sensors, thermal imaging towers, and concrete pillars erected to prevent loaded trucks from racing over, dumping piles of handcrafted drugs, and speeding back.

"It's hard keeping up with this guy," Warsaw said and tugged the rope. In slim moonlight profile the giraffe was an aristocratic specimen. "Big stride, this one. And he keeps licking my earlobe."

"Five more hours."

The borderland stirred, especially at night. A gust of warm wind erased our shared silence, and now I was unsure about my decision to pop three extended-release psychostimulants to stay tuned in. Adderall made blood pound arrhythmically inside my head. Worse was the paranoia. I grew acutely aware of every small sound. The dust trail the giraffe created looked to me like a sandstorm. Its footsteps were earthquakes, its breathing a typhoon. After a while I began feeling more naked, watched, as though I was on a never-ending trek across a stadium.

Every now and then we stopped and rested. We flashed an oval of light onto the compass to confirm our direction. Everything smelled of dry, thirsty twigs. We descended gullies and ascended the opposite banks. When we stopped to check the compass again, I heard movement.

"What was that?" Warsaw said.

Bushes rustled nearby. The giraffe shook its head and tossed warm saliva onto my neck. I turned off the light and waited for my eyes to adjust. Seven mestizo men emerged from the brush. Accompanying them was a redheaded teenager wearing a St. Louis Cardinals ball cap. The kid looked young, his face as innocent as a cupcake. The group stared silently at the giraffe as though witnessing a celestial event. One man fell to his knees and put his hands together. The kid's mouth twitched as he sized up Warsaw in blackface. I pulled the Smith Wessy from my bag and the indocumentados quickly raised their fingers. Empty water jugs hung from their necks via string. The teenager didn't flinch when Warsaw unsheathed his long, ridiculous sword. The kid looked to be about the same age as my high school students.

"We're aiming for the highway," he called over to us. He held his palms up, open, unthreatening. "There's a car waiting."

"This isn't the highway," I said. "This is the middle of nowhere."

"I think I figured that out," the kid said.

The kid walked over and brushed past me, heading for a clearing. He looked at the sky. I watched him close an eye. Shuffling around, head up, scooting to the left, he seemed to read the heavens as though decoding a complicated diagram. He let out a deep breath. "I always lead groups along the telephone poles," he said to us. "The phone company clears brush around the poles for fire safety. Telephone poles usually lead to civilization. This time, the poles brought us right here." He rubbed his cheek. "We're really off course."

I slid my finger outside the trigger guard. "I don't think the highway is far," I told the kid. "We're headed in that direction too."

"Seen any patrols?" he asked.

I said we hadn't.

"Well, they're out here."

I'd brought along extra water bottles and dispensed several, and the kid lumbered heavy-armed back to his group, called a tight huddle, and passed the bottles around. The indocumentados circled around him as he addressed them in Spanish. Warsaw and I watched how the kid interacted with his group. We watched how they followed his every order. "Maybe we should team up," I whispered to Warsaw. I watched the kid squat and draw in the dirt with a finger. "Looks like he knows what he's doing."

"But he's a Cardinals fan," Warsaw said.

I made the decision. We joined up and formed one large crowd. I followed the kid closely, with the others behind me and Warsaw and the giraffe at the rear. The kid brushed mesquite branches away and warned me before letting them go. Starlight glinted off reflector tape on the soles of the kid's shoes, which made it easier to follow him. This kid really knew the tricks. "I've seen all ages and nationalities out here," the kid said. "Men with goiters. Women with jobs waiting for them in Maine. But I've never seen anyone with a giraffe."

Inside of an hour our motley caravan went from stumbling over rocks and barrel cacti and yucca in near-perfect denseness to wandering into walls of fresh wood smoke. The glow from a considerable bonfire showed us the way, and I was amazed when we came upon an instant gathering in the middle of nowhere. Below us in a dry desert gully was a celebration. Men and women milled around. I watched necks crane back, like Pez dispensers, as people took long, celebratory swallows from bottles. I counted thirty people. In the center was a building in mid-construction. It was the size of a one-room schoolhouse. It had a roof but no walls.

One man soon spotted us. He quickly climbed the hill, his round face as shiny as wet ham, and embraced the migrants. He took one migrant's hand and pulled him down the incline. That man reached for his friend, and so on, until they were all dragged downhill like a line of angel paper cutouts.

"I've come across build sites before," the kid said to me. He squeezed the bill of his hat.

"We're fifty miles from the nearest village," I said.

"The goal is to nudge the line up to Utah," the kid said. "Take back a land that was once theirs. People figure if they build and occupy villages, they'll force the line up."

Warsaw said, "How do they get out here?"

"By carrying wood on their backs and nails and hammers in their pockets," the kid said.

"Well, that's dedication," Warsaw said.

"They've almost built the post office. That goes up and they'll construct a house. You'll have to get the army out here to budge them off the land." He sighed. "Last time it took an hour to peel them away from the party."

"Last time?" I asked.

Before starting down the gully, the kid said, "I'm just trying to earn money for college. Expensive, college."

The bonfire simmered to a gentler glow. I saw a woman with polka-dotted leg warmers shove hot coals toward unburned wood. Warsaw flashed his light on our compass and took a gander at our direction. "North is down the gully and up the opposite side."

I looked. The other side was a dark mesquite forest and beyond that more of the same. We shared some water, and then my friend went first, taking the incline carefully, watching the giraffe's hoof placement, and we descended into the rambunctious maw. People were full of mad laughter and proud of the almost-built post office. One man clutched my neck with a calloused hand and pressed a bottle to my lips. It clinked against my front tooth.

"No gracias," I said. "No gracias."

Several women hurried over when they saw the giraffe. One of them was more interested in Warsaw's samurai sword, and in a quick, fluid movement she unsheathed it. Firelight illuminated its clean steel blade. "Excuse me, that is mine," Warsaw said, but she was drunk. She swung and nearly shaved Warsaw's kneecaps off. He stepped in front of the giraffe to protect it. "Ma'am. Señorita. Ma'am," he said. The woman skipped away, swinging the weapon over her head. "Damn it," he said and he followed her with the giraffe.

Blazing fireworks burned across the inky sky, sparkling into silver flower petals. Now I knew it would be only a matter of time before BP descended on this section of land.

Another man, this one with a pencil-thin mustache, accosted me. He wanted me to sign some form with the word *sponsor* at the top. I refused. I found the teenager near the post office. Now he was playing an accordion for his original seven. "Math is my worst subject," he called out to me. "But hand me an instrument and I fall in love."

"Have you seen my friend?" I asked.

The kid shrugged and folded the accordion into a sweet note. Wind picked up and funneled into the gully and blew sparks off the fire. I heard someone yell, "La Raza!" People clapped. I couldn't find Warsaw. I couldn't find him by the group of ladies braiding bright ribbons into their hair, not by the hokey Mexicano with a fake plastic SHERIFF badge on his shirt, and not by the two academic types standing over a giant unrolled blueprint.

An hour passed. I knew we should be walking out. I knew we should be tripping over rocks with a giraffe in tow to our prearranged destination. But I couldn't find him. Sharp, unfriendly desert bushes surrounded the sad, dying fire, and soon the revelers made beds for themselves in the dirt, unrolling sheets and sleeping bags and pillowcases. Up one end of the gully, I could not find Warsaw. Warsaw was not on the other side either. I searched for signs of hoof imprints in the dirt. I came across three bare-assed men pissing names into the sand.

I retraced my steps. Warsaw was gone. It was as though the night had ingested him.

The silence was profound. I desperately hunted. Strangers shushed me as I stomped around and called out his name. People were lying in the dirt trying to sleep off inebriation. I backed into an organ pipe cactus and thorns entered behind my knee, but I was so tuned up on adrenaline and pills that the pain didn't matter. The hours went by. An elderly woman took pity on me and set an orange Arizona poppy behind my ear.

Another campesino was passed out against a palo verde. For a long while I watched the man's chin double as his head fell forward, and he snored quietly as the sky turned off-white and bloomed into aqua, his streaked eyes opening when the first burning rays crowned to the east over the Baboquivari Mountains.

I didn't have a choice. Danni had given me instructions. The radio was for listening only. There were too many voices riding the airwaves, too many unknowns, etc. BP could be monitoring from some cinder-block room at HQ. But by 6:20 AM I had no other choice. I toggled the radio's CALL button.

"I told you not to use the radio," she said. Her voice filled with electromagnetic fuzz.

"I lost Warsaw."

"This isn't the time for jokes," she said.

"Listen," I said.

She did. She told me to proceed north and wait at the original meeting spot. The hike didn't take long, and soon the van appeared below me on the sandy apron, palpitating on the rutted road. I saw her driving overland, and when she stopped beside me the trailer was covered in dust. She held up her gadget and talked fast. "I have you on the screen but no Warsaw. What happened?"

I didn't know what to say.

"Get in," she said.

It was obvious to me that Danni could not have chosen a more precarious pickup spot. Parked on top of a mesa, we had views over a dry stretch of earth. And everything had a view of us. The terrain was strafed with roads, cut like squiggly comb marks, and pocked heavily with green mesquite. Danni played with her little electronic gadget, turning it on, off, on, tapping the side. She shook it. It sounded to me like something was loose inside.

"What happened to it?" I asked.

"Give me a moment."

The van warmed. A swatch of tape fluttered over the air-con vent.

"Let's turn the air off," Epstein said from the backseat. "That chemical air dries out my sinuses." I felt it too. Chills pinched my adenoids. I turned off the air. Overhead, black crows with shiny, oily feathers circled the van, as though watching for something to fall.

By 7:00 AM the thermometer in the console read 92 degrees.

"Warsaw should be here," I said. "We should be driving. This should be finished."

I didn't see any movement through the binoculars. Our survey point gave onto flatpan bajadas that fanned out toward Mexico. At 9:00 AM, I grew more worried as the temperature climbed to 101 degrees. I flipped the air on. We were nine hours in. It would be a small miracle to drive out without being seen.

"How much water does he have?" Epstein asked.

"I have the water," I said.

"He doesn't have water?" Danni said.

"No."

Inside the excruciating span of a minute the flats jumped another degree. We sat. We breathed. We waited in the motherfucking van.

The border was a region on lockdown. The heat was punchy, the air electric. The thought of Warsaw out there without me and without water made the tip of my tongue itch. I could have burned holes in the thermometer as I stared at it. The digital numbers steadily ticked upward, sending me into silent hysterics. Sure, it was a glassy, moonless night, but what about the daytime? Nobody at our meeting had mentioned checking the daily temps. Several weeks back the paper had run a report tallying the number of dead ilegales found crisp and hyperthermic in the hinterlands—average so far this year. How could a giraffe survive? How could my friend? Ribs and femurs and coyote-gnawed clavicles were as abundant out here as rocks.

Eleven AM, 108 degrees. Heat seeped through the glass window and touched my cheek. The heat put in my mind bubbling skin, nuclear winter. I scoped the range again, more paranoid by the minute, half expecting helicopters and Air Force jets, followed by swarms of husky border cops. The dextroamphetamine in my head arranged the pieces into a grim vision: Tucson-born and finally on the business end of law enforcement guns. I saw myself splayed prostrate in the dirt as boots laid size fifteen tracks across my cheek. With me locked up, there would be no one to look after Nana. I felt panic rise in my throat. Even Danni looked worried. This was the meeting spot. I watched her watch the temperature gauge in a kind of silence that made the air vibrate.

"He has a compass. A map," she said. "He knows the general direction."

Epstein tried the binoculars, but the old man was blind, and I took them and scanned east. I scanned south, then west, then southwest. North would put him past us. There was nothing in the twin ovals except barren hardpan pocked with green-gold scrub. "We could have driven the giraffe to Nevada by now," I said.

"Save the critique," Danni said. She threw her collar up. The thermometer pushed another cramp into my side: ten minutes till noon, 110 degrees. Danni slapped her electronic tracking gadget for the hundredth time. Then, a yellow dot appeared on the blue screen.

"There's a dot," I said.

"It wasn't there," she said.

"There's a dot. I see a dot."

"I'm telling you, it wasn't a moment ago."

Thin squares divided the screen into quadrants, indicating latitude and longitude. We raced off the plateau, dropping onto a hard floodplain before moving toward the washed-out road. Danni tossed me the mechanical gadget. I prayed the dot wouldn't disappear. Branches scraped the van. We had a road, but what happened, I wanted to ask, when the road ended? Potholes the size of California could appear and swallow an axle. Mesquite thorns could rip open a tire. Then we'd be disabled. And we had to find the dot, my best friend.

Danni turned at a narrow off-road inlet. I read her the coordinates. She had skills as a driver. The van rolled over a boulder, lurched, and came down. My intestines registered the impact. Epstein clutched his seat and whooped. The temperature gauge steadied at 110 degrees. A moment later it read 111. Furnace-like heat seeped through the windows.

Danni's knuckles were white knobby balls clenched around the steering wheel. She closed the five-mile gap by maneuvering through shortcuts and worn javelina trails that ended at a grouping of ghostly-looking saguaros. The van rolled to a sudden, nauseating stop. Curtains of silt washed past the windows. Danni honked the horn. We waited, and we listened. I looked for a giraffe. Epstein's excited breaths sounded like low whistles. Very suddenly a figure leaped from behind the underbrush.

His black face paint had melted down his neck and his head was violently red. Warsaw lobbed his compass and it skipped off the van's roof. He'd unsheathed his samurai sword and dragged his dusty rucksack behind him.

"Where did you go?" Warsaw asked.

"Where did *you* go?" I asked back.

"I chased that woman from the party up the embankment, she had my sword, and it was just so dark, and she was ahead of me, and then there were these lights and those naked boys with bells on their toes and I don't want to talk about it."

"What party?" Danni asked.

"And the giraffe?" I said. My friend looked tired and sun-whipped. He licked split lips.

"He was there and then he wasn't," Warsaw said. "I don't know. I've been looking. I think I lost him."

"You should have reported this," Danni said.

"Sid has the radio," Warsaw said.

"We need to look for the giraffe," I said.

"No, no, no." Danni shook her head. "We need to get out of here."

"Who abandons a young giraffe in the desert?" I asked her.

I watched my friend go into shock the moment he collapsed onto the plastic seat. Warsaw pressed his cheek into the seat lovingly. He was burned. He was burned badly. His shaved head, his arms, his neck, even the backs of his hands hadn't escaped punishment.

"It's still out there," I told Danni. "We can't leave the giraffe. It will die."

"He's right," Epstein said.

But she jammed the van into gear and turned us around. She raced back in the direction we had just come—north—and she picked up speed. The trailer nearly shimmied off the tow hitch. The clock read 1:12 PM, 114 degrees.

I knew dehydration wasn't the worst of it. Dehydration was the first item on a deadly list that included split lips, heat strangulation, hallucinatory visions, boiled brain, all of it culminating, eventually, in heat death.

"We cannot leave the giraffe," I told Danni, but her eyes were elsewhere as she focused on the grooves in the road. She informed me, in a distant voice, that helicopters came out about now, buzzing like flies, hunting for the fallen. That right now BP cutters were tracking sign on the drag roads. And it was likely that we had tramped over a drag road without knowing it, and that, even more, we had to move because the sign cutters contacted the pilots, and that, in conclusion, the pilots were one radio transmission away from calling in the cavalry. "Okay?" she said. "Get it? We need to evacuate. If we get stopped, they'll know we've been up to something."

I knew coyotes abandoned pollos all the time and people ended up dead. The giraffe's long, innocent, young face haunted me. It had been forced into this mess. It didn't know better. It ate leaves for breakfast. The memory of its eyelashes consumed me. More than anything: it was young. A child. I would never be able to live another day knowing I'd abandoned a child giraffe in the desert. "We cannot leave him out here. Stop the van."

"Pop the glove compartment, soldier," Danni said. I noticed wetness in her eyes.

Inside was a phone atop registration papers. Behind me, Warsaw said, "Thirsty," and I saw Epstein offer his pickle jar and Warsaw gulp the juice.

The phone was prepaid and untraceable, Danni said. She'd bought it at a convenience store.

"When you make the call, that's it," Danni said. "No money. And we cut ties to El Bebé. You'll be giving up any chance of future work."

"Water fountains," Warsaw said. He kicked my seat as he scrambled to the cargo hold. When he located the cache of water bottles I heard him shriek.

"It's your decision, soldier," Danni said.

Blades of sunlight bounced off the sideview mirror and seared my eyes. The giraffe may have been just a giraffe, but it was a part of this life. We shared the same moment in time. I watched Danni shift in the driver's seat, her wet eyes, her set jaw, knowing that if I placed the call I still wouldn't be able to save it. No matter what, even if the giraffe grew old, ending its days at the cushiest zoo, I'd never be able to save it.

"I just want to teach high school," I said.

Danni finally hit the paved highway, and we tore out of the badlands, and I placed the call. A dispatcher answered halfway into a full ring.

I laid out the giraffe's general location for the woman. I studied the grid on the map and fed the woman coordinates, with latitude, with longitude, telling her what possible canyons to search. The dispatcher had a pinched, interested voice. A giraffe? She obviously thought my call was a joke. I assured her, no. This wasn't a joke. My voice trembled. I hoped she could hear it. She asked my name, asked how I was privy to this information. No doubt there was a digital box recording the conversation.

"Listen. A giraffe may die if you don't sound the alarm," I told her.

"Your name, sir?"

"Please, trust me. Please, listen, and trust me."

A long pause. "Your name?"

"George Greg," I said.

In the sideview mirror I watched the cell phone break into three solid pieces when it hit the hot, open, paved desert highway.

27 When I emerged in socks from the bedroom Warsaw was lying shirtless on the floor, feet up on the couch, clutching the FOR SALE BY OWNER sign that, the previous night, I'd parked front-and-center in the yard. A cheap electric fan blew on my friend's sun-struck head.

"Where's the coffee?" I asked him.

"Drank it."

"The entire pot?"

"I'm thirsty," he said.

"It's been four days."

"So? I can't stop this thirst."

Warsaw had spread the newspaper across the counter, and the front page showed yet another snapshot, from a different angle, of agents leading the giraffe onto a trailer. Our spectacular strikeout had made headlines several days in a row. The wires had picked up on it, and now national papers were giving the story a ride. It was not every day that a seven-foot-tall *giraffa camelopardalis reticulata* from the African savannahs was found wandering around Arizona's southern desert. BORSTAR agents had located the animal in a mesquite-lined ravine with a group of illegal immigrants that had nursed the animal with the last of their water.

"Federal agents on the front page again," Warsaw said. "No need to read the rest. That's everything you need to know. *Federal* agents. I'd punch you if my knuckles weren't so goddamn burned."

"You lost the giraffe."

"Punch you in the face," he said.

I saw passages underlined in blue ink. According to the article, the state's attorney general had now attached herself to the giraffe, apparently sensing a golden political opportunity. She wanted to find the giraffe the best home, give it a new lease on life. Wildlife sanctuaries around the country were also lobbying for the animal. I couldn't read the rest. I couldn't stand looking at the giraffe's long face. Someone might as well have set a hot iron on my brain. Yesterday, on TV, reporters had interviewed the tour guide from the zoo. Her hair looked like lightning had touched it as she shouted into microphones, "Whoever did this, prison! Prison!"

I dumped the paper in the recycle bin with the others.

"What are you doing with my FOR SALE sign?" I asked Warsaw. "People driving by won't see it."

"State your price," he said.

"Sell the casita to you? I don't think so."

"Either you sell or your grandma moves from that nursing home. Said so yourself."

I didn't need him to remind me. I would never be able to poke around the pharmacies in Nogales again. Or Agua Prieta. El Bebé's advisor could not be happy. The man was probably sending word to his minions. If I crossed the border his men would strangle me. Then they'd really get to work. My safest bet, the border town of San Luis Río Colorado, was at the western rim of Arizona, but scooting 250 miles twice a week wasn't feasible. One roll of the dice, and I lost. And if I'd lost a small cut, El Bebé had lost much, much more. Wildlife investigators were tracing the giraffe's origins. Zoologists had entered the fray. Not to mention the talk radio hosts and TV station rigs parked outside the police station. We had set a giant goose egg on El Bebé's lap. And in Mexico, problems of this nature got dealt with quickly, quietly, and permanently. I could never return to Sonora.

Watching my friend lean on his burnt elbows made mine itch. His annoying fan sounded like a mechanized hive. "I could always move into real estate," Warsaw was saying to me. "I'm sure, for some people, that's a real calling." A heat blister on his head, doused in white ointment, made the living room smell pharmaceutical. I watched the fan wash across its hideous surface.

"In the event," I said, "would you make me move out?"

"That's the best part. You come with the place."

For a moment I considered my friend's offer. "What kind of rent would you charge?"

"I don't know. A hundred. And you do the dishes."

"The dishes," I said.

"We'll be roommates."

"To whom would I write the rent check?" I asked. "Warsaw Warsaw?"

He smiled. Eleven hundred thirty square feet, in total. And the two of us as roommates. It was not the most catastrophic outcome, but it wasn't the best. For two years Juliet and I had had a decent thing. For two years I'd had what I wanted. We'd installed towel racks, a garbage disposal, and I'd left it all behind.

IT WAS GAME NIGHT, the play-offs, the D-backs and Cubs in Chicago, not that it really mattered. The only person worth watching the Cubs with was leaving me. I walked around the imperial saguaro in the central quad, killing time and stealing glances at Seymour Epstein's seventh-floor window. It was hot, low hundreds. The lights in his apartment filtered through half-closed drapes. The moon shared the sky with the dropping sun.

I paced. I searched for signs that everything would be fine, that tomorrow would come and the day after. I was comforted when I saw Ms. von Bausch doing early-evening victory laps around the lake. Her medal bounced on her chest. Management had hung enormous yellow CONGRATULATIONS banners from the swan-shaped poles. She'd placed first in the 5,000-meter race-walk. She was a woman, what was more, who refused to let everything slide.

There were others too. There were others.

Two men played a game of chess. Four women nattered on a bench. Horseshoes clinked in the pits. There was serious laughter from a third-floor window. Another shadow passed behind Epstein's window. The old man wanted my blessing to enter the final lap.

"A crescent moon," the old man said. Standing in his doorway, he wiped his hands with a dishrag.

"They call it waxing," I said.

"I enjoy new moon nights," he said. "Feels like starting over."

My stomach lurched when I stepped inside. I looked around. Boxes. I went for a faux crystal mint jar on the counter—I needed countermeasures, a sense of traction, relief from the noises banging around in my head—but the mint tasted like a pebble. I spit it in the sink.

"Don't you know where the trash is?" Epstein said.

"As if it matters," I said. As if Epstein hadn't already boxed his magazines, boxed most everything he owned, and stacked his belongings against the wall, like this was moving day.

I pretended to overlook a stack of stamped letters on the mantel. Each was ready for the mail bin. I set my postal bag on the coffee table, and the old man said, trying to turn me like a lever, "I kept the TV out. I thought we could share one more game."

I opened the drapes. The swan-shaped lamps gave the campus an eerie, magical pallor. Fountains in the lake turned from blue to yellow to blue again. The sun was falling and there was a rouge afterglow behind the mountains. Sometimes in this light I believed we were all unworthy of this land, the constant witnesses, as we were, to an environment of such daily surprise that it outstripped the beauty of anything made by human hands.

Epstein's beach cooler sat beside the couch, lid open. Inside I saw a sixer of longnecks buried in blocky refrigerator ice. He'd bought my favorite. I also noticed an open bottle on the end table. It was half finished. A bead of condensation slid down the glass.

"I thought you were off beer," I said. Epstein cocked an eyebrow. His stare told me he'd put new rules on the game. "Right. Never mind."

"Like I said. I was thinking we could watch the D-backs," he said. "Last I checked they were one down to the Cubs."

I imagined for a moment picking him up and tossing him into a barbed cholla. Then, after he relented, after he said he wouldn't leave, lifting him from the spines and wrapping him in a hug.

"The spite on your face could inspire war," Epstein said.

"Or a fight."

"You don't have that in you, remember?"

"Some things are still worth a good brawl," I said.

"And what might that be?"

"I don't want you to leave."

We sat. We looked at our dry, cracked hands. We turned them over in wonderment. To me violence in its worst form was not a punch or gut wound or gunshot, but abandonment. Abandonment trumped everything. I could understand the man's reasons, but that didn't mean I had to like them.

We tiptoed around the topic. Eventually our surface discussion boiled down to the truth: He was leaving. Permanently. It was not supposed to happen like this, only it did. I felt a shift in the power balance. The old man told me he'd like to stay in touch, write letters, keep up with my life, but our conversation was just plagiarized words from a previous exchange: how he needed this, how he wanted to move forward with his last bit of life. I had once known his symptoms, and I'd once known the cure. I'd once moved around so much that I'd lost all grounding. Epstein had been in the same place for so long that he now needed to move. And he wouldn't be returning.

I had his daughter's card, her work number, and her cell phone. I could call her, but something told me her reaction wouldn't be understated. She was as much a part of the old man's life as me, if not more. I knew she didn't deserve that phone call down the line that would incite fire in her heart, followed by the never-ending series of questions, the unanswerables. *Where is my father? Who saw him last? Where did he go?* My own father had opened a door and fallen into oblivion, and that terror should never be forced upon anyone.

"What about your daughters?" I asked.

"I've spoken with Sarah and Miriam over the past few days. Nice conversations both. They know nothing." His voice grew weary, but he caught himself. He forced out a smile. "My lawyer has their information," he stated matter-of-factly.

"And Ms. Vallance?"

"Bunny's waiting. We're headed to Lima by plane. She may return, but I won't."

"When are you leaving?" I asked and held a breath.

"When," Epstein said. He glanced at the miniature grandfather clock on top of a box. "When," he said once more. "I thought it was obvious. I boxed the bedsheets."

Epstein smiled an undersized smile, a not very interested smile, but even so—it was a smile. And to my surprise he gave me a new ball cap, one with the D-backs' Sedona red color. When he set it on my head, I grabbed his hand. His hand was dry, and warm, very warm, still warm.

The game was in the bottom of the third. The D-backs were up a run, the catcher flashing signals, tapping the inside of his thigh. Two away from taking it to the fourth. A sharp line drive thwacked the third baseman's glove—one away. The team had a deep bullpen this season. The old man and I settled into it, acutely aware of the man next to us. Important seconds passed between brief bursts of action on the television screen. Baseball was a game played in stillness. Quiet decisions were made between the catcher and his man on the mound. They trusted each other. They understood signals, air currents, the twitch of the glove, and the width of the strike zone. Depending on the sun's angle, a changeup could outperform a fastball. In a pitcher's perfect game, nothing transpired, nothing happened, no hits, no runs—a glorious void. Epstein passed me another cold beer, and I popped the lid.

"We're friends, right?" I asked the old man.

Epstein breathed hard through his nose. "Don't play dumb," he said. His eyelids fluttered as he wiped a fallen lash from his cheek. "Don't ever play dumb."

In the eighth inning, the D-backs skipped ahead by two runs. I tried listening to him breathing, tried memorizing the sound. He breathed. He still breathed. I heard him without hearing him. His breathing was felt, sensed. He would always breathe. The old man detached his tortoiseshells from his ears. Two small indentations discolored his nose. Outside, the night sky held a brilliant sickle moon. Its kind, smooth, white light seeped in, inching across the carpet. A pop fly toward left field sent the outfielder running, cleats digging, glove upward, and then the ballplayer lifted, midair, and brought it in.

MIDNIGHT AND MONA strutted through the casita's front door without knocking, as though she owned the place. She dumped an armful of dead roses at my feet, and I thought the tangled, thorny mess smelled fragrant, and lovely, like her.

"Never put them in water," she said. "With every delivery I placed them on the window's ledge, in the sun, and watched them die slow deaths." Her eyes blazed prettily, even as she drilled my chest with her finger. "I'm too old for games," she said. "Thirty-seven. I'm thirty-seven, and I know who I am and what I want, and I know what I want from a partner. Does that bother you?"

"No."

"Answer this while we're at it," she said. "A giraffe? A *giraffe*?"

"I'm not a terrible person," I said.

Her shoulder tensed to her ear. "A young giraffe, according to the newspaper."

"We're not terrible people."

"The question is," she said, "can I ignore your stupidity?"

"Can you forgive me?"

"No more prescription drugs?" she asked.

"No more."

She crossed her arms and suppressed the smallest smile. "I will be thirty-eight in December and I know what I want out of next year," she said. "A child." That little word hung in the air. "I was married before and the ex-husband left because of it. And even if I get pregnant, at my age, do you know what doctors call it? A *geriatric* pregnancy. How do you like that? Either I find someone now or say hello to the petri dish. So you should know where my mind is." Mona pushed me against the wall, and I let her. I let her. "Well? Well? You haven't run."

"I haven't."

"Listen. I'm only giving you another chance because you smell right," she said. "But forgiving you will take years."

"Beautiful," I said.

28 The long hours stretched into morning. Outside I heard the clicking cicadas making music in the soapberry trees. I sat against the headboard, watching the sun rim the picture window in a yellow, ghostly glow, knowing the only thing left of any value, other than the casita, was my grandmother's grave.

I gently turned back the covers and Mona's eyes opened. She batted her lashes against my shoulder and disappeared under the sheets, and I felt her warm breasts against my ribs. She nuzzled against me, half-awake, musky heat rising from her scalp. It was nice.

As I was getting out of bed my foot came down awkwardly on her sandal and I slammed my toe into the bed frame. "Ow! Son of a bitch."

Mona lifted up as though springboarded. "We use the phrase *son of a biscuit* instead, remember?"

"What?"

"Son of a biscuit. That's what we say."

Her bed hair was a messy nest. "Is this the part where you clean up my language with prude euphemisms?" I asked.

"Correct."

I spent the morning tidying the casita, brooming dust balls from closets, crossing out repairs as I finished them. While cleaning the spare room I found a brick of old photos hidden behind an insulation panel in the closet. It was as if no one had wanted them found. Affixed around the stack were old frayed rubber bands. The top three photos were stuck together, but the others—I'd never seen the photos before. Were they Nana's? It was a record of an unbroken family. My dad, my mom, me. Each photo surprised me. We were at Lake Tahoe. Out at Havasu. The coast of Oregon. Vacations. Back before Dad died and before Mom began looking at me with teary eyes.

In one photo, I was standing with my mother next to the gray, pounding Oregon coastline. A bandage covered my ear. I thought about it, vaguely recalling a bicycle accident on the sidewalk. I wasn't sure. Still, part of me wished I could remember my parents' reaction, what they had done. They had both been there. This picture was proof. An even larger part of me wanted to believe that after I'd fallen, they'd run up to me and taken my head in their arms, that my mother had cried, kissed my eyelids, that my father had put his hand on my mother's back as comfort, that there had been simple but profound acts of caring, that for at least one summer day on the Oregon coast a long time ago the connection between them had been undeniable and true.

Mona showed me her nasty face when she came in to report that Warsaw was sleeping on the couch. "He's here," she said. "Again." She put up her hands in exasperation and retreated to the shower. I was still in the bedroom going through the photos when Mona walked in with a towel on her head.

"You've really fixed it up," she said.

"Warsaw wants to buy the place. Says he wants to be roommates."

Her hand fell from her hip. "Or," she said, "you move in with me. You sell this house and your grandmother will be taken care of. Or we could relocate her to a nice home in Mexico. We can figure this out. Together."

"But Warsaw has money. He's serious."

"So am I," she said. Her naked toes curled against the cold hardwood. "Besides, you need to tell your friend that he needs to grow up."

MY PHONE picked up two new voice mails on my way to the backyard shed. Both Juliet. I dug a weed from the yard with my heel and listened.

"You're terrifically bad at returning phone calls. Twelve messages so far by my count and nothing in return. I don't know if you never want to speak to me again. I don't know if you found someone else. I know nothing. I'm fielding calls from Mexico now, thank you very much. Please, quit your hurtful game. One phone call, that's all I ask. And his name, since you always wanted to know, was Damon."

I closed my phone and considered this new information.

Damon.

Damon was a dog's name. Damon was the name of a gas station attendant. Damon could not possibly be the name of some man who had anointed my ex-girlfriend with disease. His name. I knew his name. My lungs burned less than they once had.

MONDAYS WERE QUIET ON CAMPUS, everyone recovering from long, busy weekends spent with family. I noticed Diego's F-150 in the lot, as expected. His truck took up two spaces.

I had three deliveries left. Earlier, Mona and I had sat down and opened the checkbook, and we'd studied the numbers. Full-time teaching began in the winter, after the holidays, four bill payments away. I had just enough in the bank. I would make it work; it would work; it could; it had to work.

Ms. Haybroke invited me inside for a cup of Earl Grey tea. Her apartment was spotless, and I watched her pinkie hook under the blue ceramic mug as she sipped. I handed her the last white bag I would ever give her and told her the news.

"The bastards caught you," Ms. Haybroke said and clutched her throat. Her reaction surprised me. "The bastards finally caught you. And all you're doing is helping people." Her eyes went wide and she looked ready to spit on the carpet.

I calmed her down by assuring her that no—no one had caught me. Everything had caught up, though, and I didn't have any heart left for the work.

"I always liked you so very much," she said. "Your grandma must be proud. Boy like you, helping us."

"I'll still be around."

"You'll visit?"

"Like always."

Diego was waiting for me in the community building, standing sentry by the afternoon supplement table. Residents came and went, selecting their favorite milk shake flavors. Branded loudly into his leather belt was his name—DIEGO. He saw me approach with my hand buried in my postal bag and he took a few cautious steps backward.

"You know what I've been told," Diego said.

"Yeah, yeah, I'm good at guesses."

He squared his hips. "Take over."

I glanced around at the handrails, at the old women, at the wobbly men, at their horrendous fashion. Giving it all up was almost worse than forfeiting the casita. It was a foreclosure on family.

"El Bebé is not pleased," Diego said to me, and then he whispered, "La frontera ya no se puede cruzar. Te quiere cubrir la cabeza con una bolsa. So I must do what El Bebé says." He framed his takeover like an apology. By the wet gleam in his eyes, he seemed to mean it. "You're getting off easy. Fausto removed one guy's pinkie with gardening shears. I watched. Fausto made him carry the stub around in his mouth for weeks." I cringed, but Diego smiled, and I wondered how much the gold in his smile was worth.

We cruised the discussion to a couch near the fireplace. I was in no mood for the changing of the guard, but the only way forward was forward. Folks still needed cheap medications. Someone needed to deliver them.

"You must understand some things," I said. I removed a folder from my bag and squared the papers with a tap. "Under no circumstances should you deliver opiates or synthetics or downers or uppers, for that matter, to Ms. Gwendolyn Wetherbee in 63G. And that means *ever*. I don't care how much she wants to pay you. Understand?"

Diego searched his pockets for scrap paper. But everything was already written down in detail. I ran through my clients, the sweet old faces. Men and women who had been dropped into this expensive paradise, a garrison of old folks who had lifetimes of memories and histories beyond anything we'd ever known. I placed the folder on Diego's lap. Names, meds, interactions, precautions, refill dates, doses. It was a good business. He was inheriting relationships. He was inheriting people's dependencies. An intimate business.

Diego stared at the folder, looking frightened by it. When he finally smiled, his gold spacer twinkled. "You care about them," he said.

"And you will too. I'll be watching."

Outside, I could feel heat rise through the brick and into the soles of my tennies. Sunlight hardened the edges on everything and heated it all from the dirt on up. Even the long horizon didn't offer relief. Not even a hint of wind. Layers of smog padded the mountaintops and settled like faint gray tarps over the valley.

From a bench under the great saguaro, I sat and watched the commerce of age, people coming, people going, visitors bidding good-bye, the deliveryman rolling foodstuffs up the dock. Light glinted off one resident's titanium wheelchair. There was a clear view, beyond the community hall, of sunlight undulating in the lake. Three gray-haired women, dressed in black, looked very much like a coven, and they strolled past me, their clean strides filled with resolve. Through the window I watched Diego chatting with Ms. Vallance, his Stetson pressed deferentially to his chest. He accepted her scrip list with his head bowed. Word traveled quickly around campus. Elderly gossip spread faster than brushfire.

The sun scored the quad into blocks of light and shadow, and I sat long enough to feel the points of my shoulders start to burn. My phone rang. It was Juliet again, 4:00 PM in Northampton. I watched it ring, and ring, organizing the words, deciding how to tell someone I had loved, and cared for, good-bye.

29 Weeks passed, monsoon season came to an end, and the stone birdbath in the yard dried. The Santa Cruz River was less a river and more a dusty coyote footpath. I managed to fix the car stereo but couldn't find any interesting tapes at Goodwill. There was no reason, anyway, to drive long distances. Mona and I fell into routines: her apartment one night, the casita the next. Nana surprised everyone with her speech therapy progress. Now, when she talked, it sounded like she had only one marble in her mouth. The fall brought cooler weather, but some days the warm distances shimmered as though vapor rose off the earth.

One night, as the sun was setting, I drove up Craycroft, stunned by the houses. I rarely visited these hidden neighborhoods, hitched up on the hills as they were. The homes were so nice that my first reaction was to scream out, each so lovely, each perfectly arranged in the natural environment as though watched over by the gods. Shadows moved sideways across the Catalinas, making the mountainside appear purple and ribbed. I drove slowly through the neighborhood. Each cactus looked placed here by a divine hand. Another night, I decided to play bingo at the American Legion Hall. Nana and Bubba had once liked to play bingo here, but now it was mostly the homeless. The homeless looked so tan.

Alejandro had installed a new exhibit in his front yard. And I'd been waiting to tell him how much I loved his latest creation. What he had accomplished was a bright miracle. The gunslingers had been removed and now there were two large feet in front of his house. They were cut from marble and ended at the ankles. It was unclear to me where he'd found such inspiration. Anyone driving past saw two marble feet, the toes unattached. Two big marble feet, and what lovely, generous dimensions.

I FELT TIRED-EYED late in the afternoon. And I was convinced someone had stolen Nana's mole.

For eighty-nine years she'd had a dark mole on her jaw. And now, somehow, it was gone. Someone had nicked it. Was there a surgeon wandering the halls with a scalpel, removing suspicious-looking moles? I questioned the charge nurse at the nursing station, but she was occupied with afternoon med charts and too busy to listen. The building's speech therapist was also behind the desk, writing on a clipboard, trying her damnedest to ignore my interrogation. I approached her about the missing mole. She returned a look, as though I was speaking an unknown language, which only fueled my sense of persecution.

It was help-an-old-fogey day at the building at the end. The helpers were teenage boys from the neighborhood "at-risk" youth home. A battered yellow school bus had dumped them for the day. The kids ran around wearing specially made T-shirts—HOMIES HAVE HEART—and they were driving everyone but the residents insane, asking how they could help, what could they do, who needed what and when. They behaved more like overachievers than at-risk youth. I watched three of them wander around passing out fresh sugar skull cookies and dead bread. It was clear the residents adored the attention. They perked up and scraped their fingers over their dentures. Warsaw commanded the operation from behind a plastic table in an activity room. A laminated VOLUNTEER CAPTAIN badge hung over his I ♥ JOHN WAYNE T-shirt. I watched him hand assignment sheets to the kids. He gave them maps of the building. The kids raced from the room, through halls smelling of flour and sugar, in search of their assigned resident.

When I returned to Nana's room, she was gone. Toilet paper fluttered from the bedposts. Either Nana had taught herself how to toilet-paper her room or one of the young visitors had exacted this prank. I tracked her to an alcove, where two nurses were quizzing her about "Frank." I saw one clutching an autographed copy of *Sunspots*. Nana's story had made the paper's cover. There was still all this business—still!—about her supposed friendship with "Frank." Bunny Vallance had outdone herself.

"Did he smell of Agua Lavanda?" one nurse asked my grandmother. "That was his favorite cologne. I read about it."

"Better," Nana said.

"Was he a gentleman?" the other nurse asked.

"Oh, was he," she said.

I watched Nana wick up the attention and pause to consider the questions before giving short, thoughtful answers. At last the nurses left us. My grandmother had grown accustomed to the building, to the staff, the residents. This was her home. I bent beside her, my knees rubbing against the wheel, and held her hands, wanting them to change, desperately wanting them to shed the dry skin, and shrink, and become thin, useful hands again. But they were cold and sharp as sticks.

"You shouldn't encourage them," I said.

In her room, we watched several nap-inducing hours of infomercials, listening to the high, excited voices echoing around the halls. Eventually the TV lulled Nana to sleep. With the help of a Nursing Assistant, we lifted her into bed.

Warsaw stepped in front of me on my way out.

"Your volunteers are driving everyone crazy," I told him.

"They need community service hours," he said. "But, listen, about your girlfriend." He tapped the side of his head. "Is this how it now works? She's speaking for you? She told me I can't stay the night anymore."

I said nothing.

"I've known you twenty years. You've known her several months."

"I'm out of the business," I said. "That's it. No mas. I'm starting up with living my life."

"I don't even get the chance to buy the place?" He wrapped his name badge around his fist.

"Listen, how about heading to the park with me? The nurses can handle these volunteers."

His nose twitched. "You have your bat?"

"The same."

We saw Mona on our way to the parking lot. When I asked her to accompany us, Warsaw set his teeth and marched to the car and waited with his arms crossed. Warsaw got in the back, and I saw his eyes narrow in the mirror as we waited for her. The look on his face was that of an imprisoned man.

At the ballpark Warsaw floated some cream puffs to warm up his arm. I took lazy swings. He retrieved the hit balls in far left field and juggled them on his return to the mound.

"So this is how it goes," he said, his eyes going like a metronome, from me to Mona, who sat sunning her kneecaps on an aluminum bench. "So now she goes everywhere you go, is that it?"

"That's how relationships work. You should try it," I said.

He spat on the dirt and ran his thumb along the ball's stitches. "Don't crowd the plate. A stray ball might hit you."

Warsaw's good pitches were surgically precise missiles. Balls whizzed past and slammed into the wooden backstop. I didn't even bother moving the bat for fear of humiliating myself in front of Mona. She was resting on her elbows and watching us try to play nice. This was the hard part, everyone getting along. Another missile crowded me out, a pitch so hard, so solidly within the strike zone that I considered dropping the bat and giving up. Warsaw wanted to prove something to me.

"Float a cupcake every once in a while," I yelled.

"This isn't tee ball," he said.

"Is not the majors either."

Even though he was the superior player, the bat felt destined. The

Louisville Slugger warmed in my hands. The sun tipped in my favor and drowned Warsaw's sightline. Several pitches drifted toward me, as though served up on pillows. I put one on the ground, another in the air, and another into center field via line drive, which made Warsaw flinch. Mona clapped.

"Lucky," he yelled.

I squared my hips and spread love into the bat. I kicked back dirt with my toe as my phone vibrated in my pocket. Thinking it was Juliet, always Juliet, I ignored it. I swung, missed. I missed another. The phone started up for the fourth time, on a 0–2 count. I set the bat against my knee and looked at the incoming number. It was from Paseo del Sol.

"I'm sorry to tell you," the woman's voice said. "This is difficult to say." It was Paseo del Sol's administrator. She spoke fast. I felt my stomach cramp. The woman kept talking. I leaned on the bat for support, remembering his face, fixed on the last moment I'd seen him. I was informed that he was alone when it happened, and his thoughts, I imagined, must have been hot with panic in those final seconds. I clutched the bat, listening to the woman and looking at the sky, at that sun, hoping it never dimmed.

"When?" I asked her.

"Earlier. This morning. Ms. von Bausch found him by the lake. Massive myocardial infarction. On his form he lists you as his decision maker."

A heart attack. Here one moment, and then the next—. The administrator told me it had happened quickly. A man walking by the lake. A bent knee. A clot on top of blockage inside a narrowed artery. Another man down. It was strange, and it was horrible, but I felt energy shimmer through my arms. I was glad that it wasn't Nana, that it wasn't Epstein. But Garland Bills would be missed.

I slid the phone back into my pocket.

"Everything okay?" Warsaw asked.

"Just pitch the ball, asshole."

The nerves in my stomach felt like they were attached to a car battery. A shadow from a light pole crowded the sun, its tip dark and limned in orange light. I felt the good, solid bat in my hands. I felt ready. So ready. I swung. The ball went and went.

MONA FLATTENED HER HANDS between squeezed knees while Warsaw studied the ground through slats in the aluminum bench. I told them the news.

"He chose you," Mona said. "There's a reason he chose you. Ultimately, it's your decision."

"But, shit. You don't need to give him the grave," Warsaw said. "You like that grave. You chose it."

"I don't have much choice," I said.

"You do," he said. "Buy another. He must have had money."

"It's a good spot. He deserves a good spot. The man had no one. His son is away. Wife disliked him. His boyfriend is dying."

Mr. Garland Bills had chosen me because I had reminded him of his son.

We looked at our knees, our feet, at the dirt on the ground. Warsaw placed his hand against his chin. "So you're going to throw him a funeral?"

"That's what's to be done," I said. "He has no one else."

"He has us," Mona said.

When I returned to the casita, I approached my neighbor's door. The sun and Mona and Alejandro's beautiful foot sculpture were behind me. Mona didn't agree with my idea, but I knocked on his door anyway. I thought the toe would make a nice gravestone. I heard a radio inside. Alejandro answered, but the screen door blocked his face.

"Alejandro, hi," I said, speaking to his silhouette. "I'm wondering, say, how much for that small pinkie toe?"

"What do you mean?" Alejandro asked.

"It's perfect," I said. "An odd shape, sure, but it's marble, and cemeteries like marble. And well, I love it. Love the whole piece. It's incredible." I opened his screen door and met his dark brown eyes. He held my gaze and didn't look away. "I'd like to buy the pinkie toe," I told him. "It's perfect. Just perfect. How much?"

THERE HAD BEEN no public viewing.

On the morning-of, Mona sat against the headboard, pillow stashed behind her back, painting her toenails luminescent aqua. The smell of her in my bed, and painting her long, lovely toes made me dizzy.

I wandered in and out, trying on Bubba's suits, gauging each fit in the mirror. My grandfather had not been a suit man. He had been a Post Man, a survivor of the Depression, someone with little need for suits. I tried all three and Mona thought I looked best in the old standard: black suit, black tie, and white shirt. It was a tight fit at the shoulders and under my arms. The suit was humorless, and if I bent over the buttons would go flying.

Seeing myself in my grandpa's clothes made me miss him. Add the frosty hair starting at my temples, like he'd had at my age, and he was almost in the room again. And then there was his old curved bed, his house, him. I kept his urn at the casita because warehousing his ashes at the nursing home seemed to be crossing a moral line. He was here. He was present. With us. I fetched his urn from the living room and set my grandfather on the dresser. "I want to bring Bubba," I told Mona. "He can wait in the car, but today I want him nearby."

Mona smiled small. Just as I allowed room for her midnight talks, she allowed my little eccentricities to share our space without comment or judgment. Juliet would have placed me on the witness stand for suggesting the idea.

I sat beside her and took the brush. Keeping inside the lines, I painted Mona's three remaining toes, dipping the brush, wiping excess polish, and applying tiny strokes. I blew on her toes. She wiggled them.

"I wish we'd known him better," she said.

"He was a quiet man."

"He helped people. I think he was a physician. That night, at your grandmother's party."

"Nobody knows."

"It's strange. Even though I didn't know him, I'm numb." She touched her chest. "Right here."

"It's not the happiest day."

"He was too young," she said. I caressed the bluest vein on her foot.

Bubba was lighter than I remembered, about six pounds, which startled me every time I lifted his urn. It was incongruous with the weight he'd had over me. In the car I strapped my grandpa into the child's car seat.

Odder things had happened. That woman in Kansas, her house peeled from around her via tornado and saved by hiding inside a refrigerator. That man in San Francisco who awoke with Gila monsters in his shower. And people claimed to see ghosts all the time. Odd things did happen. Several miles down the road, while driving to the cemetery, I spotted my own ghost: bald and naked except for white tennies. He was walking on the sidewalk.

"Oh, my *guy*," Mona said and clutched my forearm.

I pulled to the side of the road, just ahead of him, watching the mirror and waiting for my friend to catch up. He was not pleased to see us when he bent at the passenger window.

"What are you doing?" I asked him.

"I'm walking naked along the street," Warsaw said.

"We can see that. Everyone can. What are you doing walking naked along the street?"

"I don't have anything to hide."

A car passed, beeped. I saw Mona focusing on the dashboard, trying her damnedest to avoid Warsaw's bald junk pile, which hung at her eye level, shimmering in the sun like twin wrinkled apricots. I saw her glance several times, apparently compelled by curiosity.

"I decided to walk to the funeral," he told me.

"But you're naked."

"At least it's honest."

"You'll get arrested," I said.

"You know the Golden Rule. This qualifies," he said. Another car passed and someone ejected an empty beer can at my friend. It was an overthrow, and the can tumbled into a parking lot behind him.

"Get in," I said. "Look at your shoulders. You're getting burned again."

Cars had already arrived. Entire clans with sons and daughters and in-laws accompanied their eldest tribe members. Even children were here, running around the amber grass, tossing Frisbees, playing tag, yelling. The number of attendees shocked me. Mr. Garland Bills's funeral resembled a minor festival. It was incredible to think that this man, such an exemplary hermit, with few friends, could draw these numbers. The parking situation nearest the gravesite was gridlocked. So I parked on the upslope, near the golf course, on the opposite side of a sand bunker. A party was teeing off nearby. Men leaned on their clubs while eyeing their competitors' swings. One man put his ball mid-fairway.

"You're staying in the car," I told Warsaw.

He was in the back, covering himself with two fists. "I'd like to attend," he said. "I have a right."

"Not like that," Mona said.

"You're lucky the police didn't stop you," I added.

"I knew him too," Warsaw said. "I'd like to attend."

We made him wait inside the car.

I saw my grandmother being lowered from a shuttle bus via mechanical lift. Her cheeks jiggled when the lift hit the ground.

"Get me off this thing," she said to me.

"Don't worry, you're safe," Mona said.

"You gave away my grave," Nana said, impressing me more with her motor skills.

"Sid didn't have a choice," Mona said. "It was the best last-minute decision."

"I'll buy you another," I told Nana.

"That's *my* grave," Nana said. "We didn't even know him."

"He had an effect on people," Mona said.

"People whispered," Nana said.

"People whispered, sure, but it gave them something to do," Mona responded.

Mr. Garland Bills had a bearing, a surprising bearing, on others. Fifty residents and their families were present at his funeral. The only pair missing was Bunny Vallance and Seymour Epstein, and I imagined, by now, they were somewhere far away, sipping drinks from hollow pineapples.

I spotted the Activity Director re-tying one resident's shoelaces. Every molecule in the woman's body seemed designed to care for others. She was such a selfless woman, with large, wobbly eyes and a heart too large for her body and a taste for the five-dollar sale rack. She patted down an unruly collar as she walked over. "Hello, there, Mary Beth," she said to my grandmother. She bent down to touch Nana's shoulder.

"We need to thank you," Mona said to her.

"You outdid yourself," I said.

"Oh, I just put up signs," the Activity Director said. "People came because they wanted to come." She squeezed my elbow. "We're family."

Family by way of forced domesticity. Family bound by a wrought-iron fence. I was glad to see children running around. Mona watched them too. The aged outnumbered us—the canes, the wheelchairs, and the Panama hats. I loved each frail, bald, arthritic, and incontinent one. Summer had given way to fall and the leaves were changing.

The dry grass flattened under so much traffic. One man, dressed in black, and whom I'd never seen before, stood patiently at the gravesite, his hands over his cried-out face. Another man touched the small of this man's back. I'd been charged with removing Mr. Garland Bills's belongings from his apartment, placing the details of his life into boxes. Judging by how this man wept, by how his shoulders shuddered, I would give everything to him. Mr. Garland Bills's son could not be found in time. He lived in Mali. It was not my fault. He did not live near phones.

I wheeled chairs closer to the gravesite, summoning a ripe sweat, ducking to avoid Frisbees, but the jamboree eventually drew to an end when, at last, the long black Cadillac hearse arrived. The Activity Director guided the hearse into a prime parking spot, her arms lifted and giving directions. She acted like an airport runway attendant. Several strong-shouldered employees set the casket over the empty rectangular hole. The hoist winced.

I stood beside Paseo del Sol's minister, a small, animated woman with a powder-blue shirt and clerical collar. She waited with a soft leather Bible held against her chest. She wore thick prescription glasses and squinted heavily, showing everyone her gums. Mona rolled Nana alongside Barb's father, who was dressed as a cowboy. I smelled a whiff of pomade coming from his slicked-back hair. I overheard Ms. Patterson compliment Ms. von Bausch on her cut triceps. Danni Zepeda arrived late, with Diego, and I watched them park across the cemetery, on the upslope, in order to view the funeral from behind tinted windows. Sunlight bounced off Ms. O'Neill's silver necklace and raked Ms. Haybroke's eyes. Ms. Cohen wore birdcage earrings and an old-fashioned prom dress with puffy shoulders. Nearby, Ms. Wetherbee applied sunscreen to her forehead while Mr. Carter draped an arm over Ms. Green, both very much, from outside appearances, the perfect couple. A young boy blew a bubble that stuck to his nose. Ms. Parker stifled a sneeze.

"Look at everyone," Mona said. "A great spot, too."

"The best," I said.

"Mine," Nana said.

"You're a good man," Mona said.

"Epstein should be here."

"One of the better ones," Mona said.

Nana tugged my sleeve, and when I bent, two buttons popped off my suit. "You fed her Bubba's old line, didn't you?"

The Lord's Prayer was the only prayer I knew and it played out without incident. Mona docked her hand in mine while the minister held open her Bible, and the murmurings drew down, and we waited for eulogizing, to enter the atmosphere of deliverance, with the dead suspended before us, welcoming the tears, knowing tears were good, tears helped. We searched ourselves for decent memories of the man, as the wind blew, muffling our ears, even as the murmurs began again. The young boy beside me raised his arm and pointed. I looked. Where the slope peaked Warsaw was now standing, as naked as the morning was bright, on top of my car.

Barb's father jutted his chin, unholstered his plastic gun, and cocked the hammer. I watched the minister place her finger in the Bible and squint. Warsaw was holding my grandfather, Bubba. He was holding Bubba's urn, cradling him in his slick, bare arms.

"That's my dear, dead husband," Nana said.

Mona shook off my hand. "I'm telling him to get down."

I grabbed her. "No, let him." I put my hand back in hers.

"But he's standing there," she said. "On your car. *Unclothed.*"

"I know. He is."

"And?"

"Let him." I refused to let her go.

My friend was standing in sunlight, the clouds above without pattern, with his tennies undone and his shoelaces draped over the roof. Everyone stood, like him, silently stunned, and we watched this naked man in autumnal light. Bathed in sun, my friend held on to my grandfather properly, with respect. And he didn't look scared. Naked, he just stood there, pure as a child.

Mona squeezed my hand. Blood coursed through my fingers, up my neck. My heart pounded and I breathed to release the catch. The minister opened her book and recited from the Twenty-third Psalm.

"He maketh me to lie down in green pastures."

Eager gusts of wind sang through a nearby cottonwood. The tree shuddered, shedding green and yellow all around the living fingers of the gathered. Leaves fell, swept our faces, landed in our hair, and tickled our cheeks.

Another small zephyr blew. I saw a triangular leaf settle on Mona's shoulder, balancing there, neat and beautiful, green in the center and rimmed by yellow. Working against falling, stem attached to her blouse, the leaf's serrated skin rustled, refusing to disappear in the wind, fighting the rush, the anarchic and ceaseless and miraculous rush.